There is a song with the lyrics 'words come easy'. Words did not come easy to Ken Wise until rather late in his life – in retirement to be precise. Despite that, Ken felt inspired by the adventures he'd had spending the early part of his life in the United States Air Force. Circumstances then led Ken to move to Spain, where he decided to write first novel, *A Limey in the Court of Uncle Sam*.

Ken consequently became hooked on the written word. He has since written two novels, one being *Estate Agents Beware*, a refreshing contrast to his first book. *A Dream Machine to Die For* is his latest.

A DREAM MACHINE

TO DIE FOR

KEN WISE

SilverWood

Published in paperback 2012 by SilverWood Books, Bristol, BS1 4HJ
www.silverwoodbooks.co.uk

ISBN 978-1-78132-029-7

British Library Cataloguing in Publication Data
A CIP catalogue record for this book is available from the British Library

Set in Sabon by SilverWood Books
Printed on paper sourced responsibly

To Christine, my wife,
who has been subjected to countless proof reading sessions
also with thanks to my editor, Carol Cole

1

Philip Courtney adjusted his tie as he took a long look in the full-length mirror. Not bad, he thought, admiring his newly grown moustache and rugged looks. He was not sure if his mother and father would approve of this latest addition to his facial features but, if he was expected to take over the running of the family estate, he would be making the decisions, not his father. His father had always been the most domineering figure in the Courtney family household.

Philip had just completed his final year at Oxford with honours degrees in physics and history. That should make the old man happy. His thoughts were interrupted by the sound of a movement in the next room.

'Is that you, Price? You can take the trunk down. I shan't be long; just getting the old facial hairs in place.'

There was no answer. Philip idly wandered into the rather spacious lounge of the rooms that had been his home for the last four years. He had shared the comfortable quarters with his room-mate John Jefferson who had left early that morning to catch the train to London. Philip was more fortunate: he would be driving his new Avis sports car, a present from his father, back to the country estate where he would eventually be taking over as the latest Earl of Chester as was normal for the Courtney males when they reached the grand old age of thirty. He thought he had heard the swirl of a cape; he had got used to hearing this as the masters marched up and down the aisles of the lecture room. Seeing no one in the room, he was about to return to the bathroom when he noticed a rather large book on top of his trunk. Glancing at it, he thought he recognised the title of a physics book which he had lent to another graduate.

Oh well, books are not cheap and, although he had a suspicion that possibly it was not his, he placed it in his holdall. He would worry about that later. He wanted to get on his way. After all, in the year 1959, time waited for no one. Price, his valet for the last four years, finally arrived to hump the trunk down to the waiting Avis. After a few curt goodbyes, Philip climbed into his grand car and, pressing the starting button, heard the sound of the engine spluttering into life. It was the latest Avis model, just out that year, and as he pressed his foot on the accelerator the purring sound gave him a quiet, satisfied feeling. Thanks, Father, he thought. Maybe this helped make the four years of graft at Oxford worthwhile. Not glancing back as he headed for the main gates, he could not be blamed for missing the sudden pulling back of the curtains at the fourth-floor windows of the masters' quarters.

'Just take care, Mister Courtney, and mind how you go. We will be meeting again shortly,' remarked the watching master.

2

Allowing the curtains to drop back into their original position, physics master Ralph Hess returned to his desk to continue with his arrangements for the coming summer break which just happened to coincide with the departure of several of the graduates, including Misters Courtney and Jefferson. They had been a mixed bunch, he thought as he reached for the steaming cup of black coffee, which had appeared, on his cluttered desk. He would miss Courtney and Jefferson, both of whom, he knew, were from different backgrounds. Courtney was the son of an English country earl while Jefferson was an American from Boston. Although Jefferson's family were well off, they did not come close to the massive wealth of the Earl of Chester. Hess himself came from a small town in East German but he had moved to Oxford approximately ten years ago to teach physics and had been made very welcome by the University dean and hierarchy, who had recognised his considerable talents.

He had spent many hours with Courtney and Jefferson debating quantum physics and the possibilities of time travel. Courtney had surprised him as he knew that his father, the Earl, had had a massive problem getting his wayward son to buckle down to his studies due to a keen interest in the opposite sex, not to mention being the life and soul of any party. Jefferson was an easier convert who loved the unknown and had many ideas on any subject the three debated.

As Hess sipped his coffee, he noticed a pile of letters, which had been delivered, to his desk several days before. He slit open and read the top one; then continued until the final one was the object of his examination. As he read, he found to his dismay that it was from his family lawyer informing him of the death of his mother. Although it could be expected at her grand old age of ninety-three, it still came as shock as he had had no prior knowledge of any illness. His father had perished many years ago in the 1940 war so most of his life had been devoted solely to his ageing mother.

He suddenly realised that he had not been the best of sons; he had not even visited Germany for at least eight years. Grudgingly, he realised that his well-made plans would have to be put on hold and Mister Courtney would have to wait.

He hurriedly packed his bags and left by train for Dover to catch the next boat out of the country to France; and then travel by train to his hometown. He suddenly felt very agitated as he waited to board the boat. He knew the timing was ideal now to catch up with Mister Courtney but it would just have to wait until after his visit home. He needed to send off his mother in a respectful manner. He owed her that much and his Prussian father would have expected that. He would also have to delay his meeting with Jefferson in London later that month. His sense of annoyance lasted until he arrived within ten kilometres from his home when his sense of loyalty took over.

3

John Jefferson the third alighted from the early morning train from Oxford to London and straightaway headed for the Swan Hotel in Kensington, which would be his home for the next six to eight weeks. John was two years younger than Philip Courtney. Born in Boston, Massachusetts, USA, his family were quite well off, the family business having been well established in the production of paper for many years. John was twenty-one years of age, six foot two inches tall, lean and rather handsome but he had always felt inadequate when around his room-mate Philip who, with his rugged, forceful ways, always seemed to take command when the two of them went out on the town in Oxford, drinking and chatting up the local ladies. John was always the more studious of the two and gave the impression of being more intelligent, but that paled into insignificance when it came to affairs of the heart.

He wondered how things were working out with Ralph Hess. Had Hess managed to complete the task that he had mentioned he thought was necessary? John had misgivings about anything to do with Philip Courtney. Although he liked Philip, he had found him to be a little too flippant and unorganised except, of course, in his pursuits of the ladies of Oxford. Philip had little time for the female students of Oxford, much preferring the older ladies of the university town and if that meant they were married then that was even better.

'It adds to the spice of life,' Philip often used to remark. John preferred to play it much safer but that did not stop him grudgingly admiring the 'forever lady-chasing' Casanova!

John's mind drifted back to the project that he and Hess had been quietly working on for the past two years. Their secret work was now in its final stages and they were on the verge of producing a machine that would electrify the world and most likely make the two of them millionaires. John was certainly not against that. During the four years of rooming with Philip he had often felt disapproval, or maybe envy, of the way Philip had passed his leisure time and how he had spread around a seemingly everlasting amount of hard cash.

Not that Philip had been miserly with it; he had many times supported John on their forages into the nightlife of Oxford. Even so, a man has his pride and, when approached by Ralph Hess to assist him in his special project, John had jumped at the chance of using his time more aptly and not having to lean on Philip for financial support on their outings into town.

Time was passing. John was now approaching a time in his life when, thanks to his works with Ralph Hess, it would be him calling the shots. He was sure that finally, with what he and Ralph Hess were producing, his own dreams would almost certainly come true!

*

Philip's arrival at the manor turned out to be an anticlimax as far as he was concerned. Even his new moustache failed to achieve the expected response: that would have been for his father to treat him as an equal rather than just a person who treated life as one long party-going episode – which to be fair was what Philip had been doing since his early teens. Philip's father was old school with strict Victorian ways. He had not been impressed when he saw his wayward son arriving home in the early hours in a drunken state. In his father's eyes, it was just not the done thing.

Philip soon decided that perhaps the moustache was not practical anyway and dispatched it with a cutthroat razor. Even doing this had no effect on his father's attitude and he realised that his arrival home, even with his new degree, was not going to change his father's rather abrupt and indifferent attitude towards him. Philip soon reverted back to his old ways and returned to his wine, women and song, and not in any particular order. However, he found his new life rather dull. He needed excitement, but perhaps what was to follow might have been much more than he could have bargained for.

John Jefferson's time at the Swan Hotel in Kensington was cut short by a phone call from Ralph Hess. Could he come to Germany without delay? John was intrigued and hurriedly rearranged his plans, leaving the hotel to catch the next boat to Germany. It was late the next day when John arrived at the rather grim-looking house that Hess called home. Hess, who for once had a large smile on his face, greeted him at the door. John did not have to wait long before his old professor had told him some startling news.

Ralph Hess, after arranging and attending his mother's

funeral, had received a welcome surprise, which had changed his fortune, and, with it, his need and desire to catch up with a certain Philip Courtney. He had found to his delight that his mother had left him a substantial legacy, which now gave him the funds to continue with his work. With this in mind, he had contacted John in order that they could complete their dream project.

The weeks passed quickly, and the people of the local area became used to the secretive goings-on at the old house. The Second World War may have come and gone but Germany was still very much divided with the Russians and East Germans always making life difficult for West Berlin. Ralph Hess did have one major problem: this was his fondness of schnapps followed by a few large glasses of German beer. John was forced to go out and find his friend who, by late evening, had always consumed huge amounts of alcohol. Unknown to John, he was also talking loudly to anyone who would listen about his new secret work that would make him a millionaire. It was a rather silly thing to do at that time.

When he was sober, Hess was extremely good at his job; within a short time the two had produced a reasonable working machine, which, Ralph considered, was on the right track. John was impressed and had learnt more in the past few months than ever before. He had an excellent tutor in Ralph Hess.

Time had passed with little change for Philip; that is until Alice, a local landowner's daughter, caught him. Philip had always been recognised as one of the area's most desirable bachelors. Alice was a pretty young thing who had admired Philip from a distance at the church socials, which the gentry always attended at least once or twice a year. Philip had always been keen on foxhunting and he was normally attracted to the large 'horsy' type lady who regularly participated in those types of event. Alice on the other hand was decidedly against hunting foxes but she liked to attend the dances that generally followed. Philip liked the way she managed to retain that 'innocent' look which meant, maybe, that she had not been mounted by any of the randy gentry who were always ready for 'a bit of a fling' without strings, a crime indeed he had been guilty of many times in the past. With the approval of all concerned, Philip had popped the question and Alice had gleefully accepted. She was four years younger than Philip and, while her five foot four frame was perfectly formed, she was never the one that eyes were drawn to when coming into the room with other ladies of her age. Still, she ticked all the boxes when it came to marriage and the possibility of producing a son and heir, a priority where the gentry of country estates are concerned.

4

Philip and Alice were married at the local church and, within a very short time, Alice produced a son and heir whom they named Robert after one of Philip's great uncles. This happy event was just icing on the cake as far as Philip's parents were concerned. Unfortunately the arrival of a grandson eventually proved too much for Philip's ageing father who, seemingly overcome with emotion, had a heart attack and died. This gave Philip the chance, at last, to take over the family estate. When his mother passed away shortly afterwards, Philip realised that he had at last achieved his birthright. Life began to look much brighter than it had when he first returned from

Oxford. About time too, he thought. It seemed that part of the Courtney character was to accept the inevitable: he had been born to rule and, now his time had come, he accepted the role with relish. Every dog has his day; his father had had his day and now it was his turn.

Philip was sitting in his drawing room one morning, reading the newspaper, when suddenly an article caught his eye. 'German scientist found dead.' Ralph Hess, an ex-Oxford University professor, had been found dead, floating in the River Thames. Philip could not believe it and re-read the article several times in total disbelief. He was reading it for a fourth time when Alice entered the room and informed him that a John Jefferson had arrived at the door and wished to see him urgently. Philip was both amazed and pleased to see his old roommate. Soon they were congratulating themselves on their recent achievements: John for keeping in good health, and Philip proudly showing off his son and wife Alice. No change there, that was for sure.

John noticed the open page of the daily newspaper and the picture of Ralph Hess. 'It's about Ralph that I have hastened to see you, Philip,' he remarked.

Alice came in with some freshly made coffee and straightaway John began to explain to Philip the reason for his visit. 'While we were in Oxford, Ralph and I started work on an extremely exciting project with which it now seems to have become dangerous to be associated.' Seeing Philip's raised eyebrows, John went on rapidly, 'Ralph came up with an idea I was very interested in.'

'What was that?' Philip asked, with an almost nonchalant air.

'It was a project which involved the travel of the mind,' John replied. 'Please let me explain. While you were sampling the delights of the ladies of Oxford, Ralph and I carried out some experiments to see if it was possible to recall passages in time by programming one's thoughts and memories in such a way that they could be accessed, at will, at any time.'

'What, a type of thought machine?' offered Philip.

'Well, not exactly; we prefer to call it a dream machine, a machine which people could use to relax and spend time remembering some of the pleasant interludes in their life,' John countered.

'It sounds alright, but do people want to be reminded of the bad times as well as the good?'

'Well, that's the point. Our work involved working with raw crystals, which enabled us to record the nice times in one's life, not the bad. This is due solely to how we record the actual memory, which of course is meant to be pleasant for the person using the machine.' After taking a sip of his coffee, John continued, 'We realised that certain parts of the human brain are very susceptible to recording and emitting brainwaves which we in turn could recover. Ralph inherited some raw crystals from his father some years ago and they have just been gathering dust in a desk drawer until one day he took them out and noticed how they seemed to glow when in a certain light. He concluded it might be possible to change the properties of the crystals. Many experts have done a lot of work on this subject since several crystal skulls were discovered in South America. Ralph had read some of the papers published years after.'

Philip interrupted, 'Are you telling me you have actually made such a machine?'

'Yes. Well, at least, a very primitive prototype.'

Philip suddenly became very interested in John's tale. He knew that Ralph was a brilliant scientist and, if anyone could produce such a machine, Ralph was the man to do it.

As if anticipating Philip's next question, John went on, 'the problem was Ralph liked his drink and, unknown to myself, started boasting about soon becoming very rich. One day, while we were both out, the East German secret police visited our house. It was only because we were warned by one of the locals that we managed to escape and make our way to London.'

'What happened next?' Philip asked earnestly.

'Well, I went ahead of Ralph as I had my American passport. Ralph made arrangements to leave via Switzerland and eventually made his way to England. We managed to meet up just last week and he informed me that he thought he was being followed and feared for his life.'

'And the machine?'

John could sense some scepticism in Philip's voice but continued, and what he said startled even Philip. 'Well, I have it – safely hidden.'

Philip by now was half inclined to start laughing. He wanted more proof about this strange story John was relating. He knew only that Ralph was now dead and that led to his next question. 'What happened to Ralph?'

'Well, as you read in the papers, he was found dead in the Thames under suspicious circumstances. As you know, he was a strong swimmer and was not likely to go swimming in the Thames with his clothes on.' John remarked, 'I just know Ralph must have been murdered.'

Philip frowned. 'Alright, if you're telling me everything, how do I know the machine even works?'

'I know it does work because I was the first person to try it! Well, at least, with an inserted crystal in a helmet full of wires. I can only confirm it certainly seemed to work for me. After placing the helmet on my head, Ralph hypnotised me and I was able to concentrate and think about a pleasant part of my life. When he brought out of my hypnotic state, I was able to recall this past experience in a clear and vivid manner.

I managed to achieve this three or four times.'

'You're telling me that you were able to mentally travel back in time to any part of your life at will? I would imagine that many people are able to recall their experiences at will, John –'

'Yes, that's true,' John interrupted, 'but not to the depth, intensity, clarity and length that I did.'

'You mean every second and emotion that we all would have experienced?'

'Yes,' said John, 'exactly. When it takes you back in time, you go through every emotion, just as you would have done in the past and I mean all those feelings and physical form as well. The use of the crystal seemed to enhance the basic recall experience and fill in any parts that my memory may have missed or forgotten. In other words, it completed the experience of the original in full-blown colour, to the letter.'

'Isn't it true that some people might like to relive the bad times as well?' Philip, being a bit of a sadist, thought he would put that idea forward.

'Ralph wasn't too worried about that as initially you should only be able to retrieve what you put in the machine. The process is incredibly complex,' John concluded. 'Our problem has been deciding to what degree our machine is successful and if anybody with total recall could match it.'

'It does seem to me that both of you have spent a lot of time and effort on a project that is to say, if you don't mind my directness, at the least a bit iffy!' Philip added with some force.

John, smarting a little from Philip's directness, answered, 'I guess that's fair comment, Philip. However, I can only tell you that, as far as I'm concerned, I certainly recalled my episodes in much more detail.'

By now Philip was completely confused. After the initial excitement of possibly a new discovery, it all now seemed to be losing its fascination. Not wishing to appear too much of a wet blanket, Philip added that the machine could only really be judged after many more trials under intensive scientific conditions. This would mean bringing in more people, which, of course, could have a downside.

'We wanted it for commercial reasons but obviously it can be used, with some changes, for more devious uses, such as brainwashing,' John added.

Philip frowned. The more he heard, the more it seemed far-fetched.

John felt he had to elaborate more: 'You must understand, Philip, that the brain contains many memories and some people might want to use such a machine for making certain individuals reveal important details of their companies' secrets.'

'It may seem silly, John, but why have you come to me now? You certainly didn't want my help previously, so why now?'

John looked at Philip with what could only be described as a humble expression. 'Well, we were going to bring you in on it when we both left Oxford but things changed when Ralph received an inheritance from his mother. Originally we were going to ask you to give us some financial support.'

Philip looked peeved. 'Oh, so it wasn't for my brain power then?'

'Not really. We didn't think you would have the time or inclination, what with you taking over your father's estate,' John offered to soften the blow.

John then decided to come to the real reason for his visit. 'Do you remember finding a book when you were leaving Oxford? I believe it was "Physics Discovered" or something like that?'

'Yes, I do. I still have it somewhere, most likely in the library. Do you want it?'

John nodded.

'I'll go and get it,' said Philip and soon returned with the book. 'What do you want to know about it?'

'Please look inside to see if there are any drawings.'

Philip did not have to look long for as he went through the pages he found some cleverly hidden drawings between several of them. They were on very fine tracing paper which would not show up unless you examined the book very carefully.

'Who put them there?'

'Ralph. He knew the importance of the work and that it might attract some unwanted attention. It was he who hid them in the book. He left it in the lounge where you would find it while you were in the bathroom. He wanted you to take the drawings away from Oxford in case something happened to him.'

Philip did wonder briefly about his own safety but let it go.

'As I mentioned before,' John went on, 'Ralph had done a lot of research on this before I joined him. The drawings cover work he did earlier. He did try to explain it to me but it was a little over my head. I only know that the details and instructions in the drawings show the final positioning of the crystal and the wiring for the brain impulses and that they are essential to completing the machine.' John added that Ralph had not felt it was a big problem to sort that part of it out when they made the final machine.

Philip was by now totally perplexed.

John, sensing Philip's renewed scepticism, apologised. He was sure Ralph would have explained it all much better. It had been months since he had even looked at the prototype and, as far as the missing drawings were concerned, he could not even remember laying eyes on them.

Philip soothed over his friend's anxiety and suggested they look at the book and drawings in more detail. The two friends turned their attention to it lying now in front of them.

Did the drawings in the book have the missing formation? John looked carefully and finally concluded that yes, it did look promising but he would need more time to decipher the strange hieroglyphic writing. Then he remembered that Ralph had said he worked in Mayan symbols and Egyptian hieroglyphics and he had completed this part of his research before he had asked John to join him.

'We'll need some help on this,' John remarked. 'Are you with me on this, Philip?'

'Well, I'll tell you what we can do. I'll introduce you to an old friend of my father's. He dabbled in Egyptian hieroglyphics and might just be able to help you. If he thinks this is kosher, I might then be willing to put up the cash you require, for half an interest.' Philip thought he would add that last bit, just for good measure.

John agreed without hesitation; he wanted Philip on board, feeling that he needed someone of his no-nonsense ways and hands-on approach to help take this project forward.

In the past he had looked up to Philip; he always seemed to have that extra push even though it normally came when dealing with the ladies. He also now needed to convince himself that, just maybe, he had not been letting his own enthusiasm run away. A third party with some experience in this field might be just what was needed at this time.

Philip called his father's friend, Jay Browning, who agreed to meet them the very next day. John was invited to stay over and Alice went to ask James the butler to open up one of the many bedrooms and make up a bed for their guest. Even though the hall had plenty of bedrooms, Philip had found to his dismay that the finances of the estate were not as good as he had been led to believe. Consequently it was better to keep a large part of the house closed up. His father had obviously disposed of a lot of his wealth before he passed away. There was even a slight hint that some of Philip's womanising ways had been from his father's genes. Oh well, as long as nobody turned up asking for their share of the depleted estate.

Alice decided to cook dinner herself and soon produced a meal of roast chicken, accompanied by a French wine. It was good for Philip to have his friend with him again and they chatted endlessly going over old times, leaving out for Alice's benefit some of the romantic episodes they used to get up to. The three finally retired to the drawing room for brandy and coffee, a nice way to end a very unusual evening. Alice soon left the two friends to their reminiscing and went to bed leaving the two men free to relive many parts of their Oxfordshire adventures.

When Philip finally retired to his bed and his sleeping wife, he found it hard to rest. His mind was constantly invaded by strange designs and cascading rhythms that criss-crossed his sleepy state of mind. He was also totally confused as to why anyone would want to commit murder for something which Philip considered, at that time, to be a bit what you might call 'pie in the sky'.

5

As Detective Inspector Davies put down his pint of bitter, he suddenly noticed his sidekick Sergeant Jenkins standing in the doorway of the George Hotel. This was his hideaway and he wondered just how the sergeant had discovered it so quickly.

'Well, Sergeant, you've found me so what do you want?'

'I'm sorry to disturb your "relaxing" time, sir, but the boss wants to see you urgently.'

'It's been some time since we had that type of request, Sergeant. I thought he was going to allow me to retire into oblivion. By the way, how did you track me down?'

'Well, sir, it was the books of matches. You keep leaving them around the office so we knew you must come here sometimes.'

Davies could not believe he could have done such a daft thing.

'Are you coming, sir?'

'OK, keep your hair on, Sergeant, and don't let your recent detective work go to your head!' Gulping down the remainder of his pint, Davies put his glass on the counter and marched out ahead of Jenkins. He knew he had been caught out spending one of his crafty afternoons in the George and muttered 'Bollocks' to himself as he got in the patrol car, which Jenkins had conveniently provided. Jenkins knew he would receive no thanks for the smart bit of detective work but when the boss asked for the third time where the detective inspector was, he knew he had to act.

Arriving at the station, Davies and Jenkins quickly entered the Chief Superintendent's office. He found him in the company of two other official-looking men. Davies recognised them as possible Special Branch; they had that style of raincoat that seems to go with the job.

'Oh, there you are, Davies, glad you could join us.' His boss introduced the two men as Miles and Tucker and, while not admitting who they were, it was assumed that Davies knew they were from the Special Branch.

'Professor Ralph Hess, you know of him?' the Chief Constable asked.

'Oh, the man who was pulled out of the Thames a few days ago,' replied Davies.

His boss went on, 'We have pressure from the Yanks; seems they were very interested in getting Hess over to their side when the war finished but he disappeared before they could reach him.'

Davies really could not see where all this was leading. Surely they could get another German scientist. There were hundreds of the blighters coming out of the woodwork now the war had finished.

As if reading Davies's thoughts, the chief went on, 'It seems he was working on a special project which interested the Yanks very much.'

'Something about dreams or mind-reading,' ventured the nearest Home Office bod. 'We think he was murdered and we want you and Jenkins to investigate and find out what happened.'

Davies groaned inwardly. That sounded time-consuming and his retirement was just six weeks away. 'Yes, sir, I'll make some enquiries and come back to you as quickly as possible.'

Davies and Jenkins left the room and went into the incident room to look up the report on the death of Hess.

'The pathologist who did the post-mortem ventures that he was dead before he hit the water. Great, that might just indicate foul play then,' groaned Davies to himself. 'What do we know about Hess, Jenkins?'

'We know he used to work for the Nazis and at Oxford University. He came to England last month via the escape route that was in place at the end of the war. He had a room at a hotel in Kensington. I believe it was the Swan, an inexpensive hotel which a lot of tourists use.'

'Alright, then let's go there,' ordered Davies looking at his watch. He could have been on his third pint by now.

The two men arrived at the hotel and found the manager having his own nap and not too happy about being woken up. Davies could not give a damn about that; he just wanted to see the books but even more so the room that Hess had occupied. This had fortunately been secured and no one had been allowed in it since Hess had been there. Davies looked around. The bed was unmade and the bathroom had not been used as far as shaving was concerned, the bowl being nice and clean.

'Not much here, I'm afraid,' said Jenkins.

Davies was about to agree when he noticed a slip of paper on the table. The name 'John Jefferson' was marked several times with different locations against his name. He also found a name, which rang a bell: the Earl of Chester. It would seem that whoever had killed Hess had not actually visited the room, as nothing appeared to have been touched. However, talking to the Earl might be useful as the whereabouts of John Jefferson was unknown. 'Come on, Jenkins, drive me to Oxford so we can wake up this Earl. I fancy doing that!'

6

'Would you like some bacon and eggs?' Alice asked their guest who had just arrived in the dining room.

'That sounds good,' John replied.

He had just finished his breakfast and was enjoying a steaming hot cup of black coffee when Philip arrived.

'Morning, Philip, just got up?' John asked.

'Silly man,' Philip replied. 'I've been out riding as usual. This is a working estate and since we cut back on the ground staff we have to do more ourselves. Anyway, did you sleep well?'

'As you Brits say, "Like a log". What time do we leave to see Jay?'

'In half an hour.' Philip helped himself to some bacon and kidneys.

Alice decided to accompany them and, with her in the

driving seat, the three set out for the village of Hamden which was about twenty miles away. Arriving on time, they were shown into a delightful room, which was steeped in tradition with its carvings and wooden panelling.

Jay Browning proved to be an extremely likeable fellow who had a large walrus moustache that took up most of his large, ruddy face. He certainly had the manner of a scholar who knew his business when it came to ancient writing systems. The two friends straightaway took to Jay who enthusiastically agreed to assist them in their quest. However, he would require more time to study the strange lettering which covered the drawings. They left him with the drawings, which needed his attention and started making their way back to the manor.

John volunteered to drive on the way back and, with Philip in the other front seat, Alice had time to relax, sit back and enjoy the view. No one heard the shot as it entered the front windscreen and went straight into John's right shoulder with a resounding thud. He managed to bring the car to a screeching halt. A horrified Philip instinctively crouched down, cautiously peering out of the side window to see if he could spot where the gunfire had come from.

Suddenly John shouted to him, 'For God's sake, Philip, look at your wife!' Philip turned to Alice in the back seat and what he saw filled him with horror: his wife was slumped on her side, blood coming from a wound in her head. It did not need a doctor to know instantly that his precious wife of two years was dead. The bullet that had gone straight through John's shoulder had ricocheted up into Alice striking her in the forehead.

Ignoring any possible danger, Philip quickly got out and opened the back door of the car. Blood was trickling down his wife's white face, seeping into the corner of her slightly parted red lips as if it wanted to disappear from sight. Immense grief overcame him and he wept as he cradled Alice to his chest. John, looking on, suddenly collapsed. At that moment, a passing motorist stopped, saw what had happened and went to phone for the police and an ambulance.

7

'Are you awake, Mr Jefferson?'

John Jefferson felt a gentle prod from one of the nursing staff. 'You have a visitor.' He slowly became aware of the outline of a face he knew well.

'Goodness, it's you, Philip.'

'Yes, my friend, how are you?'

'More to the point, how are you?'

'Bearing up under the circumstances.'

John had been in the hospital for six weeks. Although the bullet that had killed poor Alice had done some damage as it passed through his shoulder, fortunately it had missed the vital organs. He had been heavily sedated to allow the wound to heal and there had been no infection.

Philip, realising his friend's need to be brought up to date, went on to relate that a service had been held for Alice on the estate and she had been laid to rest in the family vault. John could see Philip's eyes filling with tears as he spoke. Philip turned away in an effort to hide his emotions, and walked up and down the small ward, his fists clenched. John realised that his friend's grief had now turned to anger and, knowing him as he did, knew that Philip would not rest until he had evened the score with his wife's murderers. Philip Courtney was not the type to forgive and forget; it just was not in his nature. He had been brought up to believe an eye for an eye. Revenge would be sweet.

John had been told that he would well enough to leave in a couple of days. Both he and Philip wanted to make contact with Jay. They wanted to know if he had managed to throw any light on the strange drawings that they had left with him.

Two days later, Philip returned to collect John. They thanked the staff at the infirmary and, with John's shoulder heavily bandaged, left hurriedly to see Jay.

They arrived at Jay's home but were a little disturbed to find it strangely quiet. This was not usual as Jay had two large Dobermann dogs that were always very anxious to find out who had invaded their turf. As the friends searched for a way into to the closed house, they came upon the forms of the two missing dogs. They were stretched out in the garden as if they were just sleeping off a good meal. Philip who was more au fait with countryside matters commented that the last meal that had been served to them had been rather detrimental to their health. Poison had been administered with great efficiency as the two dogs had been trained not to take any prisoners.

Finding the door to the kitchen ajar, Philip and John entered the dim interior and, to their dismay, found the rooms both downstairs and upstairs had been ransacked. Somebody had certainly been anxious to find something and the friends could only conclude that whoever it was must have been after the drawings which they had left with Jay; but where was Jay?

They decided to call the police to report the break-in, which they managed to do using the phone box situated in the lane just outside Jay's house.

8

Davies and Jenkins, having drawn a blank at the Courtney estate, were considering their next move when they received a call about a shooting in a lane near the nearby village of Witney. Arriving at the scene, the two men found that they had arrived too late. The casualties had been taken to the Oxford Infirmary and one distressingly to the hospital morgue.

They decided to let the local constabulary deal with this unfortunate incident and returned to the office. It was two weeks later while Jenkins was going through some incident sheets that he noticed the name Courtney. Was this too much of a coincidence? They checked the details and hastened to the hospital only to be met by a formidable matron who firmly informed them that her patient could not been seen, let alone interviewed. There was nothing to do but to go away and wait.

It was several weeks later before the two men were able to return to the hospital to interview the injured man. Arriving at the hospital was another complete disaster: no Jefferson. The matron had apparently forgotten to mention to the discharge nurse that the police wanted to interview the patient. Good God, could this get any worse? As they were driving back to the station, a call came on the radio about a break-in at a house in the village of Hamden.

'Best go and see or we could be in another pot of soup,' Davies muttered.

Arriving at the house, the two policemen were confronted by two men sitting on the steps of the house with their heads in their hands. Upon questioning them, they were immediately identified as the illusive Courtney and Jefferson. At last, a bit of luck for the detectives.

'Gentlemen, good day! I do believe we have some

considerable catching up to do.' Seeing the puzzled looks on both men's faces, Davies decided to play a waiting game and hold off on the numerous questions he had for these two people. He wanted to get a clear picture of what was happening.

'We're here to see our friend Jay Browning but he seems to have disappeared,' offered Philip.

'What did you wish to see him about?' asked Davies.

'Oh, no reason, we just wanted to catch up on old times.'

Davies looked perplexed. He knew the lame excuse from this rugged individual was surely a lie. He decided to throw a few chance remarks in and see what reaction he got. He was not disappointed.

The two friends were aghast; the detective knew about everything, including Ralph Hess's death. Davies decided to get these two individuals on his own turf – he took them to the George Hotel and ordered drinks and four cheese ploughman's lunches.

Philip and John were agog. What on earth was this policeman up to – they had expected a trip to the police station, to say the least. The four ate their meals in comparative silence with the exception of Davies who slurped heavily on his pint. Thank God he could at last mix business with pleasure.

'Now, you two, we can do this the easy way or the hard way. We can talk here, off the record, or officially down at the station which you might find rather more stressful.'

Now at least they could start again with everyone knowing more of the facts, but would the two men come clean about the real purpose of their connection with Jay Browning? He would have to try to gain their confidence.

9

Dieter Geist looked on uneasily as his two companions pushed the ageing man, known to him as Jay Browning, into the darkened, damp room in the isolated farmhouse that the gang had been renting for the last three months. Dieter knew that the two men were not there to be pleasant to anyone whom they deemed to be at odds with the party's quest. He also knew that he was partly to blame for the old man's predicament. It had been Dieter Geist who had followed the two men and the woman to the old man's house just a few weeks ago. It was not he, however, who had fired the shot which, although aimed just to stop the car, had caused chaos and tragedy.

Dieter Geist, or Professor Geist as he was known in his native Germany, had been involved with his former friend and colleague Ralph Hess since the war when he had casually discussed Ralph's apparently crazy idea to construct a machine that would enable people to read their dreams. He had not thought any more about it until he was brought into the security agency of the new East German Republic. Born out of the East German Secret Service, it was of course composed mainly of Russian secret service personnel. He had been instructed to contact Hess, meet up with him and take him back to Germany.

Finding John Jefferson was easy enough after following up some of the old names which Ralph Hess had been dropping when they had had their various discussions in the past. Nevertheless, he was now getting extremely nervous about his companions who seemed quite unfazed by any deaths for which they might be responsible. He knew one to be Polish and the other he concluded was Russian. They only spoke in Russian in which unfortunately Dieter was not fluent by any stretch of the imagination. The normal way of communication with his masters was by telephone and the two men just seemed to turn up without prior arrangement. Such was the Secret Service for you.

He now had to talk to the old man Jay and get him to tell them what the strange markings on the drawings meant. The farm that they had leased was situated between Witney and Oxford and was completely isolated. It had long ago stopped being a working farm and the people who now owned it were registered 'sleepers' for the Russians.

He walked into the darkened room indicating to his two companions to stay well away. They seemed to understand this and just shrugged as if to indicate that their turn would come. Dieter hoped that this could be avoided. He had a great respect for the ageing scientist and had even read some of his published papers in the past. Jay Browning blinked and gratefully accepted the cup of tea that was offered him.

Davies knew that his only hope was Philip as he could sense that John Jefferson, the Yank, was not going to be too cooperative. He asked Jenkins to take John outside for a walk while he and Philip discussed some details of a private nature concerning Philip's late wife's death. John looked helplessly at Philip who indicated that he could handle the situation.

Jenkins and John left and Davies continued, 'Philip, we're not really interested in any fancy project you and John may be working on, but we are interested in who shot and killed your wife.'

'I've got no problem with that,' Philip remarked.

'It would help if we could understand where Mr Browning comes into all this.'

Philip decided to elaborate on the already accepted fact that Jay Browning was helping them in their project. Their visit to the house had been delayed for some weeks due to the need for John to recover fully from his injuries. At the same time, Philip had had to arrange his wife's burial, mourning her sudden and tragic death.

Davies nodded with some understanding; he had lost his own wife to cancer some years back. 'We know that perhaps, due to Ralph Hess working for the German government in the last war, we do have the Foreign Service involved in all this.'

Philip nodded in agreement without any hesitation.

Davies went on, 'If you cooperate with us, Philip, I will guarantee to give you some advance warning, if and when it comes, of any official intervention to your project.'

Philip, realising he had little option but to accept this proposal, leaned across and shook the detective's hand. When John and Jenkins returned, the four men agreed to speak again later that week.

10

Dieter Geist was not faring much better. The truth of the matter was that Jay knew very little about the basic design of the machine and, although he had taken a good look at the complicated designs, the fact was that he could not really make any constructive conclusions until he had discussed with John and Philip the actual configuration and operating method of the machine. Dieter realised that Jay was most likely telling the truth as, from his past discussions with Ralph Hess, it was certainly a very complex project. The problem was how could he satisfy his masters, get more time and most likely save Jay Browning's life?

Dieter then came up with a solution that might just work: he had to let Jay Browning go and that would enable them to get hold of the main man in the puzzle – John Jefferson.

Philip and John had returned to Philip's manor after promising to work closely with the two detectives. This would give them their best chance of getting Jay Browning back to help them with their quest. They had just sat down with two large gin and tonics to reflect on recent events when James the butler came into the room and announced that a Jay Browning was on the telephone and wanted to talk with them.

Jay dismissed his apparent disappearance with the casual excuse of having to run an errand of some importance. He completely ignored the fact that his house had been ransacked, not to mention the fate of his dogs. Philip was about to push this fact when he sensed that perhaps Jay was not alone as he was making this call. Pressed for a further meeting, Jay then went on to suggest that they should all meet at his place in a few days' time.

Philip, feeling that this was not Jay's idea, contradicted this arrangement with an excuse that John still had a few medical problems and needed to rest. Could Jay come to the estate instead? After a few muffled sounds, Jay came back on the phone and agreed, with the proviso that the meeting should be in confidence with only the three of them present.

Within seconds of finishing the telephone conversation, Philip, without reference to John, called Inspector Davies. This was getting just a little too hot to handle. John looked on with mixed feelings but, on this occasion, he had to agree with Philip's decision to inform the police.

Inspector Davies and Sergeant Jenkins had realised by now that this was not just an isolated case of breaking and entering. Although the project the two men had told them about was, on the face of it, rather far-fetched, they knew that, coupled with the death of Alice, they could not take any chances and had to keep a close eye on the two men. They informed Special Branch of the few details they had been given.

Early the next morning, John departed for London intending to collect the prototype machine from his safe deposit box at Paddington station. It was not really the most imaginative hiding place but was reasonably secure.

Philip, for his part, had recently found his thoughts drawn to his late wife and realised that he could possibly have been a better husband for the short time of their marriage. Suddenly he felt great remorse.

He looked at the picture of his young son Robert who had been the reason for his hasty marriage and came to the conclusion that, despite all the terrible things that had happened, he still had his precious son to remind him of his late wife. His feelings for Alice had been much deeper than he realised. It was strange how you didn't know what was good in your life until you lost it.

Later that day, as the sun dipped beneath the horizon, Philip sat enjoying a glass of wine. He was just finishing his second and was deep in thought, his mind dwelling on Alice and how much he missed her. He thought about the strange tale of a machine that enabled you to go back in time and reflect some of the better episodes of your life. Philip mused that perhaps it would be good if only to relive some of the precious moments he had spent with his wife. Yes, that would be nice!

Suddenly he sensed that he was not alone in the room. Straining his eyes and looking around the drawing room in the fading light, he felt great fear. He had not heard any noise but he could make out a dark shape and was about to yell out when the person spoke.

'I'm sorry to startle you. That wasn't my intention, but your man let me in.'

Philip, now fully in control, replied sharply, 'Why would he do that?' He knew his butler would never do that; it was just not done.

'Well, when I explained that I was your brother, he allowed me to come in as a surprise!'

'You're my what?' Philip was startled. Who was this lunatic who had entered his house without so much as a by-your-leave?

'Your brother.'

'Hold on a minute.' Now Philip was angry. 'You enter my home with a cock and bull story and expect me to believe it?' He stared at the stranger wondering if he should grab hold of him and throw him out.

The sudden smile on the stranger's face should have put him at ease, but Philip was now on his feet and approached the man with one aim: he wanted an explanation.

'My name is Ray Barone. I'm from Italy and I have to inform you that I am your brother, or at least your half-brother!' Seeing that Philip looked as though he was about to explode Ray hurriedly continued, 'I'm afraid that while you were away at boarding school, your father was also away from home; you might say he was playing away!'

Philip cut him short. 'OK, let's stop this nonsense. If you're trying to get money out of me with this silly story, you're wasting your time.'

Ray continued, apparently unfazed, and pulled a faded picture from his pocket. 'Do you recognise the person in the picture?'

Philip looked and admitted that it was the image of his father, although at a much younger age.

'I knew nothing of him,' Ray said, 'until two years ago when my mother told me that my father, whom I had never known and had been led to believe died many years ago, was in fact very much alive and was some kind of earl in England. My mother passed away last year so I decided to come to England to find him. I understand from the locals in the village that he has also passed away.'

Philip looked intently at the man's face and concluded that he was several years younger than himself, but, good grief, he had some of the Courtney good looks. He pulled himself together and suddenly thought he would play the man's game and ask questions to which only persons who knew or had known his father would know the answers. 'Please have a seat – would you like a glass of wine?'

'That would be nice. Ah, French, that'll be a nice change. I normally drink only Italian.'

Philip was about to utter, 'Beggars can't be choosers' but decided instead to press on and try to get rid of this arrogant, self-assured person. 'Look, my friend,' he continued, 'I really can't believe even part of your story and I must conclude that it's just fabricated. My father has never, ever mentioned your mother, and I am sure he would have mentioned visiting Italy.'

'Well, perhaps he never did. My mother worked in London at the Ritz Hotel as a receptionist. Would your father have ever visited or stayed there?'

Philip knew immediately that his father had stayed only at the Ritz when he visited London but that did not mean he had slept with the receptionist – did it?

Ray decided that the interrogation had gone far enough. He reached into his inside pocket, took out a crumpled envelope and pulled from it an easily recognisable paper: a birth certificate. A glance at it soon confirmed that the father's name on the certificate was one Earl of Chester, followed by Philip's father's full name.

Oh my God, this could not be – not now with all this other trouble going on.

'Look, Ray, you seem a nice enough fellow. What do you want and how much will it take for you to go away?'

Ray looked hurt. 'I didn't come here to ask for money. I have enough of my own. I have my own company in Italy and certainly don't need your money. In fact, judging by the look of this place, you could do with some of mine!'

With some relief, Philip decided to let the inquisition rest for a while. He invited Ray to have dinner with him and stay overnight. Ray accepted the first offer but declined the second as he was staying at the local inn in the village which suited him very well.

Philip quickly organised some food and, of course, more wine. Then the two men spent the remainder of the evening talking about and quizzing each other on their common interest: their father.

Philip found himself thinking that perhaps he just might like the story to be true, but he put this to the back of his mind as quickly as the thought had arisen. Finally Ray left Philip and returned to the village inn where he went straight to bed. As Philip had been extremely liberal with his wine, Ray Barone had warmed to his 'brother' and looked forward to meeting him again the next day as arranged.

Philip had also retired to his bed thinking that he now had even more things to think about in his already overtaxed brain! What would John think of all of this? Perhaps Ray Barone was a plant; anyone could get hold of the documents he possessed, but what about those rugged Courtney looks?

At last he tried to sleep but spent the rest of the night extremely disturbed, just like when his beloved wife had been killed.

11

Dieter Geist was not having a good day. He had been severely criticised by his employers who were not happy that he had let Jay Browning go.

'A bird in the hand was worth two in the bush' was their motto and now they appeared to have nothing. Dieter, on the other hand, was more at peace with things as they were now. He knew that the bullet, which had killed the lady, had been meant only to stop the car but he realised that this single deed would mean that the British police would be involved now and that was bad news. In his opinion, after his involvement with the inhumane SS in the war, any police force, be it military or civilian was to be feared. He knew he had to find another way of seeing his mission through; one in which loss of life would be avoided, especially his own.

Philip had risen early and already received two telephone calls, one from Inspector Davies wanting to know the latest regarding the meeting with Browning and another, which was more worrying, from Ray Barone who wanted to know if Philip was in any trouble as he had been followed back to the hotel the previous evening.

What made him think that he had been followed? Ray's answer was simple. During the war he had developed what you might call a 'sixth sense' while working as an underground agent for the Resistance.

Philip groaned; not another 'special agent'. He was fed up with all the intrigue that was already going on. Either way, he rang the inspector back just to put him in the picture, assuring him that he would enlighten him further about Ray Barone when he saw him again. Hopefully Inspector Davies would assist him in finding out more about his half-brother and confirm his identity.

John Jefferson alighted from the London train, hailed a taxi and made his way to the Courtney estate. Upon his arrival, he was surprised to see the gates of the estate closed and blocked by a large car. He paid the taxi driver and approached the gates. Suddenly he was alarmed when one of the car doors opened and a large man sprang out and walked towards him in an aggressive manner. He instinctively knew that the man was not about to ask the time of day. John was carrying his suitcase with some spare clothes and a small round box similar to a lady's hat box. He quickly realised that the hat box was the object of the man's attention and which he now attempted to wrestle from John's grasp. John struggled vainly with the man but found his assailant extremely strong and agile despite his huge size.

John was just about to release his hold on the box when suddenly his assailant gasped and released his hold on both John and the box. Looking around, John was relieved to see Philip who had his arms around the man's neck in a stranglehold. Philip had been keeping an eye out for John's arrival and, noticing the strange car, had positioned himself just inside the gates in the gatekeeper's house. This had enabled him to be quickly on the scene when the man made his first approach. Philip was certainly taking some of his anger out on this fellow; he did not know if this was the man who had shot his wife but he would make sure he knew how he felt about it. Another man in the car was about to get out when he was startled by another arrival on the scene. Sergeant Jenkins had been sent over by Inspector Davies just to make sure there would be no unpleasant surprises. Breaking free from Philip, the bruised attacker clambered back into the car pulling the door shut behind him. The car sped back across the grass almost running over the prostrate John who just managed to pull himself out of the way.

'I enjoyed that!' Philip exclaimed. 'I only wish I had hit the bastard harder.'

'Don't worry,' John said, 'you did well enough.'

Inspector Davies arrived and the four men sat down and discussed the events of that afternoon.

'It wasn't too bad,' John explained. 'The machine wasn't in the box; it was in my suitcase.' He immediately regretted his hasty declaration; he could see at once that the two detectives were now extremely interested in the arrival of the 'machine'.

'We are honour bound to inform Special Branch about this,' Davies stated. 'Look, I'm sorry about this but there are things that are beyond my control and this happens to be one of them.'

Philip surprisingly agreed but went on to suggest that, as the meeting with Jay Browning was soon, they should keep the machine, have the meeting and then turn everything over to the authorities. John could not believe his ears; there was Philip just giving away their project, in fact his project, his lovely dream machine, to some government department. He could foresee any financial rewards amounting to zero. He was not in a good mood when the two detectives left after informing them that they would be listening in on any calls that might be made on the bugged telephone lines. Philip, seeing John's dismayed look, gestured silently for him to follow as he walked across the lawn to the summerhouse, which he knew, was not bugged…

'I want you to take the machine to the Bowl Inn straightaway. Ask for a Mr Ray Barone and explain to him that we have a serious problem and you want to go with him to his home – in Italy!'

'Where, for God's sake?'

'Italy. Look, it's a long story and much too complicated to explain now. You'll have to trust me and we are both going to have to trust this Ray Barone!' Deep down, Philip did not have much faith himself in what he was saying but he knew that if they were to keep any hold on their project they would have to trust someone, and that someone was Ray Barone – whoever he was!

'Look, John, talk with Ray, tell him just as much as you need to and ask for his help. Tell him I'll explain later. I realise that he was going to stay until next week, but if he values our new friendship at all, please ask him to trust me.'

John was even more puzzled now but he said he would do as Philip asked.

'I'll see Browning,' Philip continued, 'and find out what he thinks of the drawings but more importantly get them back. He will be under the surveillance of the people who abducted him. I guess the two detectives can help me with that. I'll just have to play it by ear.' He picked up the telephone to call for a taxi to take John to the Bowl Inn.

As John left with the all-important suitcase, Philip started making arrangements for the meeting next day with the two detectives. He was a little perturbed that he actually knew very little about Ray; he suddenly realised in fact that he did not even know his brother's address in Italy. He could only hope that his gut feeling, or perhaps his brotherly feeling, was to be trusted.

Philip was mulling over his hasty decision to send John off with Ray at such short notice and without a firm contact in any way, other than the fact he knew his brother lived close to Rome. It was then that his ageing butler James, who had been with the family for more years than Philip could remember, suddenly came to him with a rather apologetic look on his face. 'I do hope you did not feel that I was out of order in sending your brother into you unannounced, but I do believe, sir, that it was quite the best and easiest way of making the introduction. I do apologise for not saying anything sooner, sir, but you have been extremely busy since.'

Philip looked at James with a puzzled look on his face. 'I did wonder why. It was rather out of your remit to do such a thing, James, and I was going to speak to you about it when I had time.'

James remained quite calm despite the thought of a dressing-down from his master, Philip. 'Well, sir, if you will allow me to continue, you see the gentleman was not a stranger to me, although it was the first time I had met him in the flesh.'

'Are you telling me, James, you knew all about my half-brother and that what he was telling me is true?'

'Yes, sir, you see I have been rather involved with your father's additional offspring for many years, in fact, since he was born. It was me that's been arranging the monthly payments to Italy.'

'I think you had better start from the beginning, James, and it might be better if you sit down while you're doing it.'

James declined the invitation to sit down; he felt much more at ease in his usual standing position whilst in the presence of his employer. This was the manner he had been taught to adopt by his father when he first took up service.

'As you will, James, but get on with it, man. I'm anxious to hear how you knew all about this Ray Barone and how I was kept in the dark all these years.'

James went on to explain that Philip's father had first confided in him when he had heard about the impending birth by his mistress. Wanting to do the correct thing, and without risking a scandal, he arranged via James for payments to be sent every three months to a bank in Rome to cover the birth and additional support for the child.

Philip realised that he now had to confer with James on

his present predicament and, after doing so, he was pleased to learn that not only did James have a contact address for the Barone family but also a contact telephone number which he could give to Philip.

'James, I could kiss you!'

'I don't think that will be necessary or in any way appropriate, sir.'

Philip was very relieved that at least it would seem he had a way of contacting John and the mysterious man calling himself Ray Barone. He had already informed John not to call him at the house due to the phone-tapping.

He spent the next few hours wondering how and where the two men were and even more about the new person that had turned up in his life; a man who could well be his brother and, if so, what effect would this have on his own life.

12

Dieter Geist entered the dimly lit room where his UK controllers had summoned him. He knew they were not at all pleased with what had taken place over the last forty-eight hours. He listened intently to the barbed comments the three men sitting there hurled at him.

'I can only report that the actions I took were the best I could think of at the time,' he retorted. 'I can also confirm that the actions taken by your two men only made the meeting which I set up impossible to take further. The British police are now involved and we cannot go near the estate. Either way, it is much better to let the two men meet and decide what their next step will be. We will then have a much more comprehensive idea how the project is proceeding. The main contact is still Courtney and he must be kept in sight at all times.'

Franz, the leader, looked at Dieter. He knew that sending in the heavies may have been a mistake. 'We are going along with you on this, Geist, but we will be putting more men on it. We know the Americans are sending men over to try to get the machine.'

Dieter hastened from the meeting to make contact with the man who would most likely have some of the answers to his problems: the landlord of the Bowl Inn, Jacob Manners, who for ten years had been in the employment of the company.

John Jefferson entered the Bowl Inn and asked at reception if he could book a room. The landlord, a Mr Manners who was very pleasant and attentive, attended to him. John enquired as to the whereabouts of Mr Ray Barone and was directed to the bar where found his quarry sitting having a drink. He approached the man and was straightaway struck by his similarity to someone he knew well. Good God, it was Philip Courtney the Second. Surely he must be mistaken but the resemblance was uncanny.

John quickly introduced himself to the man whom he concluded was of a similar age to himself and a few years younger than Philip. He sat down and decided to go straight into his tale of woe and his need to hide low for a while.

Ray Barone listened intently as John unfolded his story. He asked several questions, mainly about John's involvement with Philip Courtney, and seemed very interested in the project that John briefly explained to him. The two men then ordered a bar snack together with a bottle of wine. They were so engrossed in their conversation that they were not aware of the keen interest being shown in them by their host, the ever obliging, Mr Jacob Manners.

*

Jay Browning knew that the reprieve he had been granted was only so that he could obtain more information for his captors. He wondered what he had got into. The simple task of deciphering some drawings had turned out to be much more dangerous than he had bargained for. He called Philip Courtney to confirm the appointment for the next day and wondered if he would have companions at the meeting and what would happen afterwards. He concluded there was only one course of action: he took the drawings he had in his possession, placed them in a large envelope and addressed it to Philip Courtney at the Manor.

The following day, Jay got in his car, stopped at the village post-box and posted the large envelope, then drove to meet Philip. As he drove into the courtyard of Courtney Manor he sensed he was not alone.

John and his new found friend Ray Barone were getting on famously. They seemed to have many shared interests and John found out that Ray's family business produced electronic and telephonic instruments. Ray surprised John when, the next day, he produced a large box and took out an instrument with push button numbers on it and proceeded to phone Italy without putting any money into it.

'This will be the thing of the future,' he remarked. 'Everyone will have one of these and carry them with them all the time. They will of course be much smaller!'

John looked at the rather large instrument and thought that maybe his new Italian friend might just be a little eccentric. Still, it seemed to work and Ray turned off the machine with a single push of a button.

'Actually you might try something like this as a pressure

pad for your dream machine. It could be placed just behind your left ear lobe, which is one of the body's most sensitive parts. We are about to produce a much smaller version once the connection to the new Russian satellite has been established.'

John was not sure what he meant by this but he let it go as he did not fully understand all this talk about Russian satellites. Perhaps Ray would explain more later.

They talked earnestly for the next few hours until it was time to leave for the airport. Jacob Manners had been very obliging in offering to arrange for the taxi to take them to the airport for their flight to Italy. After watching the vehicle disappear from view, he reached for the phone and called his friend and comrade Dieter Geist. This would certainly earn him some brownie points.

Philip rose early the next day to make sure everything would be ready for Jay Browning's visit. He had already contacted Inspector Davies who had assured him that he would keep an eye out for any strangers hanging around the estate throughout the day.

Jay was welcomed warmly by Philip who was pleased to see his father's old friend, at least for now, safe and sound. Jay immediately explained that he had posted the drawings to Philip and they should be with him the following day, subject to the postal service. Jay did not elaborate why he had done this, and Philip let it go unchallenged, as he knew Jay was obviously under some kind of surveillance by his previous captors.

As the day wore on, Philip and Jay found to their relief that the presence of Davies's men ensured that they would not have any unwanted visitors. It was decided they would venture out to visit the Bowl Inn for some lunch. Philip was worried at first that this might not be a good idea as it could be leading the enemy directly to John and Ray but he desperately wanted to learn of their whereabouts. Philip knew he would not be able to do much while they were waiting for the drawings to arrive.

A quick check at the Bowl Inn reception soon confirmed that Mr Ray Barone had indeed left and returned home to Italy. The two men then left the Bowl Inn. As they left, they were pleased with the thought that at least their friends and the machine were safely on their way out of the country. It was decided that, if and when Jay was contacted by Dieter Geist, he would admit he no longer had the drawings, hopefully taking the heat off him. God knows, there had been enough sorrow already with those connected with the dream machine. Either way, Jay would only join them in Italy if required further. In the meantime, he returned home to await further instructions.

Philip, of course, had no idea that certain persons who were very interested in their project were arranging for people in Italy to be at Rome Airport to keep watch on the movements of Ray Barone and John Jefferson. Dark clouds were already gathering over the bright skies of Italy.

Inspector Davies arrived at the Courtney Estate to be informed that John and the machine were no longer there. He could only ascertain was that Jefferson had departed the previous evening for parts unknown. He was about to lose his temper when he suddenly received a telephone call from Jenkins.

'Right, Jenkins, that would seem to explain a lot,' he remarked. He turned to the rather embarrassed Philip who had found it very difficult trying to explain the absence of the machine and drawings.

'It would seem your friend John has left the Bowl Inn with a certain Ray Barone, an Italian man who was seen visiting you; in fact the same person you promised to introduce to me and explain exactly who he is, or in this case was!' Davies said scathingly.

Philip's mind raced. Although he had had plenty of time to put up a plausible story about John's sudden disappearance, he could not immediately come up with anything that would seemingly satisfy the irate inspector. He decided to give him something to work on and, at the same time, maybe get help himself with some official answers. He went on to explain that his friend John had apparently gone off with this Ray Barone who was, in turn, claiming to be related to Philip himself. He was at a loss as to why John had done this and if he had even gone voluntarily.

Philip wondered if the inspector would believe this sorry tale and if he might even suggest that he would try to find out who Ray Barone was. Fortunately he did not have long to wait as Inspector Davies picked up the phone and instructed his office to put a tracer on Ray Barone of Rome, Italy and to make it top priority. Philip was about to congratulate himself when Inspector Davies spoilt his newly found smugness.

'I do not want you leaving this house until we have some proper answers to what happened yesterday. You will not contact anyone else in this matter, including your Mr Jay Browning. Do you understand me, sir?'

Philip knew at once that he had tried the inspector's patience. He reluctantly agreed. He also realised that he would have to wait until the post came before he could make a move anywhere.

At their previous meeting, Jay had spoken with Philip about the mysterious signs and notes on the drawings and Philip knew that, with Jay's comments, John might be able to decipher the information they both desperately needed.

Philip poured himself a drink and waited for the post. He had to wait but patience was not one of his virtues.

14

Dieter Geist alighted from his flight from London and made his way to the Arrivals area where he had been informed that someone from the organisation would meet him. He would then receive an update on the latest movements of Messrs Barone and Jefferson. He groaned when he saw the familiar face of Higgs, one of the two men Geist had been introduced to at the company HQ. Dieter had taken an instant dislike to him then and here he was already in Italy. The man must have been have had a private plane or something. His demeanour did not improve when he found out that Higgs was actually the brother of the man in England and was just part of a family of people employed by the company. God, they do keep it all in the family, groaned Dieter to himself.

The grunts and short responses to his questions to Al Higgs were not much better than the previous responses he had received from Joe Higgs when he tried to find out more about the shooting of Mrs Courtney; more shrugs than spoken words. Dieter wanted to know more about the other two 'helpers', one of whom had carried out the shooting when Alice Courtney had been killed. They had apparently disappeared from the scene; maybe the company had moved them to another job or perhaps even from this planet.

They always liked to tidy things up. His heart sank as the Cadillac motor purred its way to a rather scruffy hotel in an equally scruffy part of Rome.

Whatever the organisation did, they knew how not to attract attention to themselves or their employees. He was told to wait there for further instructions. This made him more nervous; it seemed to indicate that he was no longer in charge of operations. Dieter Geist instinctively knew that was not a good thing.

*

John Jefferson felt good. He had had a pleasant flight over with Ray Barone and enjoyed an in-flight breakfast of eggs and bacon. As he left the airport, the early morning sun seemed to wrap itself around his face and body. This was perhaps something that he had missed all those years in Germany and the United Kingdom but this, this was quite nice. He could get used to this...

His thoughts were interrupted by the voice of Ray Barone hailing his car and driver that had been waiting patiently at the Arrivals entrance. John could not help noticing that the car seemed to have been parked there without any interference from the local police. Perhaps Ray Barone was more than a local businessman, but what kind of business? John was a little concerned that, although he liked Ray, he knew that Italy was spawning more things than lovely sunshine: it was also the home of the notorious Mafioso. He tried to put these thoughts to the back of his mind as the Buick automobile purred its way through the pleasant countryside on the way to Ray Barone's villa.

The villa turned out to be situated in an extremely large vineyard just outside Rome. He just hoped that the luck they had been having for the last week or two improved, especially while he was with them.

Their lunch was served on the terrace in the midday sunshine, complete with an excellent couple of bottles of vino which had been collected from vast cellars of the estate. Afterwards, Ray went to answer a phone call from England and John relaxed, speaking with Gina, one of the younger sisters of Ray's attractive wife Rena.

Oh, why do Italian ladies look so incredibly lovely with their olive skins, deep suntans and lovely white teeth? John suddenly realised that he had been missing out on female companionship for some time now; in fact the last time had been in Oxford all those years ago. If he remembered correctly, she had been the less attractive of two ladies Philip had been instrumental in picking up. Nothing could be more different now as John was here on his own, and Philip, he hoped, was stuck back in the UK. His attention to the lovely Gina was interrupted when Ray returned to the table and asked John to join him for a walk around the vineyards.

'That was Philip on the telephone,' Ray remarked as they walked towards the vineyards. 'He was calling from a payphone in the village, away from the estate and hopefully any preying eyes and ears.' The outcome of their previous actions was not as bad as they had feared and Philip was hoping to join them in Italy once the drawings had arrived at his home. He had, however, to wait a few days to ensure that the police did not follow him. Jay Browning would not join them as it was not fair to place him in any more danger than he had already experienced.

John readily agreed with that but he briefly wondered, when taking into consideration all that had happened over the past few weeks, including Alice's untimely death, whether completing the manufacture of the dream machine would make it at all worthwhile.

'Well, we'll have to find a safe way to contact Jay if we need to,' Ray commented.

For the next few days, John and Ray were deep in discussion about the 'Dream Machine'. John had concluded, right or wrongly, that he and Philip just had to trust Ray Barone. They were in his house, his country and, what was more, he seemingly had good connections in Rome. In addition to mobile phones, his company produced other equipment such as sensitive instruments and electronics.

Ray suggested that they might have to dismantle the prototype machine that John had brought with him so that they could work at incorporating some of the details they would receive when Philip arrived from England.

The three men came to the conclusion that the only way forward was to arrange for trials in one of Ray's quality control testing rooms, under strict scientific conditions with several random people taking part. Where else could they go from here? The three men were in this for good or bad!

Sometimes they took a break to join the ladies and some of Ray's workmen, who worked in the vast vineyards, for some merriment. John began to relax and it felt more like a vacation than work. He was working on his special project; in a sunny country with pleasant people including the lovely Gina. Yes, his situation was much better but for how long would this peace and quiet last?

Meantime, Philip was tidying up his estate so he could join the others. While he was eager to travel to Italy, he did not want to be absent suddenly which might attract attention from the authorities. He found that the excitement of the past few weeks had calmed down and was just a little concerned about how things were going in Italy. He had had a couple of extended conversations with both John and Ray and this had left him worried that he was not at the centre of things as he always liked to be.

Inspector Davies confirmed that Ray Barone was, in fact, a well-known businessman from Rome who had acquired his wealth by some shrewd investments from capital of an unknown source. Philip wondered if perhaps his own father had been that unknown source and Ray had been much more industrious than himself. He felt some admiration for his newly found half-brother. Inspector Davies had not mentioned Ray's parents and Philip did not feel it appropriate at this time to ask him to delve further.

Inspector Davies and Sergeant Jenkins were recapping on the events and knowledge they had gathered. 'Well, Jenkins, it does seem that Philip Courtney and Ray Barone are related. It would seem that Courtney Senior put a receptionist from the Ritz "up the spout" on one of his many forages to London. He made maintenance payments via a little known account in the name of a Mr James Baldwin, who just happens to be the long serving butler to the Courtneys. We also know that, by now, Ray Barone and John Jefferson are safely boarded up in sunny Italy. What does worry me though is what's happened to Jay Browning's captors and what they're doing now. I don't believe for one moment that they've given up the ghost.

'Anyway, I reckon we deserve some time in the sun, Jenkins. I'm wondering if I can swing it with the powers that be.' Jenkins perked up at this idea but wondered if the boss would go along with it and, more to the point would his own boss, the wife, allow it! However, his dream was soon shattered when Davies announced that he would go but that Jenkins would stay in the UK for back-up. The Yanks would give cover in Italy if Davies wanted any.

'Sorry, Jenkins,' remarked Davies as he left to pack his bags.

'Yes, sir, some people get all the luck.' Jenkins noticed that his boss did not appear too upset about him not going.

Inspector Davies was sitting down to have a coffee at the airport when he noticed a familiar figure. Putting down his coffee cup, he went over to the figure trying not too successfully to hide his large form in the corner of the departure lounge.

'Hullo, Philip, can I join you? Off on your hols?'

Philip's face was a picture of amazement and surprise. He knew he had been caught out; at least, he could not explain how, after giving an undertaking not to leave the estate, he was now at the departure gate in the airport waiting to board his flight to Italy.

Now was the time for some plain speaking and, again, poor Philip would not be having it his own way.

15

In Rome, John and Ray were at last making some progress with the dream machine. However, they had found that it was not restricted to one of emotion. In fact it would be appear to be uncontrollable; something the original designer Hess had not been aiming for. His aim had been to restrict the machine to creating dreams and emotions that were pleasant. John had been so interested in experiencing a pleasant 'dream' that the two scientists had assumed it was the end product Hess had wanted. Now, it was a different ballgame but the two friends knew they did not know everything about the human brain. Well, not yet anyway.

They realised that they would have to take a break from working on the project and await Philip's arrival with the drawings.

John jumped at the idea of having some vacation time and he wanted to perhaps spend more time with the lovely Gina. The two of them were out in the picturesque village of Lena having a glass of wine in the late afternoon sunshine enjoying each other's company when suddenly John experienced an old fear, something that he had in the past few weeks put conveniently to the back of his mind. His sense of being watched seemed to intensify but, when he glanced around, he could see nothing untoward. He said nothing to Gina but, on their return to the villa, he mentioned it to Ray. Ray said nothing but went to the phone and had a quiet discussion with someone at the other end. John assumed that he was perhaps asking for some help from some of his business contacts, a path that John did not want to pursue at that moment.

Dieter Geist was clearly enjoying the sunshine as well. He had had a couple of weeks without any pressure from his superiors and spent most of the days and evenings just keeping an eye on John and Ray Barone. He did have some assistance with that, as his superiors had sent over a listening device the shape of a fountain pen which, when pointed in the direction of his quarry, allowed him to pick up most of the conversation as long as the person was facing him. He put down the small device and shrugged his shoulders. The small talk that John was making with Gina was certainly not of any interest to him. He had not been married for all those years without forgetting how young lovers were supposed to behave. He had noticed however that, when he also observed Ray and John when they went out together, they hardly talked about the machine. He concluded that perhaps they were waiting on something or someone. Philip Courtney must be expected shortly and then perhaps he would have to make his move as he knew that his time in the sun was not going to be just a pleasant interlude.

The flight over from England was not too amenable with Davies reading the riot act to Philip and explaining that only by working together closely would he be able to provide the protection that everyone needed. Philip for his part just wanted to get to Ray's villa so that he could find out exactly what the latest was with the project.

The two men had to separate as Davies knew he would have no legal right of entry to Ray Barone's villa and anyway he had to check in with the local police to arrange help with his seemingly unwanted protection he was attempting to provide for the men. That was not going to be easy.

Philip was amazed to find a man with a card with his name written on it as he left Arrivals and stepped out into the sunshine of Rome's international airport. He found that his half-brother had sent a car to collect him. Philip was even more impressed when he arrived at the villa and saw the immense vineyards spreading out as far as the eye could see. He soon felt better when he was treated to a splendid lunch and shared a bottle of the vineyards' excellent wine. Well, this could turn out nice as long as the men with guns and their desire to take over the dream machine did not turn up.

John waited until Philip had finished his meal before he revealed his feelings of being watched. Philip took these on board but secretly hoped that he had been mistaken. Strangely, Ray never commented on this but seemed inclined to take John more seriously.

For the next few weeks, the three men worked on the dream machine and, with the help of Jay Browning's notes, managed to produce a module, which they were able to activate at will. The problem was, however, that they could not get the machine to maintain its desired connection for long.

They had also managed to reduce the wiring which had been originally placed outside the machine into a more compact form. This was mainly due to the work carried out by Ray's company which was well advanced in communications technology. The basics for using the machine were indeed very simple: all you needed to do was to relax, think of some pleasant episode of your life, let the machine take over and, with the brain activity, transport you back to that time.

The machine itself just magnified the pictures in your mind and held them in a more static and vivid state which in turn gave you the enjoyment. You were not only reliving that part of your life but actually feeling every emotion that you once experienced.

It soon became apparent that the use of hypnosis was no longer required once you had been on the machine. The crystal absorbed the connection you had built up during the first experience; subsequent connections were automatic.

The three men decided to set up a proper scientific experiment to prove exactly how efficient the machine was, and to demonstrate the full extent of its capabilities.

John further explained that Hess's initial idea was to emulate the ancient ways of the legendary people of Atlantis who apparently were able to communicate by thought waves and were well advanced in the control of the human brain. They also had managed to create machines that enabled them to move large stones at will. They built large cities which spread for miles, but the constant weakening of the subterranean caused a natural disaster and the sea suddenly broke through engulfing their splendid cities. The earth's crusts then parted and came together suddenly pitching most of the population into the abyss, and thus an extremely advanced civilization was lost. They had also been able to communicate with each other by mind transfer rather than speech which, if true, must have been quite extraordinary.

Ray and Philip both nodded, but John realised that perhaps the two brothers might just feel that this theory was a little far-fetched.

Philip, Ray and John concluded that the machine could well be used for less pleasant purposes such as brainwashing which made it even more imperative that the machine did not fall into the wrong hands. For the first time, the three men were faced with the possibility that, while the dream machine could be a commercial success, it could also mean they were introducing the world to the first portable terror machine.

The thought of this was soon dismissed by all three men, such was their desire to finish and use the machine which now seemed to have taken over their lives. Nothing must stand in the way of producing the world's first dream machine. However, they still did not have access to Hess's notes that enabled the user of the machine to retain its images for a much longer time. Philip and John decided they should increase the partnership from two to three. Without Ray Barone's input, it was extremely doubtful that they would have got this far with the changes that had been required.

Ray wanted to speed up the commercialisation of the machine. Had Hess gone into any detail at all on how he thought the machine's thought process could stay 'online' and not fade as it was doing now?

John thought for a while and said that perhaps he had, but he could not remember what had been said.

'It is a shame we can't ask Hess now,' remarked Philip.

'Perhaps we can,' John suggested.

Ray and Philip looked at John with raised eyebrows.

'If we can identify the year and approximate time, perhaps I could go back to the time in Germany, recall some of the conversations we had together and then convey them to you.'

'That would be fine but we all know the dreams you experience are of a private nature and we don't know how to get you to convey them to us, while you're having them,' Ray replied.

'That should be easy,' John went on. 'We can use hypnosis.'

'Yes, you could be right,' Ray concluded, 'as long as we can tie together the two procedures and ask you the right questions at the right time.'

'Not a lot to ask then!' Philip mused.

The three men suddenly realised that they had been talking non-stop for several hours, not even pausing for food.

'Why don't we stop for some refreshment; then perhaps we can sleep on this and talk first thing in the morning to see how we can take this further,' Ray suggested.

Without further comment, the other two men nodded agreement. The next few hours were spent in the cool evening with some excellent Chianti and freshly made pizzas and, even more so as far as John was concerned, the company of Gina.

Philip could see that at last, where ladies were concerned, John was finally in the driving seat so to speak, and he reflected on the years he and John had spent together in the Oxford drinking establishments. For once in his life, he now regretted the hectic times he spent then, not to mention the money. However, now he was more worried about what possible dangers the next days would bring.

Ray found it intriguing as he listened to Philip setting out his thoughts on the dream machine, and he also reflected on past times years ago when he was growing up while miles away in a foreign country his own father and brother were going about their own lives.

16

Dieter Geist knew that, with the arrival of Philip Courtney, things must be moving ahead and instinct told him he had to act soon if he was going to achieve what his masters expected: to obtain the machine that would further their aims in mind control. The problem was that, while he had plenty of help as far as muscle was concerned, he was short on personnel who would stop and think before shooting. He knew he had to work fast before things got too advanced, such as the application for a patent. He made a few phone calls and waited.

Philip, John and Ray had finished eating breakfast when they received a phone call out of the blue. It was Jay Browning saying he was in Italy, in Rome and could he be of assistance? The three men were thrilled that Jay was there in Italy, and seemingly available to assist them at this crucial time. As it seemed the situation had calmed down in the UK and with Jay's assurances that it held no danger with him travelling to Italy, Ray gave instructions to Jay to make his way to the village square and he would send a car to collect him and bring him to the villa. Within a few hours, the four men were united and sitting down in the sunshine. They talked excitedly about the project over a few bottles of wine. This can't be bad, thought Jay to himself, having left England where the rain had been pouring down.

Inspector Davies looked around him and wondered if by chance that the powers that be really had his state of health at the top of their agenda, such was the state of the three-star accommodation that he was in. He wished that he had managed to wangle it so that Jenkins could come with him, not that he was on holiday for one minute, but the wine with his meal that night had been exceptional and he would not have minded sharing it with his sergeant. He knew he would be able to get some assistance from the Americans who had been in touch with his superiors in the first instance but would he have control of the operation?

As he was on his way to breakfast, he was called over to the reception and handed a note with a telephone number on it. The Americans wanted him to call them. Well, the bloody Yanks could wait until after he had had his breakfast of strong coffee, boiled eggs, some freshly baked Italian bread and a warm croissant. When in Rome…and who was he to argue!

Philip had now taken over the role of chairman of the group which raised the shackles of his half-brother Ray who had assumed apparently that he would be in the controlling role as chairman. After all, it was happening on his patch. John, of course, was just happy to have the two men on the team and he knew that, as things progressed, the two brothers would reach an understanding; well, he certainly hoped so. Ray for his part soon got used to Philip's rather bossy ways. He admired the way Philip seemed to grasp the main points and, whilst he knew that John was the brains behind the project, Philip's comments were always succinct with the ability to put his finger on the main points.

With the arrival of Jay Browning, the team must surely be complete. Things were moving at an amazing rate and, for the first time in his life, Ray Barone realized that he was really enjoying life. He had a new brother and now an even wider variety of friends than he had ever had. He had always felt that something was missing from his life but even he had to admit these latest happenings were a big surprise to him.

Philip had come to the conclusion that, while he was as

anxious as the other men to advance the project, he believed that, before they tried the new approach John had put forward, it might be better to have a more in-depth discussion with all the team which by now included several members of Ray's scientific team. He was sure that, by using some of the successes the company had achieved in the last few months, the project would finally reach a sound conclusion and they would have their dream machine.

Ray readily agreed with this and arranged for the key members of his company to clear their desks and diaries so that they could attend this important meeting.

The meeting was arranged for five days' time giving the other members of the team time to see some of the surrounding area. John immediately took the opportunity to invite Gina out for a drive in the country. Gina readily agreed and soon the two were getting into John's rented car. They were about to leave the grounds when Jay appeared on the scene and asked them if they could drop him off in the next village. He explained there were a few old buildings, which he considered a must to visit. John agreed and the three left and drove into the lovely countryside.

Philip and Ray, finding themselves alone for the first time since Philip had arrived in Italy, decided to take this opportunity to talk about old times. On his arrival back home, Ray had discovered many old photographs, which his mother had conveniently hidden all those years. The two men looked at them with great interest and were soon engrossed with pictures which Philip found intriguing as he realised that this was part of his father's life that he had not known about. He felt some degree of loss as he sifted through the photos laid out before them on the table.

John, Gina and Jay sped down the country lanes which

led to the main square of the village that Jay wanted to visit. Gina admitted she had not really taken much interest in this particular village as it had appeared much too quiet for her. John rounded a corner and was suddenly forced to apply the brakes sharply. In the middle of the lane was a horse and cart, effectively blocking the road and making it impossible to pass.

The man approaching the car was certainly not a local farmer and, when he produced a gun, John's heart sank. Gina and John looked at each other helplessly and wondered what would happen next.

Jay suddenly spoke. 'I think he wants us to get out of the car. Perhaps we should do as he says.'

Al Higgs stood back to allow the three occupants of the car to get out and nodded towards Jay. 'You did well, old man. That was a smart move on your part.'

John looked aghast at Jay. 'What's he talking about, Jay?'

'I'm sorry, John.' Jay looked sheepish. 'I had no choice. They made it very clear that my family in England would suffer if I did not do what they asked. They told me that I would have to spy on you all and then set this up when I had something to tell them.' He went on, 'I'm deeply sorry, but as you know they're not too worried about killing people and things such as my two lovely dogs that I cherished very much.'

John looked at Jay and wondered if he was hearing correctly; after all they had all been taken in by Jay's sudden arrival and welcomed him into the project. They were ushered into a parked car and, with one of the gang driving John's hired car, drove quickly away from the scene. John closed his eyes and suddenly had great fear for Gina whom he was extremely fond of by now.

17

Detective Inspector Davies had finished his breakfast and travelled to the meeting place where he had been asked to meet his American colleagues. He found them very amenable and was soon briefed on their views about Ralph Hess and, surprisingly, Ray Barone. Surely there could not be much wrong with Ray Barone? Davies knew he was a well-known businessman with contacts all over the world but were they now saying he was a shady character?

'Well, Inspector, we know a lot about Ray Barone's company connections in the States and a lot of those individuals are well connected with the American Mafia and, worse still, a lot closer across the border in Scilly,' offered the Americans' leader Ben.

Davies was suddenly concerned. While he knew the Americans would be able to give him some assistance if needed, he felt that he would rather have help from someone with whom he was more familiar. When he returned to the hotel, he called his boss in the UK and asked them to send Jenkins over. At least he might have another slant on things and, anyway, one Limey against four Yanks was not good odds, even though they all appeared to be on the same side.

As Ray and Philip finished their perusal of the many photographs that had been retrieved from Ray's mother's belongings, Ray suddenly received a phone call which made the colour drain from his face. Putting the phone down, he turned to Philip. 'Gina and John have been abducted.'

Philip gasped. 'What's happened, Ray? How do you know?'

'Since John informed us that he thought he was being watched, I've had my men keeping an eye on him from a distance. When they left, I was late informing them that John and Gina were going to Lens. The guys went to the village and expected them to arrive in the square which everyone has to go through to get anywhere. Something or someone must have stopped them from getting there.'

The two men looked at each other and then Philip remarked, 'Where's Jay? I haven't seen him since breakfast.'

They checked with the one of the staff who confirmed that Jay had left with John and Gina.

'I guess they have him as well,' Ray said. 'Well, we'll probably be getting a call soon. It's obviously just a means to get at the dream machine, and we had better prepare for the worst.'

'I think it's better to wait here by the phone,' suggested Ray. 'My men know who they're looking for and they'll continue to keep up the search in the village and the nearby countryside.'

Sitting down, the two men continued to talk about the new dilemma they were now faced with. Philip, as usual, was anxious to be doing things instead of just waiting for the phone call which they both knew would come eventually. It seemed more than likely that the people behind all this obviously wanted the machine rather than just a ransom.

'Ray, I've been thinking about the dream machine. I know I haven't got the expertise of John and Jay but would it be possible to improve the performance of the machine by just adding another crystal? I mean, we all know that crystals are known to interact with each other and I understand that Ralph had more than one crystal at his disposal. What do you think?'

Ray thought for a moment. 'Well, it's certainly worth a try. I must admit I was a bit sceptical about John's idea of going back to a certain day and not knowing for sure which day they could have had their discussion about crystals. It was a bit hit and miss, mostly miss!'

'We'll try it when they get back.' Philip said this almost as if their friends had just popped out to go to the cinema. Ray felt some comfort with these words coming from his half-brother but he would be much happier when he had them all back in the villa.

18

'Glad to see you, Jenkins,' Detective Inspector Davies exclaimed as he met his friend and colleague at the airport.

'Pleased to be here, sir. Couldn't wait to get out of the rain. Seems all the roads are flooded again not to mention the Test Match being called off.'

Davies brought Jenkins up to scratch with the developments, small as they were, and the two men went to the hotel where Davies had booked him in. 'Jenkins, I've met the boys from the CIA. When I say boys, they certainly seem to be very young.'

'Sign of the times, sir.' Jenkins felt rather glad that his boss had never before commented on his own age, as he was several years younger.

Davies made a phone call and arranged to meet the Americans at one of the bars in town. He was not that enthralled with the cold beer that was on offer in Italy but it was certainly better than none at all.

Upon meeting the Americans, Jenkins silently agreed with Davies that perhaps the Yanks were just a little on the young side but that did not deter them from their enthusiasm.

'We understand that some of Ray Barone's men have been asking around the town about a missing woman and two men,' Ben, the leader of the American team, informed them.

'Don't they mean three men?' asked Davies.

'No, two men and a woman. What's more, they've indicated that one of the men is on the old side.'

Davies and Jenkins were puzzled. 'I reckon it may be time to visit Philip and Ray if we can find out the location of the villa where they're staying,' offered Davies.

Ben quickly obliged. 'If you're meaning Ray Barone, we can take you there right away. We've been keeping tabs on old Ray since we received your enquiry a few weeks ago, and anyway we know all about his links with the Mafiosi. We understand he isn't a big wheel in the company but in Italy everyone has dealings with the Mafia as they are called now, if they like it or not.'

Philip and Ray had just finished their lunch on the terrace when in walked Davies, Jenkins and Ben. After introducing Ben to everyone, Davies directed a question at Philip and Ray taking them by surprise. 'I understand you've lost a few of your party, Philip?'

Philip glanced at Ray, for once lost for words. How did Davies know about their missing friends and so soon? He never realised that Davies was playing his usual game of throwing the question in the ring to see what response he could get. He had again struck lucky!

Ray took over. 'It does seem that three of our party, including my sister-in-law have been abducted. By whom we are not sure. How did you find out so soon about this?'

Davies gestured to Ben. 'Our American friends here have been checking out certain individuals and have come up with it. Can you confirm that it is your men that are doing the looking, Ray?'

Ray had no alternative but to nod in agreement.

'How are you getting on with the dream machine, Philip?' Another direct question from Davies.

'Oh, OK.' Philip was vague.

'Can we see it please?'

The two men reluctantly agreed and Ray left to collect the machine from the company's workshops. He returned with a worried look on his face. 'It's not there, it's gone – someone's taken it.'

Philip looked aghast. How could this have happened and who could have taken it? They knew John would certainly not do such a thing. Well, that only left one person: Jay Browning, but why would he remove the machine without permission? After all, he was there as an advisor, not a partner.

Ben spoke up. 'Well, as far as we know your machine has been the centre of attention in many parts of the world and who wouldn't be tempted to steal it?'

Philip shook his head. 'I can't believe Jay would do such a thing. He was one of my father's oldest friends.'

'Well, it can't be helped this time,' Davies interrupted. 'We'll only find out if and when they contact you.'

'We were all banking on that but, now they have the machine, we're not so sure they will even bother,' Jenkins remarked. 'Now they have John as well as the machine, and he knows a lot more about the project than anyone else.'

Philip tried to inject a note of hope into the discussion. 'At our last meeting before everyone took a break, we had all agreed for John to try to transgress back in time to see if he could recall the discussion Hess and he had had about the power of the machine. We've only just concluded that a better way would be to increase the power of the crystals.'

Seeing Ray casting him a furtive glance, Philip realised that he was perhaps divulging too much information and shut up instantly. Ben, seemingly unaware at Philip's apparent change of heart, started making telephone calls to his colleagues in the nearby town.

19

John and Gina were pushed unceremoniously into a small, dark room with a tiny window that had been blacked out. A single bed was in the corner along with a table and two chairs; not much like home, thought John as he gently asked Gina if she was all right. Why he did this he was not sure; he just wanted to show he cared. They had not seen what had happened to Jay; they assumed that his quarters would be a lot more pleasant. They had noticed as they got out of the car that a box was being removed from their hire car. Their hearts sank as they realised that it was most likely that the dream machine was in there. Jay had obviously removed it from the company's testing room and secreted it in John's rental car.

For several hours they heard the muffled sounds of several people coming from the next room, the only break coming when one of the men opened the door of their small room and thrust some juice and fruit on a small tray at them. John and Gina ate the fruit and drank the juice almost in a trance; they knew instinctively that they would be here for a while and it was only a matter of time before John would be hauled in and asked questions about the machine. More time passed and eventually Gina dropped off into an uneasy sleep while John tried to remain awake and alert.

Gina woke up and found to her dismay that John was no longer in the room. Soon she realised that he had been removed for questioning. Her heart sank as she heard raised voices from the next room and she knew that John was not giving out information without some resistance. Minutes went by which turned into hours. The raised voices continued together with the distinct sounds of someone being hit. Gina instinctively knew that it had to be John on the receiving end.

She was just wondering what could possibly be happening when the door opened and John was hurled into the room bleeding profusely from wounds to his face. He had certainly had taken a beating and it was obvious that their captors meant to achieve their aim of understanding the machine and how to operate it. There was a water tap in the corner of the room and Gina managed to bathe John's wounds with cold water and some paper tissues which she had with her. The hours passed and the two prisoners tried to make themselves comfortable on the small bed. They talked earnestly about their predicament but exhaustion soon overcame them and they both fell into an uneasy sleep.

Davies and Jenkins had returned to their hotel with Ben the American who, with his usual self-confidence, assured them that they would indeed find their three missing friends. Davies was just a little more pessimistic as he had not even the remotest idea of where to look. If it had been on his Oxford turf he would have been sending out search teams all over the Oxfordshire countryside but here in Italy he knew he would have to rely heavily on the Americans, Ray Barone and his men.

The two men retired to their rooms after arranging to meet early next morning and travel to the villa to decide what to do next.

Philip and Ray also had a disturbed night with Ray almost constantly on the telephone. Philip had noticed the small handset that Ray kept using and he wondered just how this gadget worked but thought that now was not the time for him to ask questions about it. He, for his part, wanted to get out and look for his friend John and Ray's sister-in-law who, of course, he was also worried about. Either way, enough was enough and he wanted to take out his rising anger on someone. Alice's death was still very much on his mind and he was almost certain that the men responsible for that must be involved with the abduction.

The arrival of daybreak found the party of mixed nationalities in Ray Barone's large kitchen eating croissants and drinking coffee. Ray had some news: his men had heard some rumours from the local underworld. It seemed that the men responsible for the kidnappings were not local in the true sense and had come mostly from the Baltic States with the exception of an Englishman. The others were possibly Russian or East German, but whatever the nationality they were certainly a bad lot. The men's deliberations were interrupted by a phone call from one of Ben's men. A body had been discovered in the local river. They all hastily piled into Ray's car and went to the river where they found several local police and what appeared to be forensic experts all working around the shrouded outline of a body. Ben walked forward, spoke to one of his men and, after a short conversation with one of the police who seemed in charge, beckoned the group to approach.

Ray let Philip move to the front to pull back the white cloth which had been placed over the body. Knowing that Ray was obviously concerned that the body could be that of Gina, after he had looked at the body, Philip gently informed him it was not Gina, but Jay Browning.

Somewhat relieved, Ray stepped forward to take a look. His relief turned to sorrow however as he realised that the men involved in this terrible ordeal were not taking any prisoners. Whatever the men present hoped to do, they had move fast!

20

Gina and John were awoken by the sound of their prison cell door opening and even more juice and fruit was thrust into the room without any comment. Gina looked at John's bruised face in the dim morning light and her fingers stroked the marked area as if by doing this it could possibly heal it.

The two ate the food and drank the juice in an attempt to keep up their strength and flagging spirits. They had just finished when the door opened again and they found themselves gazing at the features of Dieter Geist who, up till now, had not been involved in John's previous interrogation. Dieter approached them with an almost apologetic look about him. He received only cold stares in return.

Dieter went into his usual good-guy approach, talking almost as if he had nothing to do with this disgraceful occurrence. He could have been mistaken for a father confessor such was his manner when he related the previous day's events and beatings.

'Gina, if you don't mind me calling you Gina, you must understand the men in there are no friends of mine and will stop at nothing to get their way.'

'Well, tell us something new,' John interrupted. 'We had already gathered that!'

Dieter went on with news that he knew would shake the two terribly. 'Look, I do have some disturbing news for you.'

'What's that?' replied John. 'Have you lost your comforter?'

Ignoring John's sarcasm, Dieter continued, 'Your friend Jay Browning is dead. Seems he met with an accident.'

'Oh, come on,' John said scathingly. 'You mean your goons killed him.'

Dieter looked at the two blankly and shrugged as if he had

no interest in the death, but he knew the way the company worked and showing they meant business was certainly a firm warning to anyone who tried to stand up to them. As he left the room he knew he had little control of events now and he feared for the two young persons' lives.

John and Gina remained silent for several minutes trying to absorb the terrible news. They knew that Jay had betrayed them but he certainly did not have to pay with his life.

John said a silent prayer and remembered that he had wondered whether Jay had had ideas about taking over the dream machine project himself. He hugged Gina as if to say not to worry but deep down he knew he had to play for time, and with that approach would only come more pain. He could only hope that Gina would not be pulled into that part of the proceedings.

Ben Andrews arranged for the local police to take away Jay's body. After a short visit to the morgue for a brief appraisal on how he died, the body would be flown back to the UK immediately for a full autopsy. The fact that Jay had received a bullet in the back of his head was without doubt the cause of his death. The discovery of his body in the river had no bearing on the death; it was just the usual way the company disposed of their victims. Together with the disappearance of the machine, it was not long before Davies and Ben Andrews came up with the possibility of Jay's involvement with John and Gina's disappearance. Piecing together the fact that Jay left without a word and that the machine had gone missing at the same time, they could only conclude that Jay had taken it. He may have been forced to do this, but perhaps promises of a large cash payout had persuaded him to do what he had done. Either way, he had met an untimely death which sometimes occurs when people betray their friends.

The two prisoners were suddenly surprised to see Dieter Geist come into the room again and when he invited them to spend some time outside in the sunshine they accepted without any hesitation. Dieter led them up a hill which overlooked the farmhouse where they were being kept. It was a small hill but, as they approached the top, the two could see that there was a steep drop just a few feet from the edge. No way out there, thought John as he observed the surroundings. Looking back at the house, he could see a man with a rifle slung over his shoulder standing outside. John knew the rifle could come off in second should they try to attack Dieter and run for it.

'Where are your friends, Dieter?' said John with a hint of scorn in his voice.

'Gone to town for some refreshments,' Dieter calmly replied, 'and to take advice about you two; whether to kill you now or take you to Moscow.'

'Sorry I asked. Say we're not willing to go?' John did not believe for one minute that their refusal would make any difference, but he desperately wanted to gain some time and try to come up with a plan for a possible escape.

What happened next came as a complete surprise to the two captives: Dieter had been looking over their shoulder as if to keep an eye on the guard below. Suddenly, he lunged forward, pushed Gina and sent her hurtling over the edge.

John rushed to the edge and looked over. 'Why did you do that?' he shouted, distraught and angry.

'You wanted her to live, didn't you?' Dieter calmly replied. 'Please do not try anything else as you might well be shot.'

John looked on helplessly as the guard, suddenly disturbed by the shouting, came running up the hill, his rifle now off his shoulder and ready for action.

Dieter suddenly grabbed John and wrestled him down to the ground, whispering as he did so, 'Don't worry about your girlfriend. The drop is not as bad as it looks. It's quite short and she should be alright once she hits the bracken. We have to make it look like it was her idea or we'll all be in big trouble.'

The guard arrived on the scene and looked over the edge. Seeing nothing, he turned his attention to John and, without any hesitation, smashed his rifle butt over John's head. John's sense of relief for Gina was cut short as he fell into the darkness of unconsciousness.

Dieter helped the guard to drag John's now motionless body down to the house where they threw him back into the room he had previously shared with Gina. Giving a few choice swear words in German which the guard took as anger, secretly Dieter was pleased that his ruse had apparently been successful. He had no stomach for any killings and he certainly did not want to be involved in the killing of a woman. He was after all a scientist, and already regretted the killing of Jay Browning. It had been carried out suddenly and without any warning.

21

Gina's fall into space had left her speechless and petrified, such was the suddenness of Dieter Geist's actions. She found herself falling without any idea of how far she would drop; fortunately it was not too far. The fall nevertheless knocked the breath out of her body and she remained motionless for several minutes. This in turn proved fortuitous as it hid her from the guard as he cautiously peered over the edge. Gina lay still almost not daring to breathe and after a few moments, realising there was little she could do to help John, she crawled away on all fours. She had to get help and find a phone box so that she could call home.

Ray and Rena were now almost out of their minds with worry. Gina had never been one to stay away from home for long. They knew that John would do his best to protect her but the men responsible for all this had already shown no remorse when dealing with any of their captives, let alone so-called friends such as Jay Browning.

Ray was pacing up and down when suddenly his mobile phone went off, and he wondered if Gina had been forced to give out his private number. If this was so, at least they would have some contact at last. He gave out a loud shout of relief when he realised that the person on the end of the phone call was Gina. After listening to a rather garbled account, he exclaimed, 'Gina has escaped!'

Great whoops of joy echoed around the Barone household when the news came out, and soon Ray, Rena and Philip were rushing to collect her from the town square where she was now calling from. Hugging her sister, Gina explained how she had escaped and the part that Dieter Geist had played in it.

The two men were pleased to hear that perhaps they had a friend in the camp. They now hoped that, with Gina's help, they could put in a rescue bid for John as it was obvious that the farm that the two had been held at was not that far away. Ray called Davies and Ben. Surely now they could now rescue John and retrieve the missing dream machine.

Gina was able to fill in most of the gaps of what had happened while she was being held captive with John. Apparently, the last thoughts they had had about how best to improve the dream machine had been passed by Jay to their captors and it had been that which had led their captors to seek further information from John. This had delayed the actual movement of the John and the machine to Russia. Whether Gina would have been taken along as well was anybody's guess. Everyone silently concluded it would have been most unlikely.

Gina went on to relate how John had refused to cooperate with the men and had been given a severe beating. Philip silently wished he would be able to return the compliment in the near future. These men had made it very personal and now, with the safe return of Gina, the two brothers were hell-bent on getting their own back on the men who had carried out the abduction.

Along with the local police, a helicopter was dispatched together with specially trained assault police. After a few hours however, a call to Ray from Ben revealed unfortunately that the farm was now empty with the exception of the lifeless form of Dieter Geist. Where was John Jefferson now; how long would his being kept alive be of benefit to the men who desperately wanted the dream machine in its completed form?

'This dream machine is turning into a nightmare!' exclaimed Philip when he heard that the men holding John had disappeared from the farm. 'We've now had three people murdered because of it, including Alice, and now this Dieter person has paid with his life in order that Gina might go free. Of course we're indebted to him, but maybe it was him who fired the shot that killed Alice.'

Seeing his brother was deeply upset, Ray interrupted, 'I guess we'll have to give him the benefit of the doubt on that. It doesn't sound like that he was a person who wished to hurt people and, as we understand it, he was a scientist.'

Philip nodded as if agreeing reluctantly, but added, 'The

problem is that, as it now stands, we have lost the dream machine and are now worse off than when we started the project all those months ago.'

'I cannot understand why Mr Geist was killed,' Gina who had been listening to the two men interjected. 'After all, he arranged my escape very carefully and it seems he waited until the guard was looking the other way before he pushed me off the ridge.'

Ray looked at her. 'The problem is that these men do not tolerate failure in any way and the blame was with him as he was the one that took you both out of the cellar and away from the guard's control.'

The party was sitting down having coffee when they had a telephone call from Ben who had some interesting news.

'Ray, can you come down to the mail sorting office. It seems you have a suspicious package here.' The local police had been intercepting all the mail which was destined for the villa.

When they arrived at the village square, they found a package had been set down in the middle of the car park with protective screens placed on all four sides.

'We are thinking of a controlled explosion,' remarked Ben who by now had been joined by Davies and Jenkins.

Davies and Jenkins looked at the package. 'No, don't do that,' said Inspector Davies, 'we have a feeling about this. It might not be as sinister as it seems. For one thing, we saw a similar-sized package just a few weeks ago.'

Philip gasped. 'Are you thinking what I'm thinking?'

Davies nodded. 'Yes, we've all been wondering why Dieter Geist was killed. Perhaps he had actually done one thing more before he released Gina.'

'Are you suggesting he's returned the dream machine to us?' Ben interrupted.

Davies and Philip nodded in agreement.

'Well, who's going to take a closer look so we can find out exactly what it is? Has anyone got any bomb disposal experience?' asked Ray.

Ben nodded to one of his men Niles Haines. 'Niles has. We had him trained for the last war and he did manage to disarm several bombs without blowing himself up!'

Niles stepped forward and approached the package. 'Has anyone got a doctor's stethoscope?' he asked. Minutes went by while someone was dispatched to the local clinic to obtain the required instrument. He came back with one, complete with a doctor. Everyone seemed to think that was a good idea but no one uttered their thoughts openly. They also were thinking of an ambulance, and as if by magic an ambulance appeared and parked at a respectable distance from the package.

It seemed that someone had serious doubts about the innocence of the package. Anyway, the decision had been made and poor Niles, complete with his newly acquired listening scope, approached the package and knelt down before it. Minutes went by with the party holding their breath. The silence was suddenly broken by the sound of a car backfiring. Everyone present jumped and threw themselves to the ground except for Niles who stayed put, calmly listening with the scope.

He finally sat back and said, 'It's OK. This is definitely not a bomb.'

Almost everybody grinned with relief but Ben shouted out, 'Niles, would you mind tearing off the outside packing please?' He turned to the rest of the party and almost apologetically went on, 'Well, he did say it was alright and surely it must be OK for him to do that.'

Davies laughed nervously. 'Talk about asking the man to put his money where his mouth is.'

The party waited until the box was completely unwrapped and Philip gasped his pleasure when he saw the familiar outline of the dream machine. 'Now we do know why Dieter was killed. Not just because Gina escaped; he must have mailed the package when the men left him alone with the machine.'

The men looked at each other, glad that Gina was not present.

Ray spoke quietly. 'What are the odds that John will be of any use to them now?' The others nodded in silence.

The party retired to the villa and extra guards were posted around the area to ensure that the dream machine remained in its rightful place. Gina did not say much about the return of the machine but it was obvious that the precarious position that John was now in was not lost on her. Ray and Ben talked earnestly and both agreed they would get their men to redouble their efforts in trying to find John. Ray secretly wondered to himself that they might find they were too late. He put this thought to the back of his mind though and did his best to encourage Gina to look on the bright side even though he knew that this would be extremely hard.

Philip, anxious to take everyone's mind off the failure to find John, suggested to Ray that it might be possible for his scientific bods to start work on adding an extra crystal. Ray readily agreed but felt it might have been better if they had had more of the original crystals that Ralph Hess had. Philip proposed they look in John's room. Maybe, for once, the gods would be smiling on them. The gods were not; that would have been too easy.

Everyone returned to the terrace to muse over the next step.

'Well, we do have several crystals in our organisation,' went on Ray realising that somehow they had to keep their hopes up or they would all lose the little enthusiasm that they still had.

The machine was given to Chris, the company chief scientist, complete with two guards and Ray keeping a strict eye on everyone. He knew there were many local villains who would love to earn a few thousand lire by stealing the machine.

The men were eating lunch which had now become a working lunch with all the interested parties attending. They could all be forgiven for feeling a little guilty about enjoying such great food and drink. Poor John: was he still alive to enjoy anything now? Who would protect him now Dieter Geist had been silenced?

22

The next day another letter was delivered by the police who were still vetting their post. It was short and sweet. The company were offering to exchange John for the return of the dream machine. Everyone had just one thought: they must maintain contact so that they could arrange for John's safe return. It was good to learn that at least John still seemed to be alive.

They were asked to respond by telephone at a number, which was obviously a payphone and at a specified time. The group chose Davies as the contact from their side. As they appeared to be dealing with Russians, it was felt that Davies might just be more acceptable to them than the Americans. Philip and Ray had no problems with Ben and his men as they had been in frequent contact with them and liked their 'can-do' attitude.

Either way, Davies would make the call which he duly did, only to be asked to call another number and then another. This of course made the tracing of the number almost impossible. The final request was quite startling: the party was asked to take the machine way up country – to the Lake District – Lake Garda to be precise, a beautiful area with, of course, a lot of cover for any person or persons wishing to conceal themselves. Davies and Philip were selected to make the trip north with Ben and Ray. Jenkins would remain at the villa.

Outwardly, Ray appeared to accept the news that John was still alive although he harboured grave doubts. It was more than likely that all they would receive was a bullet in return for the machine.

'I have given instructions to my staff for a duplicate machine to be made up; fake, of course,' he explained.

'Good idea,' replied Philip. 'I was thinking along the same lines myself. How long will it take to make?'

'Just a few hours.'

The duplicate machine completed and with everyone allotted their tasks, the group set out for Northern Italy and the lakes. Normally the drive up would have been extremely pleasant but the group now had real concerns about John and how they could actually arrange for his safe return.

With their own group depleted due to the disposal of Dieter Geist, it was not long before Al Higgs made an urgent phone call to England and informed his brother Joe to get on the next plane over so that they would have enough men to successfully deal with the group coming up to the Lakes.

He knew that, whatever happened, the group would not be arriving short-handed. He suspected that Ray Barone would have many men in the area and he knew that some of the men he faced were not going to speak much; they were more likely to shoot first and ask questions after. He had a quiet respect for Ray Barone and wished quietly that he had him on his side. He had been in Italy long enough to know just who ran what and where. His contact with the mob or company as they were now called had been solely for his own interests. He knew that his superiors in Moscow would not tolerate failure and he would have to ensure that he ended up securing the machine again. The disposal of Dieter Geist had not gone down too well and the company now wanted just one thing: for the machine to be sent to them straightaway and in good working order. It was something he should have done when they first obtained the machine. Another black mark had been placed against his name.

While they waited for the arrival of his brother Joe, Al flew up to Lake Garda and set his men in strategic positions around the towns which he knew the Barone party would have to travel through. If the time was right in any of these towns, he would launch an attack on the men carrying the machine.

Joe arrived next day. 'Now we'll give those English bastards a good pasting,' were his first words.

Ray, Philip, Davies and Ben arrived in the small village of Torbole which was situated close to the Lakes. They expected a message on their arrival as instructed via the last communication they had received as they travelled north. However, there was nothing.

Ray sent some of his men to the northern end of the Lakes which, although this meant the depletion in total numbers, also meant they would be in position should events move even further north. The next step must come from the gang but they also wanted to try to ensure that it did not develop into a full-blown shooting war where innocent passers-by could be hurt, something they all wished to avoid if possible.

Ray and Philip could only hope that John would survive

their rescue attempt, and he knew someone at home was equally anxious for his safe return. God, when he had made up his mind to look up his long-lost half-brother he had no idea he would be drawn into such adventure and danger. He smiled to himself as he glanced at his brother's stern face and was again comforted having Philip with him at his side. He just hoped that the outcome would be good and everyone would come out of it safe and sound.

23

John Jefferson awoke with a bad headache. It would appear that the last drink the gang had given him had been heavily drugged. Although he could hear some people speaking in a foreign tongue, he kept his eyes closed to give himself time to try to ease the pain, but looked gingerly through the slits in his eyes to see where he actually was.

Moving his head slowly around, he opened his eyes fully and saw a coffin standing upright against a wall. As he looked further he could see many others. He was obviously in some undertakers' premises; and most likely he had been transported in one of the coffins to wherever he was. He gave silent thanks that, if his suspicions were correct, the drug he had been administered had been strong enough to knock him out for the whole journey. Being in a coffin would have caused him much terror, such was his phobia of confined spaces.

Glancing around, he could see three men in the room, smoking and drinking beer. There was also evidence of leftover food which looked like the remains of pizza. He realised that he had not eaten anything for at least twenty-four hours and secretly hoped that his captors might be aware of this fact. No way would he stoop to ask them for any; his pride was too deep for that. Damn Ruskies; he hoped that soon some of his own countrymen would arrive, storm the room, wherever it was, and free him. He realised that he was feeling faint from the lack of food which was obviously causing his hallucinations about the Special Forces coming to his aid.

His mind fell back to Philip and Ray. He knew that they would surely be a more likely bet if he was to be rescued. He wondered what had happened with Dieter. He remembered they had apparently pulled off Gina's 'escape' – or had they? He realised he did not even know if she had escaped, but surely she would be with him now if she had not. His mind swirled with every thought and he slipped into an uneasy sleep, only to be awoken by a slap to the face and a cup of hot coffee thrust into his hands. Almost dropping the container, he was silently pleased to see a roughly cut sandwich on the table close by.

He sat up, sipped the coffee and eagerly ate the cheese sandwich. It just might be his last meal but, either way, he welcomed the morsel of food. He lay back, not attempting to move any further, and tried to make sense of the few words that came from the other side of the room. He knew it was a mixture of German and Russian, of that he was sure. Suddenly he realised that the men were talking about the dream machine. If he understood correctly, it seemed that they had lost the machine. He heard the name Dieter Geist – surely Dieter had not stolen the machine?

Lost in his thoughts, it was a moment or two before John realised that the men had stopped talking and were looking in his direction. He was alarmed when two of them approached him and, pulling his arms behind his back, roughly tied his hands together extremely tightly. The next thing he felt was a needle going into his arm from behind and he plunged into unconsciousness.

At the hotel, Philip and Ray talked earnestly with Davies and Ben. They knew they had to have a plan which was foolproof. Most likely they would have only one chance to effect John's rescue; that is, of course, if he was in the company of their adversaries. Ray Barone had briefed his men to work closely with the Americans and they had all taken the time to get to know those assigned to the dangerous mission of retrieving John alive and well. Philip, for his part, was anxious to get going and, together with Davies, had armed himself with an automatic weapon. Ray and Ben were also armed and it was decided to split into two with Philip and Davies taking the lead. Each team would take it in turns to take sleep breaks.

The call came suddenly at 2 a.m. The caller gave instructions in a clear English voice; with no effort taken to disguise his voice whoever he was, he seemed to have no fear of any repercussions that may follow.

'Well, the buggers show no worry about being discovered,' Davies remarked. 'I reckon they have one thing on their minds and that is to take no prisoners.'

The instructions were for two of them to take the dream machine to the edge of the lake which was approximately ten minutes' drive from the hotel. They had already taken a look around the area and knew there was hardly any cover at all there.

The two men set off with the fake machine conveniently placed in the hat box that John had brought with him when he returned from London. As they stood by the lakeside waiting, they looked around trying to take in every movement which arose through the gloom of the night air. The half moon made everything seem that much more eerie, and the two men kept a hold of their guns in their pockets.

A swirl of blades awakened their senses to the arrival of a helicopter. Davies groaned inwardly. That was bad news: the arrival of the machine would make the logistics of pursuit almost impossible. Two men were in the helicopter.

'Refuse to get in,' shouted Davies to Philip.

'Don't worry, I wasn't going to,' replied Philip.

Davies approached the now grounded machine and announced clearly that they would not be getting into the helicopter now or later without first seeing that John was alive and well.

The two men exchanged a few words with each other and then the helicopter lifted up and disappeared over the roof of the nearby hotel and out of sight. Davies and Philips looked at each other. They knew they had done the right thing by not getting into the helicopter but now the two men were leaving without even leaving further instructions.

'Strange, what do you think about that, Ray?' Philip asked, speaking into one of Ray's new mobile phones which they had all been issued with.

'I guess they were just checking us out and looking over the area,' Ray replied. 'It was just as well we all kept out of the way. We'll now have to wait for their next move. They must have some plan. They wouldn't have made us come all the way up here for nothing.'

They all returned to the hotel via different routes to try to ensure that their movements were not being observed. With one of the party keeping watch, the other three retired to their beds to get whatever rest they could. Sleep was almost impossible, such was the adrenalin that was being pumped through their veins.

24

John was now fully awake. He had woken yet again to a headache, feeling as though he had drunk copious glasses of vino which of course he had not. Chance would have been a fine thing, and again his thoughts drifted to Gina and he wondered where and how she was after her fall. He could only hope that she had made good her escape.

He was soon brought back to reality when he was roughly shaken and a hot cup of coffee and cheese sandwich was put into his hands. John wondered if his captors had any other food on the premises but he ate hungrily and drank his coffee. If the coffee had been drugged, John could not have cared less, such was his present physical state.

He was surprised to find that he was still in the same room and wondered how his friends were and where they were. He realised that being kept alive was a good sign and that his captors wanted one thing: the return of the dream machine.

He was obviously going to be the main bargaining tool. He resolved to keep his eyes and ears open and to use all his senses to find out anything about what was happening. However, his efforts were soon cut short as he drifted into a deep sleep which came suddenly and without warning. His fears about the coffee being drugged turned out to be well founded.

The next morning, Philip, Ray, Davies and Ben met over breakfast and discussed what they thought the kidnappers' next move would be.

'I guess we can only wait,' remarked Philip. Waiting, of course, was not one of his best attributes.

The other men nodded without comment knowing it was the one and only option.

'The fact they had a helicopter must mean they're familiar with this area,' Davies suggested, 'and, while there are many places helicopters can land, isn't it possible that they're holed up in or on a disused airfield?'

Ray's face lit up. 'You know, I do believe you're right. I'll see if my men can find out anything.'

'Anything is better than sitting here twiddling our thumbs.' Davies perked up.

A short time later, Ray returned with some good news. 'My men have located a disused airfield some twenty-five miles from here and they're checking it out.'

The minutes passed, turning into hours, and the four men in the room became very restless.

'Can't you call your men and see what's happening?' Philip asked Ray.

Ray gave Philip a stern look. 'And ruin any surprise that they might be setting up? These phones do make quite a noise, you know!'

Philip's face reddened at his half-brother's remarks. His face brightened however when the Ray's phone rang and he took a message. He turned to the group who were eagerly waiting for some news. The men had found the airfield and had returned gunfire with others at the field, killing two of them. Unfortunately the helicopter had taken off at the first sign of their arrival and seemed to go north. There was no sign of John.

'Is it possible that your men up north can spot the helicopter?' Davies asked Ray.

'We can do better than that. We have sensors that can pick up any flights of aeroplanes for fifty miles, something that you Brits invented a few years ago.'

Thank God for radar, thought Davies and Ben almost simultaneously.

The four men, realising that they had not eaten for some hours, returned to the hotel, collecting some bread and cheese to keep them going for the next few hours.

'I hope John's still coping with all this,' remarked Philip and crunched his way through his crusty roll.

25

Jenkins was being kept up to date by Davies and he knew that his part of the action was not going to be that eventful. He had with him one of the new mobile phones that Ray had given him and he felt quite important being able to make his phone calls without any assistance from the hotel receptionist. He was having lunch the next day when he heard an unfamiliar sound and, looking up, saw a helicopter coming in low over the hotel and disappearing behind the group of trees which lay next to the hotel.

He suddenly realised that perhaps this might be of some importance to the group and hurriedly called Ray on the phone. 'Ray, I am not sure if this is the same helicopter but, as we know there aren't many in use at this time, could it be the same one?'

'Did you see any markings at all?'

'No, they'd totally blacked out any markings as if they didn't want to be recognised.'

'That has got to be the same craft, Ray,' Davies intervened. 'The buggers have slipped back and they maybe want to outflank us. Could they be after the real machine or, worse still, be trying to take over your villa?'

Ray looked serious. 'If that's true, we can handle it, but if

91

we deploy half our men back to the villa we could be found wanting up here.'

'These men aren't amateurs. They're as slippery as a bunch of eels,' said Davies.

Not knowing exactly what Davies meant, Ben nodded and went on, 'Ray, we can't take the chance. Some of us will have to return and check this out. If they do attack the villa, you have your family there and, of course, the real machine.'

Ray nodded. 'I guess you're right. We'll arrange our own aircraft and fly south to be on hand. I'll ask some friends of mine to cover our absence until we return. Philip, you had better come with me. Ben and his men can stay here to see if they are double bluffing us.'

Ben agreed reluctantly although he had a sneaky feeling the action was about to switch to the south and he, for one, did not want to miss out on anything. This was the best adventure he and his men had experienced since the war. Whether poor John would agree with him was another matter.

Ray quickly arranged for a light aircraft and the three men left to drive the short distance to board the plane. The fact that Ray's men had not discovered any flights going south was a good sign but, as they all knew, the helicopter could easily have been flying low to avoid any radar which might have been set up.

Ray, Philip and Davies were soon back at the villa and set about reviewing the villas security, making it as safe as they possibly could, considering the size of the vineyards which surrounded it. An army of men could hide in the numerous vines which spread for as many kilometres as one could see.

It was around four o'clock that Ray received a phone call on one of his own phones from a man who spoke perfect English and who calmly announced that they had added Ben and three of his men to the number of people who were now their guests. God, Ray gasped, how the heck did Ben and his men get caught napping that quickly?

The tables had turned yet again, and the numbers game had swung back to the Russians who now held more cards. Worse still, the group still did not know the whereabouts of John. How could Ben have been so lax? They were all being completely outfoxed by people who seemed to second-guess all their movements, almost as if they were in the room at the same time.

The two Higgs brothers lounged back in their easy chairs and puffed on two large Havana Cigars. Joe puffed some smoke at Ben. 'I'd offer you one, Bengie boy, but I guess you're a bit tied up now.'

The two men laughed loudly, flicking their ash towards Ben's face. Together with his three men, his mouth had been roughly taped over and his arms tightly bound. It had been all to easy with Ben who, after convincing himself that the action had moved south, had allowed himself and his men the first decent meal for a long time. Unfortunately, as two of the men had gone to the toilet, the waiting brothers had knocked them unconscious.

The first Ben had any idea that anything was wrong was when Al Higgs appeared at his dinner table with a napkin covering his gun. By then it was too late. A Hollywood movie would have been more dramatic than poor Ben and his men's quick capture.

Ben seethed through his taped mouth. How could he have been so dumb; how the heck could he have been so lax? It was his own fault for being so convinced that the sighting of the helicopter by Jenkins had meant that they would be missing out on the 'fun'. Now, of course, they were all sitting there with egg on their faces. What would all the other men in the American Intelligence think? It did not dare thinking about.

Al and his brother felt very smug indeed. It had been Al's idea to give the impression of the switch of operations back to the south and it looked like the Courtneys had fallen for it hook, line and sinker; that was a good old Limey saying. He now held a good hand and he knew it.

He whispered instructions to two of his men and Ben was alarmed when one of his own men was taken from the room. His moans and groans through his taped mouth did not have any effect on his captors and he feared the worse for his colleague.

Ray and the group had been talking about their next move when a package arrived via the police. They feared the worst as they could see blood on the bottom of the box. Opening it confirmed their fears when the box revealed two bloody fingers of a hand which could come only from one of the Americans. A ring was still on one of the two fingers. The note in the box was quite explicit: the captors would work their way through the parts of one of the captors every day if the dream machine was not returned to them! They had many days' 'spare parts' to work with was the final remark at the bottom of the page.

Ray groaned to himself. This was not good; they had to do something but what on earth could they do without more knowledge of where the kidnappers were.

Many questions and no answers. Everything seemed to favour the Russians and they were obviously getting more short-tempered with every day that passed. Fortunately the next few days did not see any more packages with severed fingers in them, but the point had been made.

Ben knew that the Higgs brothers were not messing around

and the return of his man complete with a roughly dressed hand which, somehow had stopped bleeding, was a sign for the worst. He knew he had to do something but what, for goodness sake. The only time he was allowed to walk about was when he and his men were able to use the toilet facility and that was not often. Looking about him, Ben could see a small window which might be large enough for a man to crawl through. Their captors had got into a routine of leaving just one man to guard them when they went about their daily chores – whatever they were. A lot of time seemed to be spent sitting around playing cards and drinking. They were obviously waiting for something to happen. Ben took the building they were in to be a farmhouse. There were a lot about that region where Ben had been many times. He recognised the rustic scenery when he had managed to glance out through the open door on the occasions one of his captors entered to give them their once-a-day coffee and cheese sandwich. He, like John, came to realise when that would be and what the next meal would consist of.

Ben and one of his men managed to communicate making a plan that he thought might just work. Well, it worked in an old George Raft movie he had seen many years before.

26

Philip and Davies felt completely helpless; they did not know where to start. Ray's men were out searching the countryside and they just had to wait until their intelligence improved and they had a lead they could work on.

'This is daft,' remarked Davies. 'The gang seem to know

exactly where we are and what we're doing and, what's worse, they seem to know the countryside much better than we do.'

'They might have the upper hand now but that won't last for long,' Ray growled.

The two other men could only nod their approval, but without much conviction. Ray had better prove his words soon or they might well be receiving yet another bloody package. That was one thing none of the men wanted to experience.

Ben was dozing when two of his captors came in and removed two of his men. He was not sure whether the intention was to keep them separated or, even more sinisterly, to send a further message to Ben's friends down south. His frustration grew as he realised that there was very little he could do. However, he decided to go ahead with his 'George Raft' plan of escape; anything was better than just sitting there waiting for their captors to dream up some nasty end. He signalled to Dick, the poor unfortunate colleague who had lost his fingers that he wanted to put his escape plan into place. The plan was simple enough: when Ben was allowed his latrine break, Dick would pretend to faint due to loss of blood, etc.. Heaven knows how Dick had managed all this time to put up with the pain. Ben made a mental note to make sure that Dick received an award from the department when or if they got out of this mess. Ben was still smarting with embarrassment at just how easily they got caught.

The time came for Ben's break and, as he rose up from his chair, Dick with a loud gasp sank to the floor. The guard immediately crossed the floor and peered down at Dick with apparent concern.

Ben pounced on him from the side and brought him to the ground. Dick righted himself and, breaking from his bonds, let out a small cry, 'He's got one of Ray's mobile phones on him.

We can call Ray and tell him where we are!'

'That's just it though,' replied Ben. 'We don't know where we are; just somewhere in Tuscany!'

'If you look on that pizza menu where they got their pizzas from,' Dick continued excitedly, 'there might be a phone number or even an address of the town.'

Ben, with bated breath, did just that and, sure enough, there was not only the phone number but also the town where the pizza takeaway operated from.

Eagerly, Ben picked up the dazed guard's phone and dialled directly to Ray who just could not believe their good fortune.

Ben excitedly outlined to Ray just where they thought they were located adding the name and address shown on the pizza box. Ray confirmed that they would be able to trace them via the shop by asking the local police for its location. If they moved quickly, they could be there within hours.

'Just keep them there. Give us time to get there,' Ray ordered.

Ben laughed for the first time in days. 'Of course, Ray, we have just the one gun and they have many, but we'll do what we can.'

After tying the guard up and collecting his gun, Ben and Dick moved cautiously towards the door. 'We have to move fast, Dick, and buy ourselves some time until the others get here.'

'Right behind you, Ben.'

Opening the door, Ben's face fell when he was met by the smiles of Al and Joe Higgs. 'Going somewhere, Mr Ben? Not getting fed up with our company, are you? We'd like you to stay a bit longer and be fully rested when you meet all your friends that you have very kindly asked to join us.'

Ben's face screwed up in fury. Stepping backwards, he turned and one of his last moments of consciousness was when he felt Dick's gun as it caught him a glancing blow on the side of his head, sending him reeling to the floor. As Ben slipped into unconsciousness, he realised that he had been betrayed by one of his own men.

Dick had stepped aside, letting his former boss fall to the ground.

Al Higgs snatched at Dick's 'injured' hand. 'Well done, comrade, couldn't have handled it better myself.'

Dick smiled and finished removing the bandages from his now miraculously healed hand. 'Won't be needing these again.' He laughed.

'No,' added Joe Higgs, 'we always have plenty of spare fingers to go around.'

The three men laughed heartily as Dick tied up his former boss and, releasing the other guard, left the room in darkness.

Ray and Philip were in good spirits as they started plotting their route back up to Tuscany, which they now knew was their target area for the possible rescue of John, Ben and his men. Collecting the maps, they made their way to the car.

Suddenly Philip paused and shook his head. 'Something's not right, Ray. It's all too easy.'

Ray stopped in his tracks. 'What do you mean?'

'Well, heavily guarded Ben is allowed to overpower his guard, and then luckily the guard has one of your phones on him at the time? Come on, it stinks! They're up to their tricks again and what would be better than if we conveniently all troop up to their hideout and present ourselves for capture with everyone else?'

Davies had been listening. 'I'm inclined to agree with you, Philip. After thinking this through, it does seem very strange that they always know where we are and what we intend to do, almost as though they have a spy in the camp, and I do mean our camp.'

By now everyone seemed to have doubts about the strange phone call which Ray had received.

Jenkins came up with yet another observation: 'Well, you know those fingers that we got in the post. I just heard from the local police surgeon that, in his opinion, they were not a few days old but several weeks! The blood was not fresh.'

'So he's saying that the whole finger lark is a scam?' asked Philip.

'Yes, most likely, which would explain why we didn't have any more fingers in the post. They were only trying to scare us – and it almost worked.'

'Well, we'll never know until we get Ben and John back, will we,' Ray went on. 'We can't do anything in case the phone call was for real. We have to make some effort but at least, if the call was meant to trap us, the location must be correct or they wouldn't be in a position to take us when we turn up.'

Ray phoned his men in the north. It was decided that some of them would search the immediate area for John who would seem to have been secreted in a totally different hideaway to Ben. He must be in a place that was quiet and off the main roads. The searches from the air already carried out by Ray's men had been quite intense.

Philip was still pondering. 'We know they must be receiving some help from someone who knows exactly what we're doing or intending to do. John has been gone almost two weeks now and we're none the wiser where he is and even if he is actually still alive.'

Ray, sensing Philip's frustration, tried to sound positive but deep down he was uneasy as his brother. 'What do you think, Inspector Davies?'

By using Inspector Davies's title for the first time, it was almost as if everyone was trying to act as professionally as they could.

Davies let the sudden title thing go over his head. He also felt that things had got out of hand and, with the enemy seemingly calling all the shots and with such ease, he was not a happy detective. 'I'm of the opinion someone has to remain here in case the plan is still to take the dream machine by force. After all, that's what they really want, not us.'

Ray nodded in agreement. 'We seem to have reached a crossroads and, in this kind of situation, I believe it's better to stay put until we have something better to go on.'

The rest appeared to agree without further comment.

Ray and the group were still at the villa when Chris, who had worked on the first mobile phones, suddenly came in from the workshop with an idea that interested Ray. 'We haven't got many phone masts in Italy and sometimes we have trouble making a sound contact, but it might just be possible to pinpoint some of the calls which we've recently received. We know that the last one came from the Tuscany region and we also know they have at least two of our phones which they must have taken when they took the four Americans. It's possible that if they've made any calls from where John is being kept we might be able to trace them.'

Ray looked intense. 'It's a bit of a long shot as we can't be sure exactly within twenty miles where the calls come from, but it certainly worth a try – we'll get the men to check them out. Go to it.'

Several hours later Chris returned smiling. It seemed that, while he was not able to pinpoint exactly where the phone calls had been emanating from, there did appear to be a cluster that had come from the area they had just left, near the village of Torbole.

Ray contacted his men, instructing them to give the area in and around Torbole some extra attention. It could well be that the gang had regrouped in that area when Ray and the others returned to the villa. Ray, in the meantime, found that the length of time which was elapsing was not going down too well with his daughter Gina who had been in an almost hysterical state since her escape. He gave her as much assurance as he could be but deep down he knew that it would be some time yet before they were likely to rescue John – if at all.

27

Al Higgs and his brother Joe were very pleased with themselves having tricked Ben into telling Ray and the others where they were held, and with it, seemingly, an open invitation to rescue them. They were quietly confident that their ruse would succeed. After all, so far they had captured John and Gina, admittedly losing Gina but that problem had been dealt with by taking the life of Dieter Geist. Al knew his superiors had not been too happy with that part because they had hoped for some technical assistance from Dieter once they had the dream machine. Anyway, what's done is done; now they were up to date with things, they seemed to be reasonably happy with how events were shaping up. He knew, however, that they did not have unlimited patience and pondered his next move with some relish.

Ben, meanwhile, was in a state of shock. The world as he knew it was tumbling down around his ears. Worse still, he now found he had a Russian sleeper in his midst who had been supplying information of their whereabouts to the enemy every step of the way. Besides that, his head hurt, not to mention his pride. He just felt he wanted to get hold of his treacherous former colleague and give him a sound bashing. Goodness knows how many secrets he had given away over those years and how many agents he had betrayed.

Ben made a promise to himself that, if he ever had the chance, he would certainly give Dick his comeuppance. In the meantime, he was the one shackled to a chair and he was the one staring into the dimly lit room and feeling just a bit sorry for himself. He also did not know what had happened to his two other men who had been removed before he had tried his ill-fated escape. What an earth could he say to his fellow agents and, more to the point, all the guys back at the villa?

Davies and Jenkins were busy collating the information, which was being sent back to the villa. It was a strange job to do. It was not information where the Russians were, but more where they were not. It was early the next morning when word came through of a 'suspected' find.

Ray had given all his men strict instructions that should anything suspicious be detected they should call in and then stake out the area. It was around four in the morning when he came into Philip's room. 'Come on, chum, looks like we have a "possible". It's about thirty miles from Torbole and definitely a maybe.'

'Your men must be exhausted by now,' remarked Philip. 'They haven't had much rest, have they?'

'And they won't until we find John.' This was a side of Ray that Philip had not really seen before. Most likely it came from his past association with the Sicilian Mafia, something that

Philip chose not to think about or even consider. The thought of Ray being a Mafioso was definitely against all the breeding of the Courtney clan. They all had to be the number one and not be beholden to anyone. For once in his life, Philip could not change this particular set-up and perhaps, deep down, he did not want to. He had found a brother he never knew he had and now he was in a full-blown adventure with him which, although he was worried about John, he was quite enjoying. It was a bit like one of the detective stories he used to read about in his Oxford days: the Adventures of Bull Dog Drummond.

In the midst of all this, Ray's scientists were working on the dream machine with new vigour. They had the drawings and interpretations from Jay Browning and had reached an interesting stage of the development. They had reduced everything in size and it hardly looked anything like the original prototype which John first brought back to England.

It was sleek in design, more like a polished cycle hat and it sat on the head with ease without a wire in sight. They had replaced all the wires with connections similar to those used in the mobile phones. If John was lucky enough to ever see it he would not recognise it, but would it work correctly? Otherwise, everyone connected with Ralph Hess's dream machine had just been busy fools!

It was decided to leave the final tests until John came back. For one thing, he was the only person to have experienced the trip back in time. Secondly, both Ray and Philip had suddenly found that the dream machine had lost some of its appeal with John missing, and they both felt that, as important as the machine might be, it was more important to get John back. The final testing could wait!

28

Ben was being held in the darkened room with only short excursions out for necessary visits to the toilet. He had not seen Dick, his traitorous ex-colleague again and hoped that Dick, being a native American, might just have a glimmer of regret or remorse about what he had done. Deep down, however, he knew that most sleepers were conditioned almost from birth and had always had some grudge or financial motive for even starting out on the road to treason.

Ben was pleased when his other two men, Peter and Steve, were allowed back in the room with him. It was obviously easier to keep all three of them in one room now the trap had been sprung. Mealtimes usually consisted of Italian bread and cheese, coupled sometimes with the odd tomato which they all found to be something to relish.

Ben's need to escape was becoming more desperate but his captors did not take any chances when it came to feeding him and escorting him to the toilet. There were always three of them present. The only exception was the evening mealtime when there were only two men, one with the food which was placed on the table while the other stayed by the door.

For the last few days, Ben had been listening intently to noises such as car doors closing and had noted the times to be mostly late evenings around eight o'clock. He concluded that Al and Joe Higgs, and possibly some others, always seemed to go out then for a more substantial meal. This would explain why there were only two men left to feed the captives.

Ben had plenty of time to discuss with Peter and Steve his ideas for a possible escape. Peter and Steve could not get over the fact that their colleague of some ten years was a traitor. They also wanted revenge on this man who had tricked them all these years. They all concluded that the best time to mount an escape attempt would be in the evening at mealtime.

They listened for the sound of the men leaving to go to the local town for their evening meal. Within minutes, the door opened and their two jailers came in with one carrying the tray of coffee and sandwiches. No change there! The guard carrying the tray approached and leant forward to place the tray of food on the table before Ben. This meant the man was between him and the other guard. It could not have been better. Knowing any movement had to be quick and precise, Steve and Peter lunged at the guard standing in the doorway, hurling him against the wall before he could draw his gun which was in his belt. At the same time, Ben kicked out at the tray holding the plates of sandwiches and hot coffee. The contents went everywhere, mainly in the direction of the unfortunate guard who instinctively put up his arms to ward off the hot coffee. Bedlam broke out as the three men struggled to overpower the two guards and, within a few minutes, the tables had been turned and soon the two guards slumped to the floor unconscious.

They were free – if they could make their escape from the house. Gagging and tying up the two men with some curtain sash, they ventured out of the room. They found to their relief, and as they had hoped, that the house was empty. They looked around outside carefully and, with the gun taken from their captors, they peered into the evening moonlight. They could see an old truck sitting in the compound but nothing else. They knew that the Russians had performed many tricks on them since all this started and it would be only too easy for them to shoot them down as they attempted to leave the house. Still nothing.

The three men hastened towards the pickup, each holding their breath and fearing at any moment that a bullet would end their attempt for freedom.

29

The Higgs brothers accompanied by the treacherous Dick were enjoying the delights of a hot meal at one of the local hostelries. They were now on their third bottle of wine and very nice it tasted as well. The steak had been cooked just as Al liked it and he was turning over in his mind just how to spend the bonus that had been promised him when he had retrieved the dream machine. He would most likely spend it in Southern Italy, possibly Naples, and a firm favourite of his. Most of it would go on wine, good food and, of course, many women. He would do the usual throwing around of his well-earned cash and he would, of course, attract hordes of ladies who would congregate around him and to attend to his every need, including stroking his large bald head. Al Higgs always liked that. It reminded him of Caesar, a historic man whom Al had always admired. Of course, he conveniently refused to recall just how poor Caesar died. After all, Al Higgs was a winner, not a loser!

'What are you going to do with your share of the money, Dick?' Joe asked.

'Well, I sure can't go back to the States. Perhaps I might just stay here with you guys or even try Russia,' replied Dick thoughtfully.

'No use looking at me to accompany you,' Joe said. 'I'll be back in good old London. Can't stand this heat; alright for a while but no good for the long-term. Ladies aren't bad though,' he added, turning around and leering at one of the serving girls, who in turn gave him a wide berth. His pug nose did nothing for her and she was not at all interested in the small amount of cash the men were now spreading around. Turning back to his nearly empty glass, he refilled it from the large pitcher of beer on the table, took a gulp and settled back to daydream of better things to come. Yes, let the good times roll!

*

Ben and his men had managed to get the old pickup truck started and, after checking that their former captors were still securely bound, they headed down the winding lane that they all hoped would lead them to freedom. They had gone about three kilometres down the road when Ben who was driving brought the pickup truck to a screeching halt. There blocking the lane was a recently felled tree.

'Great,' said Ben as he looked out of the window before instantly recognising the feeling of a gun pressed against the side of his head. At the same time the passenger door was opened and his two men were also confronted with guns aimed at them.

'Won't you join us, sir?' came a threatening command from the blackened face of the man holding a gun.

The three men got out of the pickup and did as their captors told them: to kneel down with their hands above their heads.

Oh no, not this quick, not just when Ben could have done something to redeem all his last errors. He closed his eyes and wondered what was next.

'I bet you fancy a nice plate of fish and chips or maybe a hamburger?'

Ben opened his eyes and was greeted by the grinning face of Philip and, behind him, the equally grinning faces of Davies and Jenkins. He leapt to his feet and there were hugs all around, it was many minutes before the three men realised that they were at last free.

'Let's go and have a drink,' said Philip leading them back to his car nearby.

'Only if it's a big drink and I'm paying,' replied a happy and now very relieved Ben.

Philip took out his phone and informed everyone that their mission had been accomplished.

*

Arriving back at the farmhouse, Al and Joe Higgs were not happy men when they walked into the almost deserted farmhouse with no pickup and, on closer inspection, no prisoners! They found only their own two men trussed up with gags in their mouths.

Al slapped the nearest man in the face with rage and started shouting and screaming. 'Damn fools, I can't leave you for five minutes and you let them escape. I'll kill you for this.' His dreams of how he was going to spend his bonus had just taken a back seat. Now he would have to start over again. He still had John who was being held in another location so, with Joe and Dick, he climbed back into the car and sped off down the same lane that his captives had taken just a few hours earlier.

Ray was in a good mood after hearing of Ben's rescue and, having placed men at several strategic points, he waited patiently for the next part of their plan to be implemented: the rescue of John. After many hours, his men had finally located two possible sites where they thought John was located. True, they did not know for sure where he was being held exactly but had played it safe and staked out both places. Now that Ben had escaped, Ray just hoped that John had not been disposed of.

It was not long before he got what he wanted: the arrival of the limousine driven by Joe Higgs, accompanied by Al and Dick. Having been already briefed by Ben about the treachery of Dick, he knew that when they took the car they had to remember that Dick was now one of the gang.

He had also decided that they would await the arrival of Al and his two partners as they did not want to be caught trying to take a house that might have armed guards in it.

Three thuds came as the men one by one alighted from the car to be met from behind with an expertly delivered smash on each of their heads which felled them.

After making sure that the men were secured, Ray and his men approached the house and entered through the open door. They found the guards inside were playing cards obviously not expecting company and, being a hot night, had left the door open allowing the fresh air that came down from the nearby mountains to blow in. The three men inside gave themselves up without a fight.

It was quite a picture to behold when Ray entered the room that John was being held in and saw for the first time the unkempt figure who, although he had been allowed to wash, was in the same clothes he had been wearing when he was taken. With several days' growth of beard, he appeared also to have lost weight.

'Fancy coming back to the villa, John? I know somebody who's been missing you a great deal.'

John, completely bewildered, stood up and looked blankly at the vision that had entered his prison: a man whom he had only dreamt of seeing again, along with his friends. Walking to Ray, they embraced. It was several minutes before John could bring himself to tell Ray exactly what had taken place during his capture, such was his relief at being rescued.

It was not long before the two parties met up with each other and headed southwards towards the villa. Ben and John took it in turns to tell the others what had happened. Ray and Philip filled in the gaps as and when they saw fit.

John suddenly whispered in Ray's ear who, without hesitation, turned off the highway towards a small hotel, a sign for which the headlights had picked up some kilometres back. The hotel receptionist took the arrival of the somewhat dishevelled looking group in her stride, almost as if this was a common occurrence.

Ray handed John his own mobile phone. 'I think you had better put someone out of her misery.' Squeals of Gina's joy could be heard over the whole of the hotel.

After the rather long conversation between John and Gina, Ray said, 'Go to it, John, take as long as you want. When you come down, we'll have a good meal and plenty of vino.'

Both Philip and Ray were just happy to see their friend alive and in one piece. While John was in his room enjoying his first hot shower for a long time and removing the unwanted beard, Philip and Ray spoke with Ben and his two men. Soon an almost party atmosphere developed.

Meanwhile Ray's men took away their captives and placed them in the care of the local police with instructions for them to contact the Italian state police. The authorities down south would be very pleased to receive them into custody.

Philip and Ray just could not believe it that after all this time they had managed to rescue John and Ben. They all sat down to a meal to celebrate and at the same time to thank all the men who had worked so hard to make the rescue possible. Sometimes it does work out OK, thought Philip.

30

All the men had taken rooms for the night but as they talked the men reflected on their good fortune with their plans. The areas picked out by Chris had turned up trumps and the men who had scoured the countryside had been excellent. It had been quite easy for Philip, Davies and Jenkins to lie in wait for the car to come along. The only difference was they were waiting for Al Higgs to come back, not Ben.

John rejoined the group knowing that he would feel a lot better after a good night's sleep. However, with adrenalin running high, the group of men sitting around the dining table that night had little time for sleep. Ray and Philip brought John up-to-date with all the latest on the dream machine and were pleased to find that John's keen interest in the machine had not wavered one bit despite his having been taken prisoner. Leaving the hotel the next day after eating a hearty breakfast, the men drove back to the villa where John could at last be reunited with Gina.

Al and Joe Higgs were handcuffed to two agents of the Italian police and, with Dick, were being transported down to the southern area of Italy where they would be interviewed and arrested on the suspicion of murder of Alice, Jay Browning, Dieter Geist and, most likely, several others although it would take some time to collate all the evidence.

By now, Dick was very nervous. He had been quite happy to go along with the entrapment of his ex-colleagues but he also knew that the murders that had been carried out before he had shown his hand would now also be laid at his door. Talking to one of the agents, he straightaway offered to turn state evidence against the other two if he could have a more lenient sentence. It seemed there was not much honour amongst thieves after all.

Roberto Perrito was just finishing his afternoon's work in his fields and was winding his way home in his tractor through the narrow lanes when he came across an abandoned car which was parked across his path in the lane making it difficult for him to pass. Stopping the tractor, he climbed off, walked towards the vehicle and peered in, recoiling in horror instantly. Inside was a policeman with a neat bullet hole in his head, and another man also dead, with a bullet hole in the back of his head. This man would be later identified as Dick James, ex-CIA, ex-colleague of Ben and company. Of the other policeman and the two prisoners Al and Joe Higgs there was no sign. It would seem that Al and Joe Higgs still had many friends in the area and the claws of the Russian Mafia were spread right across Italy. Could this mean that there was a connection with the two Mafias of which even Ray Barone was not aware?

John's arrival at the villa was a joyous affair with Gina throwing herself into his arms and expressing words in Italian which none of the visiting Europeans could understand. This was with the exception of Ray and several of his men who turned away with smiles on their faces. It was not long before Ray received a phone call and he, in turn, had to inform the party of the escape of the Higgs brothers.

Philip could not believe it. 'You have got to be joking. We turned them over to the state police, didn't we?'

'We certainly did, but it seems that Mr Higgs and co have more friends that we anticipated and ones in high places, because someone knew exactly when and where they were being moved,' went on Ray.

The party atmosphere ceased and Gina, who had been one of the happiest, clung onto John's arm tightly. 'Ray, what an earth are we going to do now?' she asked.

Ray was about to give his usual assurances when Philip spoke up. 'We all have to leave, Ray. I think we should go back to Courtney Manor. At least we can guard that much easier than we can here. I reckon the English police will be a bit more reliable than your police here as well.'

'I totally agree, Philip,' Davies interjected. 'We should set the wheels in motion if we're in full agreement.'

'The thing is your family may not be that safe over here, Ray,' Jenkins added, 'as the mob most likely knows of your connection with Philip.'

Everyone nodded in agreement.

'Well, we have two options,' said Philip. 'We can catch a flight back, or we could go by boat which would take longer but perhaps we could all be on our guard better.'

'Also, we would have no place to run either,' replied Ray.

'For them as well. That is, if they follow us on board ship,' said Ben.

'We might have the showdown which we know is due any day,' offered Jenkins.

'Not a good idea with Ray's family on board though,' said Philip, remembering he had already lost his wife to the mob. 'I'm not so sure that we should split up. We should have safety in numbers. I vote we catch the next flight out and make it back to England.'

'Or perhaps we could split up and travel by car via France.'

'It may make it harder for them to follow us all at the same time should they discover when and where we are all going,' Jenkins said.

'God help us,' Ben interjected, 'I'm already confused with what we're all doing? Can we make a decision and get on with it?'

Ray nodded. 'Yes, OK then we'll all go by car.'

'Totally agree,' Philip said. 'While we're here deliberating we could be on our way back to England.'

The same evening, two limousines arrived at the back

113

door from the garages which Ray had close by the villa. It was decided that John, Gina, Ray and his wife would travel in one car with a bodyguard, and Davies, Philip, Ben and Chris, along with another bodyguard, would go in the other. Jenkins and another bodyguard would catch a flight later. 'What about the rest of your family, Ray?' Jenkins asked.

'They'll be alright,' Ray replied. 'I'll bring in some friends who are more than able to deal with anybody that tries to come in without an invitation.'

It was at five o'clock the next morning and just before the sun came up when the two cars with Ray and Chris driving left the villa and sped quietly along the lanes which led to the mountains and then to France. They did not stop even for refreshments which suited the men as the ladies had packed some provisions for them all. The two bodyguards were trusted men of Ray's, and with Davies the two groups of travellers felt reasonably safe.

Davies had taken the time to phone his office in England on one of Ray's mobile phones and made arrangements for extra assistance once they reached Dover and then moved on to Courtney Manor that had also received their instructions for the many extra guests.

The group were mainly silent as they crossed the Italian border and entered France. Still a long way to go and who knew what danger lay ahead before they could all reach the comparative safety of the manor.

31

Al and Joe Higgs were jubilant when they were handed over to one of the police connected with the company and the subsequent dispatch of the traitor Dick. Never did trust those people who turn on their own country. Al and Joe worked for money alone – no other reason.

Al smirked as he checked the availability of some more hired guns. He thought he would not go through the normal channels because he had a sneaking suspicion that the powers that be might be asking too many questions, and he wanted desperately to get back into the position he was in before Ben had made his escape. If nothing else, Alfredo Higgs was an extremely confident man who always bounced back when faced with these little setbacks.

He ordered his new crew down south to take their positions around the town and to observe the villa, thus enabling them to report back to him when he arrived with brother Joe in the next few days.

The party travelling through France started to relax as it seemed that they were not being followed and, while the bodyguards kept a close lookout, the group took time out to stop overnight at a hotel as they sped on through the quiet roads of northern France.

Gina and John were so happy to relax and spend some time getting to know each other again. They went for quiet walks but were always accompanied by one of the bodyguards. Once bitten – twice shy!

*

Joe and Al Higgs arrived in the village near Ray's villa and took stock of the situation.

'The place appears very quiet,' concluded one of the men assigned to the watch it. 'There are a few men keeping watch though, I recognise some of them as that Ray Barone's men.'

'Everyone has their price,' Joe remarked.

'Not so sure about these men. They've worked for the Barones for many years and their fathers before them. They're all part of the mob.'

'OK, but find something out, anything so we know what's happening,' barked Al.

It was two days before one of his men came back with news. 'It seems that the whole bunch of them left here a couple of days ago by car.'

'Damnation, I was wondering if that would happen,' said Al. 'Did you find out where they are heading for?'

'I think they're heading for England but I'm not sure. The guy I spoke to was a little hesitant even with the extra drinks we plied him with.'

'That Courtney guy's got a big house near Oxford,' Joe reminded Al. 'We had a few problems with him when we tried to snatch the machine a couple of months ago.'

'Then Oxford it is. They must be in England. We'd better take a flight to see if we can catch up with them.' Al went on, 'Somehow we have to get that machine back and get it back soon or else we can kiss goodbye to our bonus. Maybe we won't come out of this in one piece. You know what the boss thinks about failure.'

The oddball party of the Higgs brothers and their strange collection of hired help checked out of the lodgings they were installed in and headed for the nearest airport only to find that flights to the UK had been grounded due to thick fog in London. This did nothing to help Alfredo Higgs' temper and he lashed out at the person nearest to him hitting him across his head. 'That's for nothing.'

Ray and Philip's arrival at Courtney Manor was something to behold, with the Americans and the Italians marvelling at the array of sixteenth-century features. Even for Ray, this was the first time he was able to take a good look at the property that had been his natural father's home for all those missing years. James has worked wonders with all the unused rooms, making up beds and lighting the fires. Well, at least the best that he could do in the short time available.

'Well done, James,' said Philip, greeting his butler warmly. He gave him a brief rundown of what had happened, telling him to remember that things would not be the same for a while and he should treat any unusual occurrences with suspicion.

After a while Philip visited the tomb of Alice which was in the grounds, saying a private prayer before returning to the great hall for pre-dinner drinks and, of course, an intense discussion on what they should do next.

This involved talks with the local police and, of course, Ben and his men had also spoken with their embassy bringing them up to date. Men had been posted at the main gate with overall responsibility for security handed over to Jenkins who gladly took on this role with great enthusiasm. Davies was then able to return to his office to update his superiors about what had gone on in Italy.

No one came in or went out without being logged in the book; in fact anyone not giving a proper account of themselves was refused entry to the grounds.

Within days, the gatehouse lodge had been brought up to liveable conditions, meaning that the guards whose responsibility it was to check and search everyone could stay overnight when they were not on duty.

32

With Jenkins in overall charge, Philip and Ray felt a little easier, but there was still the problem of covering all the grounds which were considerable. A couple of army Jeeps were commandeered from one of the nearby American bases and soon a daily and nightly routine was established for these patrols to cover the grounds. Now they were ready for any surprises and, if Messrs Higgs and co had any sense, they would stay away!

In the meantime, John and Chris had worked full-time on the dream machine, pleased that they could draw on each other's expertise. Chris had continued to work on the machine while John was 'detained' and this had given him a good understanding of how the machine worked or at least how it should work.

Ray and Philip came up to offer assistance but the two kindly refused. They found that working on their own was best so they were left to get on with it. John was so pleased that, in the time he had been away, Chris had been able to do some great work in advancing the performance of the machine. They had also managed to change the bulky old-fashioned German army-style helmet to a much lighter metal which had been perfected during the war for the production of military aircraft. It consisted mainly of aluminium, and they had managed to mix a more soluble, flexible material. This made the weight of the machine much lighter and easier for the wearer; the original had been rather heavy for the dream seeker.

It was after one of their intense sessions that John and Chris asked to see Ray and Philip. They had some thoughts that they wanted to put into practice. John had now really got back into the swing of things and was busy trying to improve the machine even more.

They had some startling news: it was simple – if one extra crystal had improved the dream machine, what would two more achieve?

In fact they had already added two more crystals which Chris had brought over from Italy with him and had found the performance of machine greatly improved. Philip and Ray welcomed the news with interest but what John then suggested surprised them. He proposed that they could one day create a machine which would be available to even more people. The next step could be to create a dream room and, by adding even more crystals, they could draw on even more power. Of course this sounded even more futuristic and Ray and Philip warned John and Chris that perhaps they should not 'run before they could walk'.

They had to ensure that the machine did what it supposed to do: recreate and hold people's dreams. Not a small feat, that was for sure. The dream machine was certainly not finished by any stretch of the imagination but it was much better than when John had first turned up all those months ago at Courtney Manor.

As the days passed without any incidents, the party in residence at the Courtney Estate started to relax. The ladies created some special Italian culinary delights which, to James the ageing butler, were amazing. He knew of course that his master Philip had become used to the local cuisine while he was in Italy but felt that it was his responsibility to maintain some of the dignity that went back many, many years. He had long been used to being in charge of organising the general running of Courtney Manor, setting out menus for the cook. He tried in vain to stem some of the proposals from the ladies but, in the end, settled for just organising the rest of the house.

Ray and Philip took the opportunity to visit the Bowl Inn for some typical English refreshments but they were always accompanied by two of Davies's men who remained in close proximity although not encroaching on the men's privacy. It was on one of these visits that Philip caught the eye of the new receptionist that had recently arrived at the inn. Christine was just about Philip's ideal lady. She was approximately two years younger than Philip and recently divorced, and therefore, as far as Philip was concerned, single.

He, of course, had patiently observed with some envy John and Gina's close relationship; for once in his life he was the one on the outside looking in. He was pleased that John had found someone special but, at this point in his life, Philip suddenly found the lack of any special lady in his life a little disquieting. He found his visits to the Bowl Inn increasing and would drop in on his own while the two minders waited outside in their car. It soon became quite obvious that Christine was attracted to Philip's rugged looks. Philip started asking her to sit and talk with him and it was not long before she was looking forward to his visits to the pub. It did take her a while to relax in his company as she was only recently divorced.

Philip, of course, had no problem chatting the lady up and, although Christine had been warned about his past life, including the tragic loss of his wife, both of them realised that there was something much more meaningful to their relationship. Soon Christine was visiting and staying overnight at Courtney Manor.

Ray was concerned about the sudden appearance of Christine at the pub. Inspector Davies had suggested that this might have been more than a coincidence and, taking everything into account, Ray could not shake off his doubts about the relationship his brother had so willing entered into. While he refrained from talking to Philip about it, he did mention it to John and made a note to ask Inspector Davies to check out the young lady. Ray was worried about doing this but, taking into consideration recent betrayals, he thought it better to err on the side of caution. Of course he wanted his brother to have someone special in his life. As it was, he had suddenly realised that his own wife had been rather neglected, mainly due to the recent hectic events and immediately gave her some flowers which helped him get back into her good books.

John and Chris had been making good progress with the dream machine. Both had worked hard and were happy to recommend the next step: actual scientific tests with a human being. All they needed was to get Philip, Ray or perhaps Jenkins to try it under strict scientific conditions. They picked Jenkins as they knew he was the most sceptical of the group. Ben and his men now had less involvement as things had settled down.

The two men, with Philip, Ray and Jenkins could not even start to believe that at long last they could be making a product which not only worked but would make all the past endeavours worthwhile. After making their decision, they all gathered together in the main hall and asked Jenkins to be the first to experience the improved dream machine.

Jenkins appeared rather reluctant which they could readily understand; after all everyone had been talking about the machine. It had obviously been the subject of intense activity by gangs trying to steal it and here Philip and Ray were asking him to 'test' it. To Jenkins' mind it was all a bit far-fetched and risky. However, after talking with John, Jenkins suddenly shrugged his shoulders and said, 'Why not!' He declared he would attempt to experience again his very first date with a lady called Jean. They questioned him why this was so special. Blushing, he indicated that he had been a virgin up to that time.

A virgin at twenty-one years of age, they all agreed, was in those days a special event…

The dream machine was placed on Jenkins' head. Much to Philip's and Ray's dismay, it was agreed that they should leave, letting John and Chris handle the test.

It had to be a proven test which would indicate that Jenkins had experienced his dream in such a way that would give the whole event and not just snippets of what had taken place. Jenkins had to be sure that it was authentic and just as it had been before.

Time passed. The men paced the floor in the great hall impatiently waiting to see if the machine had worked. Finally the door opened and the three men entered, all looking rather grim. Philip's and Ray's hearts sank. Suddenly John, Chris and Jenkins jumped into the air, shouting and laughing. The machine had worked and Jenkins had had a successful encounter with Jean. In fact it had been so successful that poor Jenkins had been reluctant to come back to the present day!

Yes, at last the dream machine had arrived and apparently in good working order. The five men fell silent, almost unable to believe it, such had been the monumental lead up to this incredible moment. All they had to do now was to try and keep it to themselves and arrange for a hastily formed company to register the patent and machine. Not too much to do then!

33

Christine had been spending a fair amount of time at Courtney Manor with Philip and they had become quite close. Philip had managed to put behind him the terrible grief that he had experienced following Alice's death and now appreciated having a new lady in his life. Christine was quite vivacious and, with her good educational background, seemed to fit into Philip's new circle of friends, including Ray his brother. Ray for his part had still not quite made up his mind about Christine. She was obviously a nice lady but was she just a little bit 'too nice' and why all of a sudden had she appeared on the scene? Was her sudden appearance at the Bowl Inn more than a coincidence?

Inspector Davies had identified the Bowl Inn as a place to watch including the landlord there, the ever obliging Jacob Manners.

Ray's worries increased when Christine suddenly asked Philip if he would like to go with her to visit her family in Scotland. Philip had previously told Christine that the heightened security around Courtney Manor had been there since the death of his wife Alice. He had not wanted to go into great detail about the dream machine, being a little cautious about telling anyone else about the machine. Christine had accepted this, and the request would seem to have been made innocently enough.

Ray and Philip talked it over with the rest of the group and, with Ray being increasingly against the idea, Philip regretfully declined putting it down to pressure of work on the estate.

He was also eager to get on with arranging, with Ray and John, the next step of registering the dream machine.

Christine was understandably upset; she dearly wanted

to show off Philip to her family. She left that weekend for Scotland. Early the next day, however, Philip received a phone call from a man purporting to be Christine's brother who explained that she had been involved in a car crash on the way up to Scotland and was now in a local hospital, All Saints – would he like to come and visit her?

Philip was extremely concerned. He discussed the situation with Ray and, with the proviso that he took Jenkins and Mike, one of the bodyguards, it was agreed he should undertake the trip. Adam, Christine's brother, had told them he would meet them at the front entrance of the hospital and take them in to see Christine.

Arriving at the entrance of the All Saints Hospital, Philip was concerned that there was no sign of Adam. With Jenkins, he entered the hospital and approached the reception desk. He was about to ask at the desk when a man who identified himself as Adam intercepted him and invited him to follow him to the ward Christine was in.

Jenkins followed behind, glancing around as he trailed after the two men who appeared to be engrossed in conversation with Philip being updated on Christine's latest condition. He was about to follow them into the lift when he suddenly noticed a face with which he had become very familiar over the past few months: the pug face of Al Higgs and, following behind him, Joe Higgs. Both men had white coats on as if they were part of the medical profession, and both were entering the adjoining lift. Suddenly alarm bells started ringing.

Jenkins grabbed Philip's arm as he was about to enter the lift and pulled him back. Philip looked startled but Jenkins hissed in his ear, 'The Higgs brothers are here. It's got to be a trap!'

Philip glanced back and could see Adam apparently

cursing as the doors of the lift closed, fortunately without the two men. As they rushed to the hospital car park, they could see men running in their direction and they knew for certain that the mob were up to their old tricks again.

Thanks to Jenkins the plot had been foiled but they were still not out of trouble yet. As they approached their car, they could see it was surrounded by three men who had effectively trapped the bodyguard Mike inside. Philip was in no mood for asking anything nicely as he smashed the nearest man on his jaw and kicked the next man in the groin which left the passenger door clear. Philip yanked it open. Jenkins in the meantime barged the man blocking his path on his side of the car sending him spinning to the ground. Jenkins was then able to pull open the back door and jump in. The car engine purred into life and, with screeching tyres, the car raced for the car park exit. Within minutes, the mob had regrouped and two cars joined in the race out of the car park.

With Mike driving at great speed, they managed to put some distance between themselves and the cars following. Philip's mobile phone suddenly rang and, upon answering it, Philip was pleased to hear Christine's voice. On calling the manor she had been informed by Ray that Philip had driven up to Scotland after hearing about her unfortunate accident. She, of course, was safely at home with her real brother Adam and was now extremely worried. She could not understand why all this was happening but Philip explained that he was rather busy just at that moment and he would contact her when he had managed to shake off the other men. He advised her not to answer any calls either at the door or by telephone. In fact, she should call the local Scottish police as she could be in great danger.

Ray also called within minutes and said he would contact

Christine again to tell her that the local police would be arriving to give her protection. Philip and his two companions had enough to worry about with the mob trying to catch up as they sped through the countryside.

Mike was managing to maintain his lead until they came around a bend and saw to their dismay that a car had been parked right across the lane. He had no alternative but to crash through the nearest hedge. The car turned over several times, ending up on its side with the wheels still spinning. For a moment everything was quiet.

Philip and Jenkins were both dazed but fortunately unharmed. They both managed to scramble out but Mike lay motionless with blood oozing from a neck wound. Jenkins checked his pulse but, feeling nothing, they reluctantly turned and fled the scene. It would not be long before the men who had planted the car across the lane would be upon them. With Mike now another casualty, the nightmare was continuing.

The two men dived into the dense undergrowth on the Scottish moors. They scrambled, their lungs almost bursting, finally coming to a stop near an old farmhouse. It seemed an age before someone answered.

However the door was finally opened by the farmer who, after seeing Jenkins' police badge ushered them into the living room. Unfortunately he had no telephone but, after being convinced that it was a matter of life and death, he was persuaded to give them the use of his car and they drove away at speed.

Finally they met up at Witney with Ray and Inspector Davies who had driven up to assist them. Davies had concluded that the pub landlord Manners had used his knowledge about Christine's family to assist the Higgs brothers in setting up the trap. Fortunately they had thwarted it yet again. The local police managed to find Mike's body and also arranged the return of the farmer's car.

Christine was brought back from Scotland in a police escort. It was better that she stayed with the rest of the group. At least they could keep an eye on her. Ray was still pondering if Christine was as innocent as she appeared to be. Only time would tell.

John and Chris were finalising the paperwork for the registration and patenting of the machine. The hard work of getting together all the correct documentation had just begun together with the agreement that the manufacturing company, an offshoot of Ray's, would be based in the UK. The four men had now been made directors of the company: John, Philip and Ray with Chris being made scientific director working strictly under John.

The dreams of yesterday had now become the dreams of today and with it would bring much wealth for the originators of the idea, even if the main man Ralph Hess was not there to behold the marvel.

34

As each day passed, the worries concerning the mob receded. Ray and Philip tried out the dream machine with amazing results; such was the vivid recreation of dreams that occurred when it was placed on their heads: Ray with his thoughts of meeting Rena and creating his life in Italy, and Philip of his time at Oxford and perhaps some of his exploits in the past with the ladies in Oxford.

John broke the happy mood one day though. 'Who's going to try to experience a bad dream now? We know we can recreate happy events but what happens when we experience an extremely bad dream?'

Chris agreed that someone had to do this before they could offer the dream machine on the open market.

The four men looked at each other.

'I'll do it, Ray,' Philip offered. 'I may be able to recall the experience of Alice's death.'

'As tragic as that was, Philip,' John remarked, 'would that be far enough back? I'm not sure that we could accept something that recent as a good enough test. I'm sure that, unfortunately, you already have that firmly fixed in your memory.'

Without saying a word, Philip nodded in agreement.

It was decided not to pursue this bad dream experiment. They had had such a hard time getting this far; why confuse things any further. The friends took turns using the machine for more pleasurable occasions. It was on one of these that Philip came back from using the machine with a perplexed look on his face.

Ray glanced up from reading an Italian newspaper that had been specially brought over for him. 'What's wrong?'

With a sigh, Philip exclaimed that his experience on the machine had not gone at all well.

John, who had just come into the room, joined in, 'What do you mean, Philip? How did it vary from previous times? Were you not able to experience the section of life you wanted to recall?'

Philip then dropped his bombshell. 'No, I did recall something but not from the past. It seemed like I was experiencing my own future!'

John's and Ray's faces were a picture of surprise.

'But that's impossible,' John said.

'Well,' continued Philip, 'all I can say is that I didn't recognise the part of my life that I experienced. It was almost as it was set in the future. I was much older, married to Christine with Robert, you know, my only son!'

Ray sat there in a stunned silence.

John's reaction was entirely different and he pranced around the room shouting at the top of his voice, 'Yes, nice one, Philip.'

Chris then came into the room, enquiring what all the fuss was about.

'Philip has visited the future!' John told him.

It was Chris's turn to be open-mouthed.

Ray, who had had more time to get his head around it all, asked feebly, 'Are you sure, Philip?'

Philip looked hurt, reflecting his disappointment on hearing his brother's doubts. He was about to reply, 'Of course I am' when he stopped himself and instead meekly replied, 'I think I am.'

The four men sat down, each gazing into the fireplace as if to throw some light on this dilemma. The only problem was that, in the middle of July, there was no fire in the huge grate and they realised they would have to get their inspiration from elsewhere.

John was the first to speak: 'We'll have to try again with all of us trying to think of something nice that we might like to happen in the future.'

Ray looked sceptical, remarking, 'That's going to be quite scientific then, John.'

'I agree,' Philip interjected, 'but do you have any other ideas, Ray? The more I think of it, the more I'm sure that I visited the future! The funny thing was that I appeared to be in a large room with flashing lights that went up and down.'

The four men sat in silence again, each with their own thoughts, each seeking to come up with a plan that would prove once and for all that what Philip had experienced had been true and not wishful thinking or a figment of his imagination.

35

After a few hours, Philip finally suggested he should attempt to recreate the last trip he had experienced on the dream machine. The problem was he could not recall how he had managed to advance into the future rather than into the past.

John then came up with a theory that sounded quite feasible: Philip should think hard about Christine and, if he could remember the actual place, with luck he might make the connection again. Philip said he could recall thinking about Christine before he actually went on the dream machine. As usual, the three men waited in the lounge while Philip went into the room to place the dream machine on his head; a simple procedure that all the men had experienced.

They did not wish to influence or disturb the thought patterns which must materialise for a successful trip on the dream machine. The use of the word 'trip' had been first used by John, when Jenkins had tried the machine some days before.

As Philip retired to the 'dream room' as it was now called, the waiting trio talked earnestly about the latest developments and soon doubts seemed to cloud their initial feelings of optimism.

As usual, John brought up the first plausible doubts: were they now almost playing God; they might well be in a position to dictate the future, or at least someone could.

'Well, that might not be so bad,' replied Ray. 'It could be beneficial to our governments if they knew how things would be in, say, six years.'

'Oh, come on,' John responded. 'We also have some dodgy people in our governments that might totally misuse the machine.'

Chris and Ray nodded in agreement.

Their fairy-tale ending was again being threatened by doubts on how to proceed, but deep down they all knew that they had no choice than to just carry on.

Poor Ralph Hess must be turning in his grave, John thought. He would have jumped at the chance to tackle this problem. After all, he had been a scientist first and a teacher second. Half an hour passed and the waiting trio started to wonder how Philip was doing. John suggested that they look into the room to see how he was faring.

What they saw filled them with trepidation. Philip was apparently still in his dream, but he certainly was not in a calm state, tossing and turning, and breaking into a sweat as with every move he was evidently experiencing some dramatic and distressing event. His distress continued as the three men watched; fear for their friend rising with every minute that passed. John was about to suggest that they try to wake Philip when he gave a great sigh and apparently dropped out of his present dream, or had he?

The three men took it in turns to gently call Philip's name and Ray mopped Philip's brow with cold water. They applied smelling salts, still to no avail. They were all now getting desperate and Ray suggested that they call Philip's doctor so that he might be able to bring him round. The apparent problems of the dream machine were forgotten as they tried to bring Philip back to reality.

Would he still be in the past, the present or the future; they just did not know. Removing the helmet, they moved him from the dream room and made him as comfortable as they could in his bedroom.

Doctor Brown, Philip's doctor, arrived. He was rather taken aback at the high security as he entered the grounds of Courtney Manor. It was almost as bad as getting into Fort Knox, he remarked as he was taken to Philip's bedroom. He found Philip lying on his bed with cold towels on his head.

'When did this happen?' he asked.

The waiting men looked at each other. They knew they could not possibly tell the doctor the truth, but were they placing Philip's life in danger by not telling him about his time on the dream machine?

Ray told the doctor that Philip had been drinking quite a bit the night before and that they had put him to bed and he had been like this when James went to wake him that morning.

Doctor Brown was an old-fashioned doctor who took everything in his stride and he gave Philip a thorough examination.

On completion, he pushed his glasses back to the top of his head and, shaking his head at the same time, he gave a sigh. 'Well, I can't find anything wrong with Philip. If I didn't know better, I would say he's just asleep. He certainly isn't in a coma but he doesn't seem to respond to anything. I think all we can do is to let him rest and we'll have to see how he is in the morning.'

The waiting men nodded in agreement, thanked him for coming and he was shown out of the high security grounds. The friends resigned themselves to the fact that they would just have to wait until Philip woke up, if he ever did. God, that prospect was not worth thinking about.

Christine had now arrived and was asking questions. The men felt that they had to tell her enough to make her understand that Philip had been testing some new machinery that they had perfected. Of course this did nothing to allay her fears. From the fierce looks she gave them, they could see that she was not happy that Philip had been subjected to such danger.

She remained at his bedside eventually falling asleep, her hand clasping Philip's.

36

Al and Joe Higgs had gathered their depleted forces together and relocated back to Oxfordshire where they suspected the dream machine must now be kept. Finding Courtney Manor a heavily guarded fortress, they knew their work would be cut out. They were sitting having lunch at their new headquarters, the Swan Hotel, discussing their next move when the arrival of two men from the company took them by surprise. Jason Noble and his brother Robert strode into the room arrogantly and over to where the brothers were sitting, thumping a bundle of notes down on the table.

'Here, you two, is your money. You are relieved from duty,' sneered Jason.

'What do you mean?' Joe looked with dismay at the rather small number of notes lying on the table,

'You're finished, you're kaput!'

'Oh yeah, and who says so?'

'Franz,' Robert calmly replied

Joe looked at Al. They knew that, if Franz had said it, they surely would be finished. Basically he was their boss and they knew he had not been too pleased about how things had been going.

'This can't be right. We were promised much more than this,' said Al, nodding at the few notes lying in front of them on the table.

Jason and Robert Noble both leant across the table placing their faces within inches of the Higg brothers. 'Then you should have done better. What do you expect for so many cock-ups?'

'If you can do better, be my guest,' snarled Joe, standing up.

'That's what we're here for,' Robert replied, leaning forward, his face almost touching Joe's nose.

Joe and Al looked at each other. Even though they had the other men with them, they knew that if the big boss Franz had sent these two over then their involvement in retrieving the dream machine was at an end.

'You can both vacate your rooms. We're moving in and taking over. You're lucky to get anything, let alone keep your kneecaps.'

Cursing, the Higgs brothers left the hotel and made their way to the next town. They were unsure what exactly they could do but they both agreed that they would contrive a plan that would get them into the good books of their boss.

Christine had just finished a cup of tea that had been brought in by the ever helpful James who had also taken his turn at the bedside of his master. Philip was apparently sleeping soundly and, to all intents and purposes, looking very healthy.

It was a shock to Christine when, just as she put her cup down, he woke up and asked her what she was doing there and where his morning cup of tea was. He could not understand the joy on Christine and James's faces as he sat up and started to get out of bed.

James gently pushed his master back down and politely suggested he stayed there while he fetched the others. Ray and John entered the bedroom and, crossing over to Philip's bed, grabbed his hand which only served to make him even more confused. While Ray explained to Philip what had happened, John rang the doctor to inform him that Philip had woken up. The doctor said he would come straightaway and check Philip over. He arrived within thirty minutes and, after giving Philip a thorough physical examination, shrugged his shoulders, suggested that it must have some kind of sleeping sickness and left. Job done!

Philip tucked into breakfast with great vigour. After all, he had missed almost the whole of one day. With his greatly relieved friends, he talked about how and what might have caused this apparent bout of sleeping sickness.

'But was it actually a sickness?' John remarked. 'Well, you know Philip was attempting to recreate a part of his life that was yet to come.'

'Yes, of course,' replied Ray. 'What's your point?'

'Well, having made and achieved his goal, what reason would he have to cut short his dream when it basically was the first time he was experiencing it?'

'Of course, it was an almost endless dream which at that time Philip was just going through the motions of experiencing.'

John's face turned serious and he went on, 'If this is going to happen every time anyone attempts to go into the future, either intentionally or unintentionally, they'll be in trouble.'

'Not necessarily,' interjected Philip. 'Did I not come out of it when you removed the machine from my head?'

'Yes and no,' Ray replied, 'but only because we were there and removed the machine from your head. It took nearly twelve hours for you to come round.'

'I reckon that we'll overcome this in time,' John joined in. 'Maybe we can just solve it by using an alarm clock that can be set for one hour's time. After all, it is a dream we're talking about.'

Philip and Ray nodded in agreement.

'It is puzzling though we don't seem to have any trouble coming out of and finishing any of the pleasant past dreams,' Philip added. 'It's almost as if the machine is able to control and limit the length of the dream you're experiencing. I guess we can't be sure about all this and we'd have to make some provisos about it if we're ever able to market the damn thing that people will have to set their alarm clocks if they wish to travel to the future. It could well be as simple as spending more time on the machine. The brain stores up the knowledge we feed into it and the more we use it the better the memory bank should be.'

It was Ray's turn to look downhearted. 'You know this is one of the most amazing discoveries of the century and it seems that we'll to have to rely on the use of the common-or-garden alarm clock! Wonders will never cease!'

37

Davies had been taken some days off but, upon his return to work, was brought up to date on what had been happening at Courtney Manor and was intrigued to learn about what had happened with Philip. This, of course, was strictly top secret and not for public exposure but, as in all secrets, someone managed to leak to the press that the people at Courtney Manor had perfected some thought machine. Fortunately the information was rather sketchy and, by laughing it off, the authorities just denied any knowledge of it.

Davies was at his office desk when the phone rang. Answering it, he was surprised to receive a short message: 'If you want to find the men responsible for the murder of Alice Courtney, you should visit the Grand Hotel in nearby Oxford and visit rooms 110 and 111.'

After consultations with their superiors, Davies and Jenkins decided to follow up this unusual call. With members of the Flying Squad, they left for the Grand Hotel in Oxford and presented themselves at the reception desk at three o'clock in the morning. Warning the receptionist to refrain from calling the occupants of the rooms, they went up the stairs and approached room numbers 110 and 111. Using the usual method of a ram first to smash down the doors and asking questions later, they rushed in simultaneously to be greeted by the very surprised faces of Joe and Al Higgs.

Al had a lady with him in his bed, Gwen, a buxom blond, whose charms were obviously exposed to gain maximum attention from any client who wanted to spend time relaxing with her. She was released within a few minutes and went on her way, pleased that payment for her work had been secured before the early morning call by the police.

Both men gave themselves up quietly and, after being bundled into the waiting police vans, they soon realised that, as usual, the company had alternative ways of settling scores. Inspector Davies immediately phoned Philip to inform him of their capture. Who would or could be charged with Alice's death was uncertain however as there were no witnesses or weapon. It was more likely that the two would be sent back to Italy to be charged with the deaths of Dieter Geist and Jay Browning. Still, the police had the Higgs brothers inside and it would take a good lawyer to get them out now.

*

The next important thing to do was to find out what Philip had been experiencing before he came out of his latest dream. He certainly had been experiencing some distress and the way he had wrestled on the couch was as if he was fighting with someone. Philip was at first puzzled when Ray and John kept insisting that he had gone through a rather disturbing experience. He tried to relax and finally details of the dream came back to him and started to relate to his waiting friends what was appearing to him.

Apparently the dream had been short, despite the seemingly long time Philip had spent in his trance-like state. The location of the event in the dream had not taken place in the mysterious round room where he had been in the first dream, but at Courtney Manor. The manor was being attacked by men, their faces blackened and guns blazing.

He was walking in the grand hall with Christine when they had surprised a man who had broken in the house. He had grappled with the man and was on the ground hitting the man who was returning punches. John had suddenly appeared and pulled Philip off him. It was it this time that Philip had apparently stopped dreaming and gone into his extended sleep. In the dream, all this was taking a much longer time to experience and, it must be said, was rather more painful as the punches they were all experiencing had felt very real.

The listening men gasped at the revelation that the manor would be attacked and on such a large scale. The problem was when; what was the date that Philip had dreamt of. They decided to contact Ben and Davies who normally took turns in running the security side. Davies said he would advise the standby team although he had to admit he was not sure how he was going to put the whole team on red alert because of some dream that Philip had experienced.

Ben just returned from his break in the USA was more up for it. He now knew that the machine worked and had trust in what Philip had related but he too was not sure how the alert should be put into practice. Still, he went round his men and the other police and asked them to be extra vigilant. Everyone now knew what was coming but not when.

Days went by and everyone starting wondering just how far ahead Philip's dream had been. It could have been days or even weeks. There was nothing more to do other than wait.

After some discussion, it was decided that the ladies, with the exception of Christine, should return to Italy, as having them there if they were attacked could place them in danger and if they left there would be two less people to worry about. They were accompanied by some of Ray's men who would also take the opportunity of seeing their families back in Italy.

38

With Ray's help, John and Chris had managed to write up the scientific paper which set out the aims and functions of the dream machine. This enabled them then to prepare for the next important steps of firstly obtaining the patent for the dream machine, and secondly presenting it to the scientific world so that it could be accepted as the real thing rather than four cranks literally dreaming up some machine which tricked people into thinking they had regressed. They worried about the 'future' part as this was of course not only new to them but, at this time, without any firm data as to just how it had actually occurred. The first thing to do was to get the patent registered.

Chris and John were reasonably happy that they could accomplish this and they worked many hours putting together a synopsis which they hoped would be accepted by the scientific community. Of course, the only other thing they could do was to manufacture the machine and be damned, letting the machine prove itself. However, they all agreed that they preferred the first option.

Inspector Davies was called into the chief's office and informed that, while they appreciated everything he had done, he would now return to normal duties as, as far as they were concerned, there was enough manpower now to guard the manor. Davies was rather upset about this as he had become completely immersed in the dream machine project and had made some good friends there. He had spent a rather eventful time in sunny Italy, again making some good friends, and he could only imagine that a return to normal duties could and would be rather dull to say the least. He was given one week to prepare a detailed report. Jenkins would also withdraw from the project. Still, an order was an order and, with great reluctance, the men informed Ray and Philip of the proposed changes.

Ray and Philip were extremely disappointed. They had grown to like the two policemen and, what was more, they respected them as true professionals who had helped them out of more than one difficult situation. Philip reacted in his usual volatile manner saying that he would call the powers that be and get them to change their minds.

Philip was in the grand hall with Christine when he heard shouting and the sound of gunshots. He caught hold of Christine and they ran to the window just in time to see men dressed in dark clothes and with blackened faces shooting into the windows and at anything that seemed to move. A gun battle was taking place between the attackers and some of Ben's men at the top of the building. It appeared that the attackers had the advantage. Philip had a feeling of déjà vu but had no time to dwell on it.

Telling Christine to hide behind one of the many long curtains, he started to look around for any of the intruders. Ray and John had come out of their rooms and were shouting at Philip to close all the doors and keep away from windows. Where were the guards? Where were Ben's men and the police that they knew had always been placed around the manor? Ray and John joined Philip and they headed for the room that held the dream machine, hoping they would get there in time to protect it. Ben and his men were indeed extremely busy, after having a quiet time for several weeks with nothing to do but to check on the perimeter fences. The problem was that the men attacking had not come through the fences or even via the front entrance. It was a hair-raising experience with many shots being fired by the attackers and the guards returning fire.

It was obvious that the company who had launched this latest attack had caught the occupants of Courtney Manor completely by surprise. Somehow they had found out everyone's routines.

As Philip and John arrived at the dream room and opened the door, they could hear the sound of glass breaking and they realised that someone was breaking the large windows at the side. Rushing in, Philip approached the intruder, his face blackened, dressed in army fatigues. He was picking himself up and looking around. Philip did not wait for the man to see him; he rugby-tackled the man to the floor before he could straighten up. The two men struggled to gain the advantage.

John ran to the fireplace and grabbed a poker. He soon

found he had a use for it as another figure appeared at the broken window. Seeing the blackened face, John knew he had to hit first and ask questions later. He hit the man hard in the face and the man gasped and fell to the floor where he lay motionless.

Philip meanwhile was enjoying himself as he smashed his fist into the attacker's face and then punched him hard in his stomach. He only stopped when John managed to gently pull him back with some soft words: 'OK, Philip, he's out cold and won't be bothering us.'

He reluctantly let the man drop back to the ground and looked around for more attackers. No one else appeared at the window so Philip and John collected the dream machine and headed for the door. Entering the grand hall, they found to their horror that one of the intruders was standing in the middle of the hall holding Christine.

Robert Noble had managed to sidestep the guards that had emerged from the breakfast hall by hiding behind the many large curtains that adorned the grand hall.

Christine, alarmed by the commotion coming from the dream room, had broken her cover from behind the curtains. About to enter the dream room, she was suddenly pulled back by someone who immediately put a gun to her head, at the same time placing his large hand across her mouth.

'Not a sound, missy, or it will be your last,' whispered Robert Noble. He figured that this lady must be one of the wives of the men at the manor.

One thing Robert Noble knew well was stealth, from his time in the American Special Services during the war. This was before he was attracted by large sums of money offered by the company in New York. His brother, also an ex-army officer, had soon joined the company and he also knew how to make his way around places quietly. As he held Christine close to him, he suddenly heard a door open and, to his delight, saw two men, one of whom was carrying a box that could well contain the dream machine. As they came into the hall, Noble tightened his grip. 'Come in, gentlemen, I'm very pleased to see you.'

Stunned, Philip and John suddenly felt very exposed.

Noble waved his gun in the direction of the box. It was obvious what he wanted.

John looked at Philip and, without any comment, placed it on the floor.

'Push it over towards me and no funny business or she'll get it.'

It was just like a scene from the old Elliott Ness and the Untouchables but it was happening now and, for the second time, one of Philip's ladies was in danger.

Noble smirked as the box was slid across the floor towards him. As he bent down, he pulled Christine down with him, keeping her between the two men and himself. Suddenly, he found himself being hurled headfirst towards the two men. What he did not know was that Christine had also been in the Special Forces some years ago. She took advantage of Noble slackening his grip of her and, with his body leaning forward, she just helped it on its way with a first-class jujitsu move.

Philip and John were almost as surprised, but Philip rushed forward to disarm the now prostrate Robert leaving John to rescue his beloved box.

After making Noble secure, Christine and Philip hugged each other before their attention was drawn back to the continuing mayhem outside. Philip was worried about Ray. He had not seen him since the attack had started. Also, where was James, his ageing butler who surely would not be able to stand up to these fierce attackers? Arriving at the kitchen, he was greeted by an almost comical sight: there was James sitting on top of one of the attackers' heads, a glass of sherry in one hand. Sitting on top of another felled man was Ray, also with a glass of sherry in his hand. The two grinned, said, 'Cheers' and then laughed.

Philip's and John's mouths dropped open and, while they were pleased to see that the two men were safe and sound, they were concerned that the two appeared completely oblivious to the mayhem going on outside.

'Don't you realise there's a war going on outside?' asked Philip.

Ray, still sitting on his man, seemed quite undisturbed by this comment and, pointing with his sherry glass, replied, 'Not quite, Philip. The commotion outside now is the Flying Squad rounding up the rest of the intruders.'

Evidently James and Ray had hidden themselves in the large kitchen and, as and when the attackers had appeared in the room, had dispatched them with two of the extremely large and heavy saucepans.

A good job done by all with special attention to Christine and James!

39

It was an extremely cheerful group that sat down to dinner at Courtney Manor that evening. Included in the party were Davies and Jenkins who had obtained special permission to have the night off. Ben and his men were also relieved from the evening guard duty.

Christine found herself the centre of attention from Philip and Ray who toasted her with champagne. James was seated at his master's right-hand side, but felt just a little out of place at this special event. However, Philip would not take no for an answer. Tonight was a special honour which James found extremely to his liking. Getting up to get the master's coffee too was not permitted and James finished the evening feeling a little tipsy.

Ray and Philip also finished up just slightly drunk, and why not: at last they had seemingly reached the end of a nightmare that had cost several lives and caused much heartache. Ray's call to Italy to his wife gave John a chance to talk at length with Gina and for once the world seemed at peace, at least for that evening.

Sitting in his vantage point, a large tree overlooking Courtney Manor, Jason Noble who had seen his brother successfully enter the manor just a few hours ago was cursing. How could their carefully made plan fail this time? That damn Courtney family must have charmed lives; how could it happen? Twenty well trained men had been dropped by two helicopters, and still the attack had failed. He could not believe it as he witnessed his brother being led away in handcuffs and the rest of the men bundled unceremoniously into waiting police vans. This could not have happened – but it had. He knew there was nothing he could do about it. Cursing, he dropped down from the tree and made his way back to his car and Oxford.

John and Chris had finished their report on the dream machine and the friends were now ready for the next step which was to go to London and register the patent. Being in charge of the new company, it would be Philip and Ray's responsibility, but

John would be going as well to answer any technical questions that would almost certainly be asked.

The four men had come to terms with the last attack. Surely now the mob were a spent force. They were at last feeling more confident. With the two brothers Joe and Al Higgs safely behind bars and now the latest leader Robert Noble also behind bars, surely the mob would now give up.

Philip was surprised to receive an unexpected telephone call from his solicitor in Oxford. He wanted to know if the partners in the firm could meet him at his office as soon as possible.

Philip, Ray and John drove the short distance to Oxford for the meeting. They imagined he wanted to recheck everything before they left for London.

Sitting in his office, Reginald Simpson came straight to the point: 'When you asked me about registering the patent for your machine, I naturally assumed it was your own machine.'

'That is correct,' answered Philip.

'Well, can you advise me who Ralph Hess is?'

'Oh him,' John interjected, 'he was my last partner who unfortunately was murdered some while back.'

'It seems his next of kin, a certain Karl Hess, has recently made a request for the registration and the patent for the dream machine.'

'But that's impossible,' continued John. 'I've never heard of any Karl Hess and certainly didn't meet anyone by that name when Ralph and I worked together in Germany.'

'Well, as I see it, you have to explain this prior registration of the patent and prove that the dream machine is yours and not this Karl Hess's.'

Ray, John and Philip looked at each other in total disbelief. Who was this Karl Hess and where had he been all this time? Ralph had never ever mentioned having a next of kin.

'Well, you'll have to go up to London, taking all your paperwork with you and, of course, the machine. I'll go with you if you wish but I would imagine you will only need me once you have established the ownership of the machine.'

Thanking Mr Simpson, the three friends left his office and returned to Courtney Manor, their heads filled with all kinds of notions and tribulations. Surely this could not be true. It had to be a mistake.

Well, thought Philip to himself, everything was going too smoothly. This machine has maybe had a curse on it from the start. Either that or someone or something does not want us to produce it in the first place!

Jason Roberts knew that any more attempts to secure the dream machine by force would not be possible. Too many people now knew of the last attempt and it seemed everyone in the UK police force was guarding the damn machine. The company whose tentacles had spread all over Europe and Russia would not take defeat lightly, as illustrated in the past with the sudden disposal of Dieter Geist and Jay Browning.

40

Al and Joe Higgs had been held at the local police station before the Home Office ordered that they be deported. This was quickly arranged due to the fact the police could not charge them with Alice's death. With so much political pressure from the Italians, it was obvious that the authorities would not grant them bail.

Al and Joe Higgs, after hearing that they were to be

deported back to Italy settled in their seats at the Crown Court to learn their fate. They recognised a familiar figure in the public gallery – the face of Jason Noble, who smiled at them as if to give his reassurance. They glared back for as far as they were concerned they were only in this predicament because of him and his brother. They had heard from one of the guards in the police cells that the latest attempt to secure the machine had failed miserably and they gave silent thanks for that. The Noble brothers were finding it much harder than they had imagined. The hearing was short and sweet: deportation within two weeks with no appeal possible. The two brothers held their heads high as they left under guard for their next stay – the deportation centre near Heathrow Airport.

Philip, Ray and John gathered all their papers together and, with the machine, left the safety of Courtney Manor and drove to Oxford to catch the 8.30 a.m. train to London. They took turns in carrying the 'hat box' which had by now been adapted by Chris and John and was lead-lined for greater protection. The problem with this, of course, was that it made the box much heavier.

They would go first class as that allowed them more room and would also enable them to keep an eye out for any trouble. The train left Oxford station on time and, by the time it approached Reading, the men were more relaxed and talked quietly amongst themselves. It was anyone's guess as to what would await them in London at the specially arranged court where they had to prove ownership of the dream machine. However, one thing was certain: they would not give it up without a fight. Who was this person claiming to be the brother of Professor Hess? It was complete mystery to them. Hess only seemed to have had his mother alive at the time he was working on the dream machine.

*

The car that arrived at the deportation centre was large and spacious and the two men who got out were smartly dressed. They handed official-looking papers to the guards on duty there. These papers stated that the two men should take custody of the two Higgs brothers without delay.

The brothers were surprised to hear that they were leaving so soon as it had been understood they would be in the deportation centre for at least two weeks. Either way, they were soon released into the custody of the two immaculately dressed men and, when leaving the centre, were surprised to see the car was being driven out of Heathrow Airport instead of going to Terminal Two which was the usual point of departure for Europe. Al Higgs started to feel uneasy at this sudden change of direction and he questioned the two men who up to this time had remained silent. One of them just told them to relax and enjoy the ride which would not be long.

One hour passed and the car sped down the motorway and finally turned off at the Oxford exit which the brothers knew well. They started to feel much better. After all, this must be part of a plan to get them released and the two men must be part of it. The company, after hearing about the last failed attempt, must have realised that they were their only hope and were giving them another chance.

Pulling into a farmyard, the two brothers started to get out of the car only to be told to remain where they were. It seemed that this was purely to collect some refreshments.

As the two men who had collected them went into the farm, Al turned to Joe. 'I'm wondering if this was such a good move after all, Joe. I reckon we should get out of here.'

Joe agreed and reached for the nearest door but was

alarmed to find it firmly shut. The explosion that suddenly followed was very loud.

Soon afterwards, the men emerged from the farmhouse, checked what was left of the burning car and left quietly in another car that was parked at the back of the farmhouse. The company were just tidying up any loose ends in their usual inimitable way.

Philip stood up, yawned and stretched his arms above his head. 'I reckon I'll go and get a coffee. Anyone else fancy one?'

'That would be nice,' answered Ray.

'Me too please,' added John.

In the buffet car, Philip purchased the coffees and made his way unsteadily back to the carriage. The train lurched and swayed in different directions making his hold on the coffee rather precarious. He arrived at the door to his compartment but was surprised to find that it appeared to be jammed. Placing the coffees on the floor, he yanked the door hard. Suddenly it seemed to release and Philip almost fell through the opening.

What confronted him filled him with horror: a man was holding a gun on John and Ray.

'Come in, I've been expecting you. Please come in.' Jason Noble beckoned at Philip with his gun. Then, turning his attention to John, he asked calmly, 'Now if you pass me the machine, I'll be on my way and no one will get hurt, except maybe your pride.' He laughed as he said those words.

John and Ray had been taken completely by surprise by his sudden appearance.

Philip took a step forward; he for one was not going to give the dream machine up without a fight. Jason Noble calmly released a shot which lodged itself just above Ray's head. It was enough to stop Philip in his tracks.

Ray looked at John and gestured for him to get the machine from the overhead luggage rack. John stood up and placed his hand on the handle of the carrying case. This could not be happening again after all their hard work, sorting out all the problems with the operation of the machine, not to mention the deaths that had occurred. With a grim but determined look on his face, he turned and, with a superhuman effort, hurled the heavy boxed machine out of the open window which the men had opened previously to get some fresh air.

'If you want it that badly, go and get it!' he shouted at Jason.

'You damn fool, why did you do that?' Jason yelled and hurled himself towards the carriage door as if to try and stop the dream machine. Leaning out, he was just glimpsed the machine falling down the steep viaduct and into the River Thames which ran beneath the bridge.

Philip, although shocked at John's action, was equally upset about his brother being shot at and sprang into action. 'I agree, John. If he wants it, let him go and get it.' With that, he bent down and picked Jason up by his ankles and, with an almighty heave, hurled the unfortunate Noble through the narrow open window. It was fortunate that the man was leaning out of the window at the time which made Philip's task that much easier. Miraculously missing the passing upright supports of the bridge, Jason plunged over the edge of the bridge and into the River Thames below. The screams that followed were soon muffled as the deep waters in that part of the River Thames engulfed him. It was doubtful that anyone could possibly survive such a fall.

The train continued on its way with the three men standing in shocked silence.

'Well,' John said after a moment, 'perhaps it was just not the right time to allow the peoples of the world to dream too much!'

41

Several years later...

Kevin Scott dragged himself out of bed. He had been out the night before drinking with his mates. This was a practice he had followed every weekend since the age of fifteen. At least now, at the age of eighteen, he could be recognised as a legal drinker, although being of legal age had never bothered him before. Martin, his father, did not worry about what his son got up to. He himself was a frequent visitor to his local public house, the Hotpot Arms, which was located close to his home in Newbury, Berkshire.

In the past, Martin had worked for the Thames Water Authority and, as with most public authorities, had found plenty of time to relax and drink most lunchtimes. This was fine until he continued this practice every evening before going home. His wife, Joan, soon got fed up with this, left him and went off with his best friend Albert. This did nothing to alter Martin's demeanour and, finding that he had been left with their teenage son Kevin, (Albert not wanting to take over that particular responsibility), just made him meaner and inclined to drink even more.

He tended to take out his unhappiness out on his young son, hitting him and generally making the youngster's life a misery. This was only stopped when Kevin grew to Martin's own height thus making it impossible and not at all advisable for him to continue the practice. Martin's tactics changed and he started taking his son to the pub with him. An uneasy truce between them ensued.

After a quick wash, Kevin left the decrepit house they called home and made his way to his daytime job. He stopped briefly at the local baker's and collected his breakfast, generally consisting of a sausage roll and a pie. A cup of coffee was next when he arrived at the local supermarket Macy's where he worked as a shelf stacker. With his head pounding, he went about his work with little more than a grunt. His workmates knew better than to be too talkative to Kevin after one of his Friday nights out. He only managed to keep his job because of Sarah the department head's daughter's interest in him. She had to beg many times with her father, Roger, not to sack her wayward beau.

When Kevin arrived home that evening he found the house in darkness as usual and pottered around getting himself some soup. He cursed his luck for having a deadbeat father who did not seem to care if he was there or not. Martin had held down a very responsible job years before and had been in charge of the Thames waterways from Tower Bridge stretching right back past Oxford. He had managed the whole waterways and, when problems arose, Martin Scott was always there to correct and manage the situation.

It was on one of these occasions that one of the workers on the dredgers had brought back a strange box which had been recovered by one of the boats. It was extremely heavy and coated with slime and grime that had attached itself to the outside. Nobody had been able to open it. Martin looked at the heavy box with a certain amount of distaste. Surely it was not part of his job to clean it up? He was about to detail one of the men to do the job but, on looking around, found that they had made a hasty retreat. They knew Martin only too well.

Looking at his watch, he soon found an excuse to delay this particularly nasty job: it was nearing his lunchtime – that is, if you are fortunate enough to be able to start taking your lunch at eleven thirty in the morning. He placed the box in the lost property department. There would be plenty of time to sort it all out when he returned. However, returning several hours later, Martin now had other things on his mind than dirty old boxes and he went about his usual practice of locking the office door and getting his head down for a couple of hours. The box remained in the lost and found department for the next ten years.

It was only when Martin was informed that he could expect a thorough departmental inspection that he hurriedly started to tidy up the effects of his department, which of course included the lost and found items.

The re-discovery of the dirty old box left him with a dilemma: there was no paperwork. This was not surprising as he had neglected to fill out the proper forms due to his haste to get to his 'important' lunch. As for dates and times, he did not have a clue. The one person who could have assisted him with this problem had long ago left the employment of the Thames Water Authority. So Martin did what he considered the best option open to him: he placed the heavy box in his car boot and took it home. Arriving home, he removed it from the car boot, imagining it probably held a typewriter or something like that, and placed it in his basement. It remained there untouched and uncared for for another five years.

Andrew John Jefferson Junior had always followed in the footsteps of his father, John Jefferson. He had always been an upstanding member of the local community.

He had also inherited ten million pounds from his father who died in 2003 in a tragic manner, nevertheless leaving his only son well cared for financially. No one had ever come up with any acceptable reasons why his father had died in what appeared to be a suicide pact.

His father being a devout Christian made it even harder for Andrew to understand why he would ever carry out this act. It had happened in Italy where his father, uncle and friend had moved to many years before. Andrew was in England running the company that had been set up by his father, uncle and friend. The circumstances had been surreal with the three men as usual retiring to the 'Dream Room' as it was called, a room used solely by the three close friends. It seemed that, after drinking a toast, they had each placed loaded revolvers to their heads and pulled the trigger. The horror of discovering them was catastrophic for their wives and the remaining relatives.

The three men had been friends for many years with Philip and Ray actually being half-brothers, due to Philip's father's dalliance with Ray's natural mother at the Ritz Hotel in London, England. Andrew's mother was Italian and, with Ray being brought up in Italy, after a short time Philip and John had gone to live in Italy after John had married Ray's daughter Gina. Philip, the Earl of Chester and master of Courtney Manor Estates had a son called Robert by his first wife, Alice, who had tragically been killed many years before. As he became very close to Ray, Philip had sold his large estate and crumbling manor house to a property developer and, with the proceeds, went to live in Italy with his new wife Christine. John had continued to live there after his marriage to Gina. Philip and Christine's arrival had made the original threesome complete. There had been talk that in the past, while in England, the three men had been involved in some foolhardy project concerning mind travel or such like but, as time passed, it had been dismissed as idle talk. After the deaths, Christine and Ray's relatives locked the Dream Room up securely and it had never been opened since.

Andrew Jefferson was married to Bridget, a young lady

he had met while at Oxford University, who had trained and qualified as a doctor specialising in psychology and, later, diseases of the brain. Bridget was two years younger than Andrew and they had yet to start a family due to the couple's busy work schedules.

They lived in a large house just outside Oxford which had always been a favourite part of the country with his father John and his friend Philip. Andrew had been running the company since it was set up in the late seventies. The company manufactured electronic equipment and mobile phones. He chose to lead a quiet life and, with Bridget, had always worked hard to keep his rather large house in good order.

After the death of the three men, their surviving relatives had been left extremely well off but still kept up the charitable contributions that the men had always been renowned for. This was much to the relief of the local mayor and community. Robert was the sole heir to Philip's fortune, having moved to Italy with his father. He had married a local Italian girl, Jeanette, and they had produced a son whom they had called Roberto. He now ran the huge vineyards but kept in touch with Andrew and his wife in Oxford. Robert knew more about the Dream Room than he chose to reveal but always changed the subject when anyone tried to find out what exactly had happened that fateful evening. His usual response was that he was not there when it happened. This was not true as it had been he, after hearing the shots, who had entered the room and discovered his father and two friends slumped in their chairs. The sight would haunt him for the rest of his days; never had he been faced with such a distressing scene. He had loved his father and he had been told about the strange happenings that took place all those years ago on a certain train journey to London. His silence did nothing to help throw light on the three apparent suicides, and, strangely, the remainder of the family including Philip's wife Christine and Ray's wife Rena also maintained their silence.

Robert Courtney's quiet life was about to change. It would not be long before this terrible part of his life would be coming back to haunt him and his family.

42

Kevin Scott was bored with life. He was bored with everything to do with his work and, if he was truthful, even with his girlfriend Sarah, a fact he tactfully did not inform her of. He lurched around his old house that had not had a coat of paint since it was built in the 1960s. He turned out the cupboards looking for something he could sell to enable him to go out the coming weekend. Finding nothing, he continued down the creaky stairs that led to the basement. Surely his father must have something he could sell enabling him to 'do the town' in the manner he richly deserved. Again he found nothing.

He was about to climb the stairs when on a shelf just above eye level he noticed an old box, clearly dirty but possibly an antique and, by the shape of it, an old typewriter. That could be of interest to Jake Lot who owned an antique shop in the nearby village.

Hauling the heavy box upstairs was not too much a task for Kevin and soon he was cleaning off the outside with a wet cloth, but where was the catch to open it up? He was about to throw the box on the floor when he stumbled across a cleverly concealed catch underneath which, after dousing it with oil, sprang open with ease. He raised the lid with a triumphant shout but, gazing inside, he was met by a sight that caused him to curse: a bicycle helmet! What an earth could he do with a bicycle helmet and, more to the point, what would Jake Lot do with it?

He looked at the helmet and found that, due to the box's lead lining, it was actually extremely well preserved. It must be at least forty or fifty years old, perhaps even older; maybe it was not such a bad find after all. He decided to take it down in the morning to old man Lot and see what it was worth. He would keep his find to himself. If his father knew what he had found he would certainly claim half or, worse still, take all the proceeds for himself. Hiding the box under his bed, he started to think about how much he would ask the old man for his special helmet. It may have belonged to one of the wonder cyclists who won the Tour de France. His mind relaxed as he drifted into a deep sleep.

Next morning was a day off for Kevin and he had arranged to meet Sarah for a day out in the nearby village but that was not for two hours so he decided to take out the old box and see what else he could discover: perhaps a date on the box, or even on the helmet itself. His father had retired to his usual bar stool in the Hotpot Arms and by now was most likely on his third pint.

Kevin polished the outside of the helmet with a soft cloth. He did not want to scratch it or he would not get a good price. He wondered if it would fit him so pushing back his wavy hair, he placed the helmet on his head. He found it fitted him quite well; it was a shame he did not have a bike or he could take the helmet for a ride. He laughed at his quip.

He had not been a good scholar at school but, over the years, he had become extremely streetwise due mainly to his father not leaving enough money for important things such as food. Yes, Kevin had surely had to make his own way through his early years and one thing he did know was how to turn a buck as the American saying goes.

He was not sure what and how it happened; one moment he was thinking of his father out drinking, his imminent date with Sarah, when suddenly he was experiencing a nightmare of such clarity he yelled out loud. He was with his mother who was telling him to be a brave boy as she packed her suitcase and, with a tap on his head, went out of the door to meet the waiting Albert Jones. The tears that cascaded down his cheeks were real enough and he wiped them away with the sleeve of his coat. His coat! What the heck was happening? It was the old blazer that he wore when he started junior school. It was the exact green that he had always hated and here he was wearing it.

Kevin pulled at the blazer and he knew he wanted to take off his school cap which was pressing down on his head. The next minute he was plunged back into his own room and sank to the floor with some force. What an earth was happening to him? He could not understand what was going on. His vision of his mother's departure was exactly how he had remembered it, but her assurances and her touch on his head had been even more vivid than he could remember.

An hour passed before Kevin could even look at the helmet again and, putting it back in the box and placing it under his bed, he left the house to meet the waiting Sarah who was already at the meeting place, the new Burger King which had only just opened that week. Kevin was strangely quiet all through their lunch and Sarah was starting to wonder if she had done something wrong again, and would Kevin start his usual bullish behaviour. That was the part of Kevin's attitude that Sarah hated: he always seem to take his displeasure out on her.

*

Roberto Courtney had decided he wanted to meet up with his cousin Andrew and, after arranging the time off with his father, booked his flight to England. Arriving at dawn he found to his pleasure that the sun was shining and, what was more, the forecast was for pleasant weather all the week that he planned to stay with Andrew and Bridget.

A car outside Arrivals hooted its horn and Roberto recognised his cousin Andrew who eagerly collected his case and placed it in the boot. The two men laughed and talked as if they had never been away from each other, but the truth was they had not seen each other for at least a year, such were the trials of running a large vineyard and, in Andrew's case, a large company which was an offshoot of Roberto's grandfather Philip, Uncle Ray and Andrew's father John's original company in Italy.

The trio had evidently found it better to relocate the whole company to England to escape the intrusions of the Mafia, old acquaintances of Ray's. It was not that he had been ungrateful to his old friends but, now he had his new half brother as part of his life, it was agreed that it would be better to move the business to England. Chris, the original company manger, had also moved to the United Kingdom but, after he suffered a heart attack, it was decided to let him return to Italy with a substantial pension to see out his remaining years.

Arriving at Andrew's spacious home, and sitting down to relax, Roberto started to regret that he had never married. Of course there had been lady friends who had flocked around him, but the truth was that Roberto was gay.

Andrew and Roberto followed an old Courtney tradition of coffee and brandy in the large drawing room which all the old houses in England seemed to have retained. Although his father had been an American, Andrew found he liked the life of the English gentleman and it seemed to suit his inherited wealth. Just how all this wealth had accumulated had never been explained but Ray Barone was already extremely wealthy from his communication and technology companies and Philip had benefited from the sale of the estate. What remained unanswered was how that wealth almost trebled within just a few years?

Andrew suddenly turned to the issue of the three men's deaths. He wondered if Roberto had any answers.

Roberto smiled. 'You know, Andrew, I brought this up with my father only last week.'

'What did he say?'

'Well, to tell the truth, he did seem to want to talk about it all, which was unusual for him. He normally refuses to discuss it.'

'Please go on, Roberto,' Andrew encouraged him.

'If you recall, they had this special room called the Dream Room which was only accessible to the three of them; not even their wives were allowed into it. Well, this wasn't entirely true. Several times Christine and my father actually got to go in there having a coffee and such like. The room was quite extraordinary: it was completely round, about twenty feet in diameter and had a large round table in it with three very large chairs, obviously very comfortable. Red leather, my father remembers. The room itself was unlike any other room in the villa. It had to have been built specially.' Roberto paused as if to see if Andrew was taking this all in.

Andrew leaned forward as if to catch his every word.

'The other strange thing was that all around the top part of the room were these strange portholes from which lights seemed to glimmer, sometimes very bright and other times dim. It was almost as if they were in some kind of suspended state.'

Andrew nodded eagerly, indicating for Roberto to continue.

Roberto shrugged his shoulders and then said, 'Nothing.

That was all my father could tell me.'

Andrew's face fell, his curiosity now even more whetted, he was extremely disappointed. He persisted, 'Can't Christine, Gina or Rena shed some light on this mystery? They must have some knowledge of what their husbands were up to.'

Roberto nodded. 'I'm sure they did, but they just remark that too much sorrow has occurred in their families already. They don't want any more and to talk about it would cause them such grief.'

Andrew thought for a moment. 'Look, Roberto, I'd like to come back to Italy with you and get to the bottom of all this. I must have inherited my father's gene for knowledge and I really can't rest until we finally get some answers.'

'I'm glad to hear this.' Roberto smiled. 'I was hoping you might want to do that. Perhaps together we can find out more about this.'

'I have to sort out a few things but I'd like to bring Bridget. Before we go, there will be a few things to arrange.'

The two cousins finished their drinks and retired to their respective beds.

43

Kevin could not rest. He had returned early from his evening out with Sarah which was extremely unusual because he nearly always stayed over at the apartment she shared with her father. Sarah was rather worried about his behaviour; he was restless and could not concentrate on anything they talked about. She even wanted to bring up the question of marriage but realised that, until she found out exactly what was troubling Kevin, this was just not a good time.

On his arrival back at the house, Kevin checked if his father was in and, finding he was not, went straight to his bedroom. His father was out as usual, most likely chatting up one of the bar girls at the pub. Kevin reached under the bed and pulled out the box, removed the helmet and gingerly placed it on his head. Then he waited – nothing. He tried again and again – nothing. Frustrated, he tried yet again but all to no avail. He sat back in his chair and pondered. Had he imagined the previous episode? Had he been that drunk from the night before to imagine the incredible experience? It had been the most incredible happening of his young life.

The helmet seemed to relax him and he drifted off in a deep sleep. He woke up with a great fear, for there in front of him was another part of his life he had forgotten: the first time he had been picked on by the town bullies. He had been ten years of age at the time and was just walking home. There had been six of them and they surrounded him and demanded money. With three of them holding him down, they removed the ten pence piece he had on him at the time. It was all he had and was the result of getting his father some fish and chips. Not that his father had given it to him; Kevin had found the ten pence on the ground outside the chippie. He fought and kicked out at the thugs holding him down, shouting and screaming at the crowd looking on to help him. No help came and finally he was left on the ground, without his ten pence and feeling very let down by his fellow town folk.

This was total recall. Now he remembered all the faces of his attackers, the time, the date and even the youths that held him down. He knew some of them but had put all this behind him, choosing to block out the incident entirely but it had obviously had a negative impact on him at such a young age.

How and why could he now remember it so clearly? It was some time before Kevin concluded that it must have been the helmet on his head that had made this possible. He spent the next few hours trying out his new found toy and, the more he used it, the more excited he became. This had to be a dream though; it could not be happening to him. After all, he had always had nothing, not even winning ten pounds on the national lottery which he occasionally bought a ticket for. A dream indeed!

He was just about to call it quits for the evening when he had another experience that amazed him. He suddenly had an image of his father falling down the embankment alongside the railroad. He saw everything: the trip, the fall and people running after his father to pick him up and asking him if he was alright. His father obviously was because he just resumed his walk back to his home. Kevin suddenly heard the sound of the front door opening and, quickly putting the machine away in its usual hiding place, went down to see if his father was alright. After questioning Martin, he was slightly upset to find his father was indeed fine and did not even mention his fall. Kevin retired for the night – well, one out of ten was not that bad. Obviously he could not have total recall correctly every time.

Next day Kevin went back to his job and, while he kept remembering now and again his experience with the dream machine, he still could not come to terms with how and what was happening to him when he placed the helmet on his head.

He decided to stay sober that night so he could be in complete control of his senses. Cancelling his date with Sarah, he returned home to play again with his newly acquired machine. Once more, the hours passed and again Kevin managed to conjure up several instances from his past. He found he could do this by simply thinking about certain times in his past life which were of interest to him. The more he used the machine, the more he seemed to perfect the experiences he had.

It was much clearer and most precise and he came to the

conclusion that the 'helmet' he had discovered in his basement was indeed magical, although that seemed a little far-fetched – it had magical powers which only he could use. He had one further piece of news before he retired to bed that night: his father came in cursing. It seemed he had fallen down the embankment on his way home and had the bruises to prove it!

Kevin did not have much sleep that night. Not only could he see into the past, but he could also see into the future. There was only one way to find out and the next day he rushed to the newsagent's and bought himself a ticket, using the numbers he had managed to 'dream up' that very morning. He waited eagerly Saturday Lottery, checking his numbers with great anticipation. Yes, he had won the lottery; he had managed to win the grand total of ten pounds! Even more confused, he went and joined his mates in the local public house, returning home that night extremely drunk and falling quickly into an alcohol-induced sleep.

The next morning a fuzzy and bleary eyed Kevin exclaimed, 'Bloody machine, I wish it would make up its mind. Whose side is it on anyway!'

44

Martin Scott had, for many days, been wondering what his son Kevin had been up to; normally he was coming in in the early hours of the morning. He constantly had to complain about his playing of loud music which is normal for young men of his age. He went to seek out his son and, finding his room empty, was about to leave when he noticed a strange box sticking out under the bed. He pulled it out thinking that it did seem familiar and, opening it up, was rather taken back to see this strange helmet which he at once took to be a bicycle helmet. He pondered: could he sell this strange hat to one of the local cycle shops? He was just about to tuck the heavy box under his arm when, turning around, he was faced by his son Kevin who appeared to be a little angry.

'I was just coming to find you.'

'Well maybe, but you can put that back on my bed,' said Kevin sternly.

'Oh come on, Kevin, we can make a few bob on this,' argued Martin.

Kevin was perplexed. He knew he could not reveal that he knew the real powers of the machine so he craftily pretended to agree with his father.

'OK, but I'll take it down and sell it. Then you can have half.' This seemed to satisfy his father who relaxed his hold on the heavy box and placed it on Kevin's bed. He left the room; he was rather late for his meeting at the local pub anyway.

Kevin knew he had to do something and do it soon. He waited for his father to leave and then started to throw clothes into a suitcase. He knew he couldn't go far with his present finances so, leaving the house, he headed for the one person he knew would be sympathetic to his needs: his girlfriend Sarah.

He received a warm welcome from her at the apartment but not from her father Roger, Kevin's immediate supervisor at work. He had long ago put Kevin down as a loser of the first order and, seeing the suitcase, he straightaway whispered in his daughter's ear that he did not want Kevin staying at his house. Sarah was angry at her fathers' response to her boyfriend's plight but she knew she could not go against his wishes. Taking Kevin into the kitchen, she asked him what on earth was going on, to which Kevin lied and said his father had kicked him out without any money.

It was soon evident that the only way Sarah was going to help was to give her wayward boyfriend some money so he could at least get somewhere to stay that night. Kevin gratefully took the money and headed for town, finding a reasonable bed and breakfast. He was pleased that he was on his own as this would allow him to sort out the problem of the helmet which to all intents and purposes was behaving more like a machine and a machine that operated independently.

Roberto and Andrew left for Italy with Bridget's promise to catch up with them as soon as she could arrange a break from her heavy work schedule at the local hospital.

Arriving at the villa, they grabbed something to eat before arranging a meeting with Roberto's father, Robert, at the villa. Andrew let Roberto take the lead because he at least had had a prior discussion with his father as to what actually took place that fatal day.

Robert started, 'I guess it's about time you both know the truth, but I'm not sure you will even understand what happened that fateful evening years ago.' He suggested they all adjourned to the Dream Room to start at the beginning.

The men entered the room which Robert opened with a key card similar to those used by the local hotels. The lights came on automatically and the temperature seemed to be controlled at a pleasant level. The walls of the room could be likened to a planetarium and glistened in the subdued lighting. Inserted at shoulder height in the walls were thirteen porthole- shaped lights. Each circle appeared to hold a round globe, about twelve inches in circumference. Three chairs were placed equidistant from each other around the table and the men were surprised to see that the circle of lights that had been glowing upon their entry into the room now started to glow even brighter.

Robert then asked them to be seated. They sat down in the luxurious chairs which were made of deep red leather. The round table was made of some kind of metal which had a kind of reflective coating on it which was smooth to the touch. It gave the impression that it was also extremely strong. Inserted in the table in front of the three men were three black computerised panels which consisted of numbers which glowed in the twinkling lights. In the middle of the table was a large circle.

Robert asked the two men to put on the headsets which consisted of dark Polaroid-type glasses with large side arms that were designed to grip tightly against the side of the head. He explained that these side arms had concealed microphones and headphones enabling the wearers to listen and talk to each other. This was an offshoot from the technology of Ray's mobile phone company. He then asked the two men to press down on the lights which shone the brightest on their individual panels. Robert did likewise. They did as requested and immediately the round circle opened to reveal a globe similar but much larger to the ones in the walls of the room. As the gap in the circle widened, the globe rose to a position which completely filled the space. The globe seemed to consist of pure crystal similar to the Crystal Skull that had been found many years before.

It was completely transparent except for a mist that seemed to swirl around this strange crystal at irregular intervals. It seemed as if it was just waiting for something to happen. Robert had seemed to have been in control of the procedures, but even he jumped along with the other two men at what happened next. The room was suddenly filled with bright darting lights that emanated from the thirteen circles of lights which cascaded towards the globe in the centre of the table that was now extremely bright.

The orbs from the circle streamed towards the globe, and

they seemed to enter the centre of the globe now shining with a greater intensity. The three men jumped up out of their seats, terror showing on all their faces. As they stepped behind their chairs, the bright lights immediately retracted, retreating into their original circles.

Andrew was the first to talk: 'What the hell happened there?'

Robert calmed down, explaining that he had been following instructions left to him on a disk left by his father. 'I've never actually done any of this before because I knew that there had to be three persons present to activate the system.'

Roberto turned on his father. 'I think you'd better explain before we go any further. Exactly what is happening here and, more to the point, how?'

Robert suggested that they should adjourn to the lounge and have a drink, promising to tell Roberto and Andrew everything he knew including how the Dream Room had evolved from something that had once been called the dream machine.

Kevin looked at the estate agent's particulars. It was a nice house; rather smaller than he had envisaged but he knew it would have to do for the time being. He had finally managed to work out how to use the machine to his best advantage. It was a simple matter of going forward a couple of days into the future at one of the large stocks and shares markets, noting what state the shares were and then placing his bets accordingly. Of course, he made many errors to start with but once he had learned the ropes he was able to read the signs better. He had borrowed even more money from his long-suffering girlfriend Sarah, before he eventually became self-sufficient..He had realised that the machine seemed to recognise what he wanted to do without much effort. Surely it was not capable of reading his mind; he dismissed the thought and was just pleased that he was getting the results he wanted.

His softly-softly approach had gone unnoticed by the usual authorities and, by spreading his 'bets' around by moving around the country, he had managed to build up a nice little profit. This was enough to buy the house which he was now looking at with his even more adoring Sarah.

They moved into the property which had been on the market for some time. Martin, his father, had been too busy to notice hardly that his son had not been around since the evening he had staggered back from his night out at the Maypole Arms. Sod him, he thought as he looked around for that helmet which might provide him some extra cash. No use, that bloody son of mine has sold it and kept the money himself. Not to worry, I'll get rid of his CD player and such like. If he could have seen the new furniture and stereo systems being delivered to Stoke Manor in the nearby village of Witney he would have choked on his pint.

Sarah was in her element and for once her father, after the initial shock, had come around to the fact that perhaps he had misjudged his daughter's boyfriend. However, how he had suddenly acquired all this money was a mystery to him. He just hoped it had not come through him dealing with drugs.

Robert suddenly suggested that they invited Rena, Gina and Christine to join them; three very important people who had remained silent for reasons best known to themselves. Maybe they would agree however now to tell the men what exactly had happened that fateful day. Time had been gracious to the ladies and, despite the tragic deaths of their spouses and their own advancing years, they had remained fit and well in the Italian climate. As they lived at the villa, it was not long before they were located and all of them readily consented to join the men who were now outside on the terrace.

They waited until the men had retaken their seats before suggesting that the men each pour themselves a glass of vino, as they might need it. This caused even more anxiety. Rena explained what had taken place on a certain train journey to London, leaving nothing out, including what Philip had done to a man called Jason.

'When they found that they had lost the dream machine they were devastated although they didn't seem to be so bothered about the fact that Philip had thrown Jason out of the window. By the time they arrived at Paddington Station, they had decided on a plan: first they had to return to Oxford by the next train, and secondly, they had to leave the UK for a sunnier climate; in other words, return home to Italy. Philip knew he would have to tidy up things up in Oxford but, for John and Ray, it was much easier for them to pack their bags and catch the next flight out to Italy. Philip at once put up the estate for sale and, taking his butler James with him, followed as soon as the sale was completed. It was indeed very fortunate that property developers at that time were eager to obtain large plots of land to build houses and Philip soon found that he was soon able to book his passage for both of them.

'You must remember that day, Robert, because you were not at all happy about leaving the estate and all your friends. Within a few weeks of arriving home, the three men knew they had only one option: they had to rebuild the dream machine.

'They still had the plans prepared by John and Chris, but they decided to rethink the whole concept. They realised that they would have a fight on their hands registering the patent in the face of opposition from Hess's brother, if that was who he was. They also knew this would involve giving up all their secrets just to prove it was they that owned the machine. John then came up with some thoughts he had expressed some years before: he suggested that they turn the machine into a room.

'His plan was simple and what he proposed left Philip and Ray temporarily lost for words. It was to build a machine which would be placed in a room that would become the machine itself. Your Uncle Philip was the first to comment as usual. He said, "Not a lot to ask then." That was typical of him.

'Ray was his usual non-committal self but, after some thought, said that he liked the idea. However he was doubtful that they could do it. Chris then joined in and agreed with John – it was certainly worth a try! Then Philip said it would take a lot of money and remarked it was a good job he had sold the estate.

'It took six years for them to complete even the room itself. It was extremely difficult to obtain the right materials for it. You see, they didn't want anyone to know what they were doing. The room would have to be circular and would have to be secreted away somewhere in the villa, away from prying eyes.'

Andrew and Roberto looked at each other. Andrew slowly shook as head; what on earth was coming next?

45

Kevin's luck was running out. His sudden wealth had not gone unnoticed and the newly promoted Inspector Ken Morris had checked out this new man on the block who seemed to have money to burn. There appeared to be no drugs involved, no crime as such, no misappropriation of any public funds. As a matter of fact, this young man had never been on the dole. He had been in a few scuffles with the police in the past but to all intents and purposes he was as clean as a whistle.

He was making his money on the stock market and that

was not illegal in any way, unless of course he was short-selling which would come to light sooner or later. In fact, he was a little bit too good to be true. The inspector had filed his report with a proviso that someone keep an eye on this new entrepreneur.

The money continued to come in at an incredible rate. Kevin just put it down to luck and the good nose that he had always had. He used to brag: 'I just put my thinking cap on!'

He was now a millionaire four times over and rising. He and his father had made up, and Kevin, feeling sorry for his father, had set him up in a new house with a small income.

Martin, for his part, was happy enough but not for long. Soon he started to wonder what would happen if Kevin and Sarah were to meet with an unfortunate accident. Who would get the money? He dismissed this thought – how could he think such things. He knew that Kevin had been more than generous to him. He would not even consider this scenario – well, not for now.

The ladies were continuing their story about how the dream machine had become an even larger commodity. The room was eventually ready for the next and most difficult step: the actual installation of the dream machine; but what would it consist and how would it work? While this was going on, Gina had also been busy producing a son whom they named Andrew and who smiled as this was mentioned.

'John and Christopher had worked out what they considered a simple plan: they would install raw crystals around the room placed so they would produce beams of information,' Christine explained. 'These would connect to a larger crystal that would be located in the centre of the room. The thirteen outside crystals rotated like a vortex situated in the outside skins, the velocity of which produced the energy that made the machine work.

'Years of difficult negotiations had gone before but it seemed that when large amounts of money were involved, nothing was impossible. The men amassed large amounts of raw crystals from South America and it would take many years until the room was ready for testing and, hopefully, use. How it would all come together was anyone's guess.'

By now, Robert and the other two were impatient to learn just how the machine or, should they say, the room worked. Not having the knowledge as to how the original dream machine worked, they just could not understand what the room was used for! Robert then filled in some more information about how the room worked from the information on the disk his father had left him. It was still rather vague as far as Andrew and Roberto were concerned, but they were finally able to grasp the basics of how the machine performed.

'As we said before,' Christine continued, 'it took ages for the room to produce the correct and desired effect. They had numerous problems getting the beams of light in the correct sequence to connect with the main crystal.'

Robert could not contain himself. 'But what does it do when it's working?'

The answer took their breath away: 'It told you of the past but more importantly it is also able to inform you of the future,' Gina answered.

Andrew wanted more answers. 'How do you work it and how do you control the actual machine?' He had been sitting silently taking in everything.

'It took years to sort that out,' went on Rena. 'They found the only way they could operate it was with the three of them being in the room at the same time, something which they had not done with the original dream machine. This is why you have three seats in the room and the panels are set exactly so they alone could control the functioning of the room.'

By now the three ladies were growing tired and, seeing this, Robert, Roberto and Andrew decided to call it a day even though they had many more questions to ask them. Sitting down that evening talking amongst themselves they could have been mistaken for the original three men that started on their quest to produce the first dream machine.

The next morning, the family reconvened in the lounge next to the Dream Room.

Eagerly waiting for the ladies to start, the three men sat in silence.

Rena started. 'We have told you how the Dream Room came about and now we'll tell you what's been happening since its creation. Our husbands were quite secretive about what they did in there but we found it best not to ask too many questions.

'It was then that the people started arriving at the villa to see them. We were never told why these people came, but they always spent some time with the men. They visited frequently at first, but then they seemed to come just now and again. They came for the knowledge that your fathers gave them, knowledge that they all seemed pleased to receive. I did ask Ray what exactly was happening but he just assured me that everything was fine and that what they were doing was helping humanity. I didn't ask again. I don't believe they asked for or received money from these people. We did, however, always seem to have plenty of money to go around as you all know when you received your inheritance early.'

The three men nodded in agreement. Andrew by now was eager to ask the big questions and he finally did, gently directing it towards all three of the ladies. 'But what happened?

How did it go so wrong?'

Roberto also spoke: 'Why did Grandfather die?'

The three ladies all shook their heads, looking perplexed. 'We don't know,' they chorused.

The meeting concluded and the family retired to have lunch. Afterwards, while the ladies took the opportunity for a siesta, the men retired to the terrace and sat there in silence.

Andrew spoke first. 'I do not believe my father would have taken his life for nothing and not left a message. I believe the answer is still there – in the Dream Room. I'm going to find out exactly what happened. Do you both agree?'

The other two men nodded their agreement.

46

Kevin and Sarah had produced a daughter Louise and, shortly after, a son whom they called George. Kevin had now come to terms with his new found wealth and become quite a nice person. All those evil thoughts he had had about mankind had gone; all the disappointments of the past had long disappeared with all the money conveniently erasing every one of them. He found that his love for Sarah was much deeper than he thought and he went about making her as happy as he could. He even gave his father-in-law a good position in one of several companies he had set up. He was also now the owner of the local football club and, not surprisingly, had plenty of new friends that came around in great numbers.

He recognised some the old school bullies and would drop some hints now and again by casually lighting up a cigar with a ten-pound note just to see the look on their faces. Now Kevin was the King, and when the King spoke or lifted his hand, everyone sat up and took notice. Yes, King Kevin had reached his rightful place and he intended to stay that way.

He would retreat with his growing family to his one of his many villas, some of which were located in the Caribbean. In fact he owned two or three of these islands; they could not always remember which ones though. Yes, life was extremely good, and reaching the point that the use of the dream machine was now very limited. After all, Kevin had more money than he could ever spend.

He was out driving alone in his Porsche when he suddenly came upon a car that appeared to have broken down and was blocking the road on which he was travelling. He was about to stop when a shot came from the right-hand side and struck Kevin on the side of his face. As he struggled with the controls of the car, a second shot struck him in his left shoulder causing him to lose control and the car to swerve violently off the road and down a steep embankment. The Porsche turned over and over and Kevin was thrown out of the car near the bottom of the slope. Darkness overcame his senses and he slipped into unconsciousness.

Two men came to the edge of the embankment, peered over and casually remarked that one of them would have to go down there and make sure he was 'finished off'. They could see flames coming from the wreck and knew that the car could explode at any time. They started to argue about who should make this rather precarious climb down. Suddenly they heard the sound of an approaching car.

'I reckon he's had it,' remarked one to the other. 'Let's go and get our money.' With that they got into their car and sped off.

Mitch and Terry Wise were out with their girlfriends. They had just been to get a burger and now were taking the girls for a Sunday drive in the country. As they rounded the corner, they could see some skid marks on the road that seemed to go only one way: over the side of the cliff. Pulling the car to the side of the road, Terry got out and, looking over the side of the embankment, could see the now burning car.

'There's got to be someone down there,' he shouted. 'Call the emergency services and ask for ambulance and police.'

Mitch reached into his pocket and pulled out his mobile phone which his father had recently given him and phoned the police. The two men stood at the top of the cliff and looked down. How could they get down there and see if they could find anyone? They started over the edge.

'Be careful, the car could blow up any moment,' cautioned Debra, Mitch's girlfriend.

Terry and Mitch picked their way gingerly down the deep slope, stopping only to see if they could see anyone in the burning wreck. It was clearly empty and the two men hastened by and continued down the slope. It was an opportune moment when they both tripped and fell to the bottom as, at the same time, the car's petrol tank exploded. The blast went completely over their heads. Getting up, they could see the sports car was now completely engulfed in flames. The two girls at the top of the embankment were now almost hysterical and were shouting for the two men to come back up.

'Don't worry,' Terry called up to them, 'we're both all right but I'm not so sure about this poor fellow who we've just found down here.'

'Any sign of that ambulance?' Mitch shouted up.

'Yes, we can hear the sirens now,' Lisa, Terry's girlfriend answered.

Within minutes, the ambulance and the police arrived. They, in turn, quickly arranged for a rescue team to be called in. However, the rescue team, upon reaching the injured Kevin, decided it would be impossible to move him straightaway because of the other wounds that they immediately identified as having been caused by gunshots. This was not an accident. It was more like attempted murder – or even murder if the man died.

Terry, Mitch and the girls were warmly thanked by the police. Having established that there was nothing more they could do to help, they continued on with their afternoon drive. They would certainly have something to tell their mothers and fathers when they finally arrived home.

A helicopter managed to land and was standing by. After the medics had finally managed to stem the bleeding from the wounds, the rescue team carefully lifted the desperately injured man back up to the main road and into the waiting helicopter.

One of the police attending the accident suddenly announced, 'Do you know who this man is?' Without waiting for an answer he went on, 'That's only Kevin Scott, one of the richest men in England – perhaps in Europe!'

'Bloody heck,' replied one of his colleagues. 'The man has certainly made someone mad. Who could have done this?'

After putting the children to bed, Sarah had given instructions to Betty, the cook, to prepare Kevin his favourite meal: corned beef salad, one of his favourites from the old days. She smiled when she heard the phone ring. That would be Kevin giving her some excuse why he was so late coming home. He normally always tried to get back before the children were put to bed. She could not get over the change in her husband. After all, before they married she was not even sure she could continue loving him, such was the mean disposition that he displayed now and again.

Answering the phone, she could not understand what some woman was telling her. She was asking Sarah to come to Oxford Infirmary to see her husband who had been in a road accident, and what was more she should come as quickly as she could.

Replacing the receiver, Sarah felt like she was in a trance and she walked out of the house without even telling the nanny or the cook where she was going. Tears streamed down her face as she recalled what the woman at the hospital had said: 'Come as quickly as you can.' No, that couldn't be right – not now with everything so perfect. God, she could not believe it.

It would be several hours after arriving at the Oxford Radcliffe Hospital before Sarah was allowed into the private room in which her husband Kevin lay after coming out of intensive surgery. She approached the bed, fearing the worst, but she was unprepared for the sight that greeted her: her husband was lying there with tubes coming out of almost every part of his upper body. He had an oxygen mask on his face that was deathly white, enabling him to breathe. She cried silently to herself as she held his hand gently and just sat there in silence.

How could this happen to her husband, a man who had turned from an ill-mannered lout to a loving husband, who had found happiness after many years? The fact that they had many millions of pounds in the bank might. However, what was money if she was about to lose the only man she had ever loved?

47

Chief Inspector Ken Morris had arrived at the crash scene and, looking over the edge, he could see the burnt out sports car that was being pulled back up to the road. After about an hour inspecting the accident site, he was about to leave when his deputy Detective Sergeant Steve Pearce came up to him. 'This man certainly had some luck, sir. It seems he was thrown from the car just before it exploded. The two men found him about ten feet further down and they were lucky themselves when the car exploded again.'

Morris looked at his sergeant. 'And that was lucky?'

'Well, it was if you take into consideration that the darn car blew up into hundreds of pieces, sir.'

'Yes, I take your point. Do we know anything about the poor sod?'

'Well, sir, it seems he is a local bigwig called Kevin Scott.'

'Hold on a minute, Steven, wasn't he shot as well?'

'Well yes, sir, I was coming to that.' Pearce could feel his face growing redder by the second.

'I know that man. I've actually met and interviewed him about his sudden wealth. Seems he's exceptionally well off and that occurred in a relatively short time as well.'

'Well, he's been taken to the Radcliffe Hospital in Oxford. He's already had an emergency op, and his chance of survival is about fifty/fifty.'

As Pearce was driving him back to Oxford, Morris could not help thinking of a past shooting that his uncle, Sergeant Jenkins, had related to him when he and his boss, an Inspector Davies had attended all those years ago just outside Witney, when a Mr Philip Courtney lost his wife. His uncle had become a close friend of Philip's and the two other men since he had retired and had spent some time with them in Italy. Ken Morris's uncle Clive Jenkins had related to him many times the strange case of a dream machine which had been invented over forty years ago and had ended in tragic circumstances with many deaths before the machine was finally lost on a trip to London. Morris had joined the police at a young age and had now worked his way up to be an inspector after his uncle had recently retired.

Arriving at the hospital, he was shown into the private room by the Staff Nurse who politely informed him he would have no chance to question the gravely ill man and it would not be proper for him to quiz his grieving wife. Morris looked perplexed: don't these nurses ever think we have hearts, he thought as he gazed at Sarah holding her unconscious husband's hand. It did not look good for the self-made millionaire. He left the hospital and went back to his office and did what he often did in these cases: he waited.

The news that Kevin Scott had come out of his coma was extremely good news both to his wife Sarah and to Inspector Morris who wanted to talk with this unfortunate man. He arrived at the hospital just as Sarah was leaving for a few well-earned hours of rest. However, he found he still could not talk with Kevin who continued to slip in and out of a deep sleep. Doctor Brown who had performed the operation on Kevin had explained to Sarah that this was a good sign as he would heal more quickly whilst sleeping. Sarah accepted this. She wanted her husband back to his normal self and home with her as soon as possible.

The policeman caught up with her as she was about to get into her car and he gently asked if he could visit her at home to talk about the incident. She readily agreed but informed him that she did not any idea why someone should attempt to kill her husband. Morris arranged for the visit next day after she had again returned from the hospital. With Martin, Kevin's father, now taking turns to sit with his son, it was a little easier for Sarah to get back to some normality with the children asking when Daddy was coming home. It was nice to assure them that he eventually would be coming home but not just yet. In fact it would be some weeks before that would be possible.

Meanwhile, in Italy, Andrew, Robert and Roberto were resuming their efforts to find out exactly what had occurred all those years ago in the room known as the Dream Room.

Rising early, Andrew, Roberto and Robert entered the Dream Room and, without activating anything, sat at the table with the intensity of the surrounding lights going up and down, almost as if they were eager to be activated.

Robert turned his attention to the three black panels and noted for the first time that it resembled some of the modern mobile phones that the company had produced over the years. What was quite interesting was the particular four numbers glowed brighter than the others, all different on the three individual panels.

'Let's have another look at these panels,' he said, running his hands over each of the other numbers but avoiding the ones that glowed the brightest.

Roberto looked at his and Andrew also gave his close attention. The numbers went from one to nine plus zero which of course gave the possibility of choosing all kinds of combinations.

Andrew came up with a suggestion: 'How about each of us try certain numbers making sure that we don't repeat them. If you look closely at each panel only four numbers on each of the three panels stand out.'

The other two men nodded their agreement. Robert said he would go first. 'I'm going to try just four numbers; and I'm going to try the four numbers on the four corners of my panel.'

He pushed gently the four corner numbers and waited for a response of some kind. Suddenly something that resembled a TV set similar to that which drops down from the ceiling in aircraft when they want to show an in-flight movie appeared from the centre of the ceiling.

The three men quietly marvelled that they had not noticed any joins which would have shown that some item had been concealed. Within seconds, the screen illuminated and the rugged features of Philip appeared looking quite serious.

He spoke in a serious tone which gave the three waiting men a deep sense of foreboding. Their fears reduced a little when Philip introduced himself and said he hoped he was talking to the heirs of Ray, John and himself. This had obviously been his aim when he gave Robert the disk that led them this far.

Philip went on to explain that the room had been built for the good of mankind and a lot of time and money had been spent perfecting it. It would seem that, after a relatively short time, the information gleaned from the three men's use of the machine was of great importance to other parts of the world. Indeed the visits in the past by certain dark-suited men were the result of invitations by the three men for other scientists and politicians to visit them. The invited guests were never allowed into the circular room but remained outside being entertained by the three spouses. Christopher had been there to supply some of the technical support but his part of the proceedings was curtailed when he suffered some more heart problems and had been forced to retire. The information given to the waiting guests would seem to have been solely for the particular country they represented and not for general release to other countries. Perhaps this was to ensure that the passing of the information was carefully controlled at all times. There evidently were no two-way discussions; the visitors were just informed about any future happenings that might affect their particular country. It was possibly the first case of fortune-telling about countries rather than individuals.

Philip now appeared to be reaching the conclusion of his statement but what he said just before he disappeared from the screen made the three men sit up with amazement: 'We have agreed to share with four countries, including Russia and China, the secrets of the dream machine. We feel at this time with all of us getting older and with the passing of each year that we cannot just stop giving out this very important information. We have supplied the technicians and the drawings for each country to build their own dream machines. Eventually there will be another six countries that will be invited once we are assured that the original four are conducting themselves correctly in the use of the machine. We have taken the precaution of building into the plans an override system which will enable us to disable any dream machine that may be used incorrectly. You will hear later how we have done this task and it will be part of your duties when you finally take over as keepers of the dream machine to monitor this. We will talk more when you have had time to absorb what we have told you and to look at the additional paperwork which will be given you after my broadcast has ended.'

With that the image on the screen faded and the TV disappeared back into its original position. Even after close examination, the three men could still not see any join that would show just how the screen was concealed.

'How are we supposed to receive the paperwork Philip spoke of?' Andrew asked.

As if Philip had heard his words, a drawer opened near Robert and a file consisting of around fifty sheets of paper made from almost silk-like material slid into view. Robert picked up the file and left the room, their minds swirling as they tried to digest all the information that Philip had related to them. It had been really eerie seeing him again after all these years, and that only added to the suspense the men felt. They could not comprehend just how this all came together. After all, it seemed that Philip's recorded message was made when everything was normal but what had happened afterwards to cause the men to take their own lives? They may have had some of their questions answered but, at the same time, they had been charged with new responsibilities and that would seem to be more than they bargained for. It was obvious that their way of life would never be the same again.

Inspector Morris and his sidekick Steve Pearce drove through the large wrought-iron gates that led to the grand manor house that was the home of Kevin and Sarah Scott. The name of the house was previously Stoke Manor but the locals had renamed it Stocks Manor after knowledge of him playing the stock markets got out.

Sarah answered the door and invited them in. Making them comfortable with a cup of tea, she answered their questions about the current status of her husband's health. Morris and Pearce were genuinely pleased to hear that Kevin was definitely on the mend.

'Did Kevin have any enemies you can think of?' Inspector Morris asked her.

'I guess he must have, but none I can bring to mind.'

Morris and Pearce nodded. 'That's normal when successful people make large amounts of money. There's always someone that is jealous,' Morris continued. 'We were thinking more of a disgruntled employee or someone like that.'

'No, no one, the only people we employ are domestic as Kevin keeps his side of the business private with only his stockbroker in London knowing what he's doing.'

'We'd like to look around, Sarah, if you don't mind.'

'No, of course not, look wherever you want. We don't have any secrets that I can think of.'

The two men thanked her and went about their way checking meticulously every room. They found that the house contained around twenty bedrooms, several lounges, a snooker room and gym. They were about to conclude their search when they came upon a room at the top of a landing which was locked securely.

'Go and ask Sarah for the key,' Morris ordered Pearce.

Pearce came back with Sarah, who looked puzzled. 'Kevin has the only one. I'll go and see if it's in the bag of personal effects that the hospital gave me.'

She returned within minutes, smiling and holding up a large key which she thought might fit the old locked oak door. It fitted and the three entered the room. For a millionaire four times over, the room itself was certainly not grand by any means, just having a round table, two chairs and a filing cabinet. Morris was about to ask for the key to the filing cabinet when he noticed a strange object on the top.

'Good God, what have we here?' he exclaimed bending over the box which was lying on the top of the cabinet. Pearce looked blankly at the object and shrugged his shoulders. Sarah looked equally blank and shook her head.

'Do you know what it is, sir?' asked Pearce

'I can't be sure; it is very heavy. Let's look at more closely.'

Morris looked under the box and unclipped the latch which enabled them to take off the cover. 'The inside of the box has been coated in lead and there's what appears to be a machine that looks like a cycle helmet. Good grief, I've seen something like this before. It was a picture in a book which my uncle had some years ago.'

Pearce looked expectantly at his boss.

Morris ignored the look and turned to Sarah. 'I'll need to talk with Kevin as soon as he's able to answer some questions.'

Nodding at the box, he continued, 'And I think it's best that we take this back to the office until Kevin can explain more about it.'

Sarah nodded her approval. The old box was no interest to her and she could not think of any objection that her husband Kevin would make; not for that old thing.

The two men drove back to the office with the heavy box. Peace looked strangely at his boss. 'OK, sir, I give up. Why on earth are you interested in this old box, and why are we taking it back to the station?'

'Steve, you have your new camera at the office. Take some detailed pictures of this machine as soon as we get back. All I can tell you is that this could be a very special machine and I think I may have solved the mystery of Kevin Scott's immense wealth.'

Pearce looked again at him but Morris would not comment any further. All he wanted to do was to talk with a certain someone as soon as he could.

Although Kevin was slipping in and out of consciousness still, he was improving each day. Sarah had been coming in every day and she could see the progress her husband was making, and when he started making a few jokes she knew for sure that he was indeed on the mend. It would however be several days before she recalled the fact that the nice policemen had visited the manor and removed that old box. She was of the opinion that such trifling things as old boxes were not of interest to her now recovering husband. Yes, news of the children would be of much more interest to him. Morris did check with the hospital to see if he could interview him but was told to check back again in a day or so.

48

Robert, Roberto and Andrew had been patiently going through all the paperwork that they had been given by their deceased relative. Andrew seemed to have more of a grasp of the data due to his involvement at the plant in England. He still found it difficult when it came to the how the room actually worked, and the three men had to go over and over it again before they could understand the basics of the workings of the room and the strange lighting. Contrary to their initial hopes, talks with the three ladies had not been very fruitful as they had never really been involved with the room from day one.

'I reckon we need to look at the room and its workings in more detail,' remarked Robert.

'I'm not so sure,' replied Andrew. 'I'd like to try to get a better idea of what has happened since Philip recorded that message.'

Roberto nodded in agreement. Robert shrugged his shoulders, admitting defeat.

One thing the men had agreed on was that anything they did with the Dream Room was with their total agreement. They had imagined that one of the reasons why the dream machine had worked so well was that the three men involved before had always worked as one. Robert suggested that they again ask the ladies if they could recall any of the team of men that would have been involved with the visits to other countries.

Meeting the ladies in the lounge later proved of some help with Gina remembering that there were many visits to several countries including the USA, Russia and France. She had been responsible for arranging the hotels and expenses, but the majority of these were covered by the parent country that was receiving the information to build the new machines. This had been happening two years before the three men's deaths, which made it around 2003. The three ladies retired for their normal afternoon nap.

'Does this mean the building of the machines is still going on?' Roberto was curious.

'Maybe we can get even more information from the Dream Room,' suggested Andrew. 'I mean, perhaps there are some more hidden TV panels, or do you think it was the only one.'

Robert shook his head. 'I have no idea and, unless they have the same sequence of numbers at each corner, it could take ages for us to hit the correct ones!'

Andrew continued, 'From what Gina has said, it does seem that there are at least four countries actively building a dream machine presently. Roberto, we must ascertain exactly who is building them. We should be able to do this by going back over the records and seeing where our personnel are based and how long they have been based there.'

Contacting the personnel department was the first place to start and the men found it easy to get the details of all the men who had been sent to each of the four countries, including the United States – right up to 2005 when the information ceased.

They checked and rechecked but found the same results: there was no trace of their men – they had not returned from Russia, China, USA and France. Even their families who had gone out with them had not returned.

The three men looked at each aghast. What could have happened? What had gone wrong? How could thirty family units have just disappeared?

Robert frowned. 'I don't like the sound of this. How could all these men apparently just leave the company without anyone saying anything about it?'

Andrew approached his mother, asking her if she could throw any light on the matter.

'When your father suddenly received all these requests from the men to be allowed to move permanently to Russia and China, they were very worried but when the men insisted they had to agree to their requests. Those who didn't wish to be transferred permanently just returned, also over a period of time. When questioned, they said they were offered great sums of money on the understanding that they stayed in the countries they worked in. In other words it was almost like a modern-day defection.'

'We must try to find out more about this,' Robert added. 'I suggest we go to the Dream Room and see if we can get the information there.'

Roberto and Andrew agreed. Entering the Dream Room, the three men found it quite easy to activate the TV screen again, using the four corner numbers.

It was Ray's turn to appear on the screen and he came straight to the point. His voice was rather strained and they could see that he was extremely worried. It soon became evident that Philip, John and Ray had been betrayed by three of the four countries that they had invited to join in the Dream World project, as they had named it.

One by one, starting with China, the men they had sent there had requested to be transferred permanently. They could only imagine that either the money offered them had been immense or that they had been forced to make the request. They had no way of knowing. It seemed that the ones that came back of their own accord had not been threatened but, according to Ray, all the ones that stayed were key personnel and the ones coming back could be easily replaced by home-produced staff. He went on to say that even France, one of the first countries contacted by Philip, seemed to put pressure on their workers to stay there permanently. Ray concluded that they were much closer to Russia than they wanted to admit.

The American government were the only government that still worked normally with Philip and Ray and no pressure put on the men they had sent over. However, they also expressed their concern about what the other three countries were doing. It was strange that the United Kingdom was never mentioned. Many questions needed to be answered but unfortunately this was a one-way transmission.

'We sent men over to see the people we had worked with from the start,' Ray continued, 'only for them to return empty-handed reporting that all the men originally in charge had just disappeared. Not one man in their original set-up was now in charge. In fact, both the Chinese and the Russians even denied any knowledge of the Dream Room! And top-level visits from Italian and EU politicians failed to get the two countries to admit any knowledge of the Dream Room.

'Philip went over and was not even allowed into Russia or China. We have no choice now but to think about deactivating the machines. However, it will not take them long to overcome this with the help of our own men still working for them. We are trying other methods to keep their machines from coming online but, while it took us years to perfect, with the drawings we gave them they could still be up and running in three years.

'If they realise it is possible to bypass our centre and create their own by joining up the three rooms together they can make one and end up with an even more powerful machine than our own.' Ray did not elaborate any further as to how this could be done.

With that, the screen went dead and retreated into the ceiling again.

The three men sat in stunned silence, their thoughts racing as they pondered these last mind-boggling events. They realised that, when the last bulletin was made, the problem was still ongoing and that the three originators of the Dream Room were trying to solve the problem. However, Robert, Roberto and Andrew had no idea if their relatives had succeeded, or was the threat from the three other countries still present?

49

Kevin Scott felt good for the first time in weeks. He was sitting up, taking normal meals and recovering fast from his injuries. He was eating his lunch when Sarah came to visit him. Just as he was enjoying the last of his cups of tea, she dropped her bombshell. During her usual update of things that had happened at the manor, she remarked causally that the detectives on their last visit had taken away the old helmet stored in the room at the top of the house.

Tea sprayed from Kevin's mouth as the enormity of what his wife Sarah had casually announced sank in and he exploded, 'They've done what?'

'Well, they were checking to see if they could find any clues as to why anyone would want to shoot you. It wasn't possible to talk with you as you were in a coma,' Sarah offered timidly. She quickly realised that Kevin's reaction meant only one thing: the removal of that old machine was more important that she had envisaged. She could be in for a bumpy ride – again.

Reaching for his clothes that had been placed in the bedside locker, Kevin had no problem getting dressed such was his haste and intention to get out of that hospital.

Sarah fearfully pressed the button for the nurse who arrived within minutes.

'What are you doing?' she asked Kevin. 'You're not ready to be discharged yet.'

But Kevin was not listening. Finally dressed, he stormed out of the room and headed for the hospital entrance doors. There he came to a standstill. He had no car and was forced to wait until Sarah caught up with him. However, home was not where he wanted to go – he wanted to go to the police station and would not stop until he got his precious money-making machine back.

He knew full well he could not reveal just how important the machine was to him but, with his anxieties at full strength, he kept his foot down on the accelerator until he arrived at the police station. His hasty arrival at the sergeant's desk was blunted however when, on demanding to see Inspector Morris, he was politely informed that the inspector was out – out of the country, Italy to be precise.

Inspector Morris walked up the path which led to his uncle's house and upon knocking on the door, it was opened by Glenda, his uncle's wife, and was shown directly into the garden where he found him lovingly tending the numerous plants. The old inspector was pleased to see his nephew and protégé, having been his mentor for many years before taking his retirement. Asking his wife Glenda to get them some tea, he enquired as to why the sudden visit after all this time.

Ken removed the pictures of the machine which had been taken by Pearce from his briefcase. 'Uncle, I think these could be self-explanatory, but can you confirm what this looks like to you?'

Clive Jenkins examined the pictures carefully. 'Good God, where did you get these and, more importantly, have you got this machine?'

'Yes, we have.'

His uncle shook his head again in astonishment. 'I haven't seen it for many a year, maybe thirty or forty years. I think the best I can do to help you is to give you a copy of the book my old mate Mike Davies wrote when he retired and left the force, it was called 'A Dream Machine – To Die For.'

'You mean all this has been documented in a book?'

'It certainly has. Admittedly it was written as fiction which got around any legal problems. He wrote it under a nom de plume, but both he and I were very much involved in it.' Clive laughed. 'I guess no one would have believed us anyway. It wasn't exactly a best-seller.'

He got up from his seat and walked to the bookcase. 'Here's a copy. I suggest you read it. It'll save me telling you all about it. You've recovered something which is most likely the marvel of the century and I suggest you should return it to its rightful owners who actually reside in Italy, or at least their descendants do.' After a moment's hesitation, Clive continued, 'The three men who invented this machine unfortunately died under tragic circumstances.' He said no more.

'Uncle, I can't take this machine out of the country,' Ken answered. 'It could still belong to this man Kevin Scott quite legally.'

'Well, I can only advise you that that may not be the case. I do know how the machine was lost and where, but if you put this in the public eye you could end up with many problems on your hands. It won't hurt to leave the machine under lock and key over here and go to Italy with these pictures to show the relatives. Please, Ken, treat this as high importance and a matter of national security. If you don't, you may live to regret it.' Again, his uncle chose not to elaborate any further.

Ken could tell by the stern look on his uncle's face that he was not joking. He left him feeling rather more confused than he went in, but he knew his uncle would not have uttered words of caution unless he had good reason. Ken decided that he would do as advised: leave the machine under lock and key and go to Italy with the pictures and see if he could get some more answers. Kevin Scott was still in hospital and could wait.

50

Inspector Morris arrived in Rome and made his way to the villa following the detailed instructions given to him by his uncle. His phone call ahead had been greeted with a non-committal response which only added to his puzzlement. However, he was welcomed warmly by the ageing ladies. Rena, Ray's widow, suggested that the inspector met with the three men. They would be very interested in what he had to tell them.

Joining the ladies in the lounge, Andrew, Robert and Roberto greeted Morris with sound handshakes. They had all heard about his uncle's help in the past to their fathers and grandfather. He laid out the pictures he had of the recovered machine. Andrew and Roberto sat in silence looking at the pictures.

'Good God, do you actually have this now?' Robert exclaimed.

'Yes, I believe this to be the original dream machine that your fathers and grandfather produced. I have it at the Oxford police station.'

The three men questioned the inspector as to how he had obtained the machine and he explained to them how he managed to acquire it. It might be that Scott had some kind of claim on the machine but how he came about it was not clear at this time.

Morris told them that his talk with Kevin's father had been

more enlightening because Martin Scott just came out and said the machine was his, and that he had found it years ago in the River Thames. He omitted the fact it had been recovered whilst he was in the employ of the Thames Water Company. His information, however; meant that the history of the machine could now be linked with the actions of John when he threw the machine over the bridge to stop Jason Noble from obtaining it.

'I am not worried about Kevin Scott and any claim that he might make to get the dream machine back; I reckon he would have too much to explain if he went to court,' Ken concluded.

The men thanked the inspector for the information but then went on to reveal even more startling revelations. The machine, although extremely very valuable, paled into insignificance when compared to the magnitude of the new Dream Room. Feeling rather obligated to him, they asked him to accompany them into the Dream Room.

Inspector Jenkins was dumbfounded as he stood in the middle of the round room, lights glowing in anticipation. They explained in detail how the room worked, what had happened and, more to the point, what could be happening even now.

Morris's attitude changed from one of lively interest to some degree of concern. He knew that what the men were telling him was a real threat to mankind. He sat with Robert, Roberto and Andrew for several hours and they finally agreed a plan of action: the inspector would return to the UK and endeavour to see the Prime Minister himself and make him aware of the threat of which possibly he had no knowledge.

Kevin Scott was incensed. He paced up and down in his lounge and Sarah was getting concerned that he would suffer a setback with his health which had up to now been improving daily. His disposition was not helped in any way when he received a visit from his father who firmly informed him that he, Kevin, had stolen the machine from him.

Kevin, thinking his father knew more about the machine, confessed he had made his money by using the machine. Martin Scott looked at his son with a blank look on his face. Kevin knew he had said too much. How could he have been such a fool? Now his father had him at a disadvantage yet again and Kevin knew that he could well regret having blurted out the truth about the dream machine. His father was not one to let it go. However, the situation now was that the police had the machine and it would take some hard talking to get it back.

They both finally agreed that they would meet later that week after Kevin had tried to retrieve the machine from the police.

Kevin sat waiting impatiently for the inspector to arrive and he was disappointed to see that he was not carrying the machine. Inspector Morris and Sergeant Pearce were invited to sit down and, after the usual pleasantries of enquiring about Kevin's health, they got down to business.

Morris listened to Kevin's rather angry request for the return of his old machine. Evidently, it was a family heirloom, an antique passed on by one of his grandfathers. He omitted the fact that his own father was involved and had in fact found the machine in the River Thames.

The inspector leaned back in his chair, looking steadily at the man who by now was sweating rather profusely. 'It is a little hot in here, Kevin. Are you feeling alright? Do you want to rest for a while?'

Kevin instinctively knew that he was being set up for a fall, realising that he was getting into a dangerous position. He knew that he could lose everything if Morris knew enough about the dream machine and its uses. He also knew that what he had been doing with the machine and making all his millions was definitely illegal. His manner changed quickly and he tried to appear nonchalant.

Morris, realising that Kevin had switched tactics, considered quickly his next step. He knew he did not want this to come out in the papers and he also knew that he had more pressing things to do in London that very week. 'Well, Kevin, I think it would be better to wait until you're feeling better and we can talk again. The machine is in a safe place so you shouldn't worry too much about your "family heirloom".'

Kevin reluctantly agreed and, with a sense of helplessness, bade farewell to his visitors.

Walking to the car, Steve wanted to know what had just happened in there. For the next few hours, Ken Morris briefed his sergeant about what had happened all those years ago, what was happening now, and what they had to do in the next few days. Morris smiled to himself. Why should he have all the worry? It was Steve Pearce's turn to be gobsmacked as he sat next to his inspector as they drove to London.

It was Martin Scott's turn to be incensed. Soon after his arrival at his son's manor they had a heated argument and, not receiving any credible answers to his questions, he turned back to his usual way of threats and more threats. In the heat of the moment, he even admitted to Kevin that he had told the police that he had found the machine years ago. Kevin ignored his father's comments. He could do nothing about how things stood at that moment. All the two could do was to wait.

He was about to tell him to get out when his father uttered something that made his senses reel. Looking at his son, his face full with rage, Martin said, 'I wish I'd finished you off properly!'

Kevin looked at his father speechless. Sarah who had been sitting quietly beside Kevin gasped. 'Oh no, Martin, please don't say it was you who arranged for Kevin's shooting?'

Martin Scott's face coloured. He realised that he had said too much. 'Of course not, it was just a figure of speech.'

Kevin looked at his father and just could not believe what he had heard. 'I think you'd better leave, Dad, and I don't think I want to see you again.'

Martin left the manor in great haste and, not looking back, got into his car and left.

Kevin and Sarah just sat in silence. Kevin knew that in the past things relations had not been that smooth but, over the last few years, they had improved and now they got on quite well – or so he thought.

Kevin looked at Sarah with tears in his eyes. 'I know Dad was always having a go at me but I thought what we've done for him over the past six years might have made things better between us.' He continued, 'But to try and kill me – that can't be right.'

Sarah looked at her tearful husband. 'What are you going to do?'

'I don't know.' Kevin shook his head. 'He certainly had hate in his eyes, and what if he tries again?'

51

Andrew, Robert and Roberto had much to sort out. In addition to Robert's daily tasks of running the huge vineyard, Andrew had to think about his responsibilities back in the UK. They made some hurried adjustments to their working schedules and started making plans to visit the Italian authorities at the highest level. It was about this time that Andrew's wife Bridget joined them after finally being able to prise herself out of her busy work schedule. It had only taken a month but Andrew for one was extremely pleased to see her. A petite, pretty and extremely intelligent woman, she was an honours graduate from Oxford University, outstripping in performance both the Courtney and Jefferson men who had gone before.

She was welcomed by the elder lady members of the family and made to feel at home. Andrew, who had no secrets from his wife, went over in detail what had been happening over the past few weeks, leaving nothing out. He wanted another person's input to the situation the family now found themselves faced with. What better person than his own wife whose opinion he always valued.

Bridget spoke also to the three ladies, making extensive notes as she usually did at work. She was careful not to upset them by being too exacting but she wanted to see if they knew more than they realised; anything that might shed some light on why the three men took their own lives.

It was at one of these sessions one evening that Rena revealed she and Ray had been talking whilst enjoying a nightcap before retiring to bed. She admitted that Ray had been deeply distressed about the Dream Room, and the harm that they could have possibly done by being too optimistic when sharing the secrets with the people they had invited to the room. It had obviously been too soon; they had put their trust in people that they had been dealing with, people who shared their scientific interest in what the Dream Room was forecasting. However, their masters above them must have had other ideas.

The general feeling emanating from all three men was that they had been fools; bloody fools to let out the secrets of the room to outsiders.

Rena then said an alarming thing: that Ray and the other

two had mentioned that maybe it would better if they were not there and took the secrets of the Dream Room with them. Was this the start of a possible suicide pact? Why had she not mentioned this crucial remark before? Was it because, being a Catholic, she would never admit that her husband could have been contemplating suicide?

She went on to explain she had spoken sternly to Ray about such thoughts and he had promised her he would not do anything silly. Perhaps this was a promise he was just not able to keep?

Bridget had a lot to think about as she typed up the report she intended to show the three men the next day. She also had some lengthy sessions with Robert as he had had meetings with his father Philip. They both concluded that it had to be something of gigantic proportions for Philip to even contemplate taking his own life. Robert could only remember Philip as a man who took life very seriously and had much to live for after his marriage to Christine.

The next morning Bridget sat with the whole family setting out how she chose to look at the facts she had been asked to investigate. The three men and the ladies had welcomed her views on this matter; anything that they as a family could come to terms with.

After going over all the details in chronological order, Bridget came to the main reasons she thought the three men had taken their lives. There were three:

1. Obviously the three men were in total despair at what they had done.
2. They had experienced some event more frightening than could be imagined.
3. The machine had told them what to do.

As she read out the third option, there was a loud gasp from everyone.

'That's impossible.' Christine was the first to react. 'We know the machine does not order anyone to do anything.'

'I realise that,' went on Bridget, 'but who knows just what years of continuous usage of the machine can do with one's mind. It is just possible that the machine gave them solutions, one of which they concluded was the best option open to them!'

'We cannot rule this out.' Roberto looked at the other two men.

Bridget then made another suggestion: the three men had to go back into the room and see if there were any other bulletins from Philip, Ray or John. Perhaps the third chair would produce the answers the group were looking for. Had it been by accident that the three men had taken seats that seemed to produce bulletins in the correct order of events? This was most likely by design as the three men knew that their relatives would not take the risk of confusing them with details of events which would prove to be out of sequence. It would not have been too difficult to arrange the bulletins in the appropriate order.

It was agreed that Bridget would sit in on the next meeting but in a chair which was out of the triangle. She had a small portable light to see by in case the room was plunged into semi-darkness as it sometimes was.

Andrew, being the only one not to have operated the four corner numbers, did so, and all present were pleased when the television screen appeared again. This time it was John talking also in an extremely serious manner and Andrew was taken aback by the strain that clearly showed in his father's face. This was not how he remembered him and it was good that his mother was not in the room to witness the scene. John spoke slowly and what he said shook everyone there.

Bridget stopped taking notes, the pen frozen in her hand. John was clearly upset. 'By the time you are see this broadcast it is most likely that the three of us will be dead.'

The waiting group could not believe what they were hearing – it seemed they were witnessing their relatives' suicide note.

'It is apparent to us that we have managed to do what years of threats by nuclear bombs have failed to do: we have put in place events that will lead to the destruction of this planet. Through our naivety and our constant practice of playing God we have managed to do just that. No one else can take the blame for this and it is only right that the three of us should pay for this with our lives. We now know that the other four countries may realise that we intend to decommission their machines through a safeguard device. It's very fortunate that we thought of doing this as we would have been helpless to correct this problem. We don't know how long it will take for them to figure this out, which is why we are forced to take this drastic action.'

Bridget had managed to regain the use of her writing hand and was scribbling down the words.

'We have been advised by the machine that the world will come to an end within a relatively short time. It has advised us of the date. We will give you this date at the end of this transmission.'

Finding it too distressing to watch his father, Andrew turned away.

John went on to inform them that messages from each of the men to their wives would follow. These were of a private nature and would remain on the screen

Robert, Roberto and Andrew looked at each other and nodded their agreement for this to happen. It would allow the wives to have a private moment with their husbands and might just give them some closure on these tragic events.

John now seemed to be concluding his message. 'After we have said our goodbyes to our wives, we will leave on the scene the information we have been presented with by the dream machine. In the past we have had one hundred per cent accuracy from it so we have no reason to doubt the truth about what it now tells us.'

With that the screen went dead and, as the following sequence indicated it would be solely for Rena, the four left the room to enable Rena to enter and say her goodbyes to her husband. It was an hour and a half later when Christine, the final wife called into the room, came out, tears streaming down her face.

The four men re-entered the room and looked at the message on the screen. It read: *10.30 p.m. December 22nd 2012*

That was only three years from now!

52

Inspector Morris and Sergeant Pearce, completely unaware of the amazing events at the villa in Italy, had arrived at Number Ten Downing Street and been ushered into the private office where the Prime Minister was waiting.

'Thank you for seeing us so promptly,' said Morris.

The Prime Minister, David Carson, smiled and gestured for them to sit down on the seats before him. 'If you don't mind, I've invited our Secretary of Defence, Secretary of State and the Chief of Armed Forces to join us.'

Morris was amazed at the array of senior politicians present.

The Prime Minister went on: 'We know a lot about the activities of the two Courtney brothers and the American,

Jefferson. We were privileged to have a private meeting with them a few years back. Well, at least, some of our scientists did. We were extremely impressed and deeply disappointed when we were not asked to join the group of selected countries that were allowed to build their own machines.'

'Yes, sir,' Morris said, 'we wondered why the UK was not asked to be one of the first four, and why Russia was included instead. We just could not fathom that out.'

'Well, it seems that the company just did not trust the UK government of the day as their security was not what they considered satisfactory – they kept losing papers in their cars, etc., so they waited to see who would get in next.' The Prime Minister smiled as he said this. 'We tried to make amends at once, but it wasn't easy as we had the same lot of civil servants as they did. It was just as well we still had good relations with the Americans because, about three years ago, they informed us about what was going on and agreed to share the details with us. It was also good to receive a phone call from Philip Courtney a couple of months later offering to send over some key personnel which would enable us to catch up with the other three.'

'You mean we have a fully operational dream machine?' Morris could not believe what he was hearing.

'Not quite,' cautioned the Prime Minister, 'but the room should be operational within a month. We're testing it now and first impressions are that it should work fine. Now, tell us more about this portable machine.'

It seemed that the British government knew just about everything and, when informed that the machine was safe, did not pursue the subject again. It was just as well, Morris thought to himself or poor Kevin would be having his collar felt and he definitely would not like that. Morris had some small amount of admiration for Kevin and wondered if, faced with the same circumstances and taking into consideration Kevin's deprived background, he might have been tempted to do the same.

The meeting lasted two hours and, with a promise from the PM that they would allow the two policemen access to the British Dream Room, the two men left the offices of Number Ten. It made some sense for the two men to see the British room if only to see how it matched up to the Italian one. It was also agreed that Andrew should be invited to the UK and to bring the documents that Philip and co had left.

Andrew put down the telephone. 'We have some good news, if you can call it that. It seems that the Americans, when they heard that the Russians, French and Chinese were acting up, invited the Brits to get involved and helped them build a dream machine in the UK. In fact is seems that Philip, Ray and John sent over more men to assist in the manufacture including poor old Christopher who was yanked out of his retirement and sent over, only just managing to get down the steps of the plane.'

The three men smiled at the prospect of the extremely old man managing that trip to the UK. He did however have much more experience than anyone else, other than John, and he managed to reduce by three months the time normally taken to line up the thirteen powerful crystals with the central one. Experience does count in some cases, it seems.

Andrew and Bridget finally left Italy to return to the UK, Andrew to the secret location of the Dream Room and Bridget back to her position at Oxford Infirmary.

Morris took the opportunity to return the portable dream machine to Andrew who promptly placed it in a safe deposit box. It was best to leave it there and not on public display, at least not until they had concluded their business with the British Government.

Andrew, accompanied by Morris and Pearce, entered the British Dream Room in Aldershot, one of the British government's top security places. They were amazed at its advanced stage. The only thing different was the absence of the TV panel that dropped down when accessed by the four corner numbers of the three desk panels. It seemed that none of the new dream rooms would have had that. How that was manufactured and installed would remain a well-kept secret. Were there any other secrets which the new rooms did not have? Andrew secretly hoped there would be.

53

Martin Scott knew he had blown it and he wondered if he would shortly receive a visit from the old Bill. He waited at his usual place of residence: the third bar stool from the right at the Maypole Arms. He drank steadily. If this was going to be his last drink for sometime, he wanted to enjoy it. Three hours later he was still sitting there with now his ninth pint of the local brew. No sign of the police, no hand on his shoulder; it might be they could not find him, but surely his ever loving son would inform them where he was normally to be found. Still, there came nothing.

He went back rather unsteadily to his rather grand apartment which his son had purchased for him some months before and sat down looking at the blank television wondering what to do next. He could not believe his son had not informed on him. He had tried to kill him, for God's sake.

His consumption of all those pints of the local brew took its effect and soon he was snoring, his mouth half open. Martin Scott was very drunk, but extremely lucky nevertheless.

Kevin and Sarah had discussed at great length what to do about his poor excuse for a father. Kevin had decided not to do anything at that time and, with some reluctance, Sarah had agreed. As long as the man kept away from them, she could just about cope with that. Kevin knew he would not be able to explain what value the dream machine was to him or that it had made him a multi-millionaire. No, now was the time for him to relax and enjoy the wealth he had created over the past five years. Sarah knew deep down from snippets of information she had from Inspector Morris that her wayward husband had been up to something not quite right, to say the least. No, she too would put everything on the back burner. Now was not the time to rock the boat.

Shortly after returning to his home near Oxford from the visit to see the British Dream Room, Andrew was surprised to receive a request from the Prime Minister for a further visit to Number 10, and this time to bring Bridget. It seemed that the government wanted some clarification on the documents that Andrew had left with them after the last meeting.

The pair arrived at Downing Street and were ushered into the Prime Minister's office where there were several cabinet members present and, after the usual pleasantries, they got down to business. Andrew informed the cabinet members there about how Martin Scott had recovered the original machine from the Thames and how his son, Kevin, had possibly used the machine to make his fortune. The Prime Minister then gave further instructions: to ask Morris and Kevin Scott to come to Number Ten at the same time.

Andrew and Bridget left Downing Street and London to return to the peace and quiet (they hoped) of the Oxford countryside.

Meanwhile, Inspector Morris made his way to Number Ten.

Waiting outside the PM's office, he was astonished to see Kevin Scott being ushered to the seat next to him. He felt this was not the time to ask questions but guessed from the worried look on Kevin's face that he had not come there of his own accord.

Morris was the first to be called into the office. Coming to the point, the Prime Minister asked him if he thought he had done the right thing in giving the portable dream machine back to the Courtneys and Jefferson.

It took several minutes for Morris to explain that, as far as he was concerned, he had just returned it to its rightful owners. They were apparently the original people that developed the machine, and, if it was not for them, nobody would have a Dream Room. For some reason, Morris stopped short of informing the PM that the machine was actually still in the country. Why he did this was a mystery.

The Prime Minister was in a good mood that morning and seemed inclined not to press the point. As far as the establishment was concerned, the inspector had not acted against orders, mainly because no one had even known about the machine officially.

The PM questioned Morris extensively about Kevin but, other than how he discovered the machine at Scott's house, there was nothing else Morris could tell him that he did not already know.

Then, when Morris had been shown out, Kevin Scott was ushered in.

Lance Walker and Igor Spence sat in the lounge of their local Burford hotel and looked at their depleted funds. The high cost of the luxury hotel and continuous attendance by Jenny and Liz, two of the local ladies, was now telling on their pockets. The money given by the gent in Oxford two months ago for their services on the hill had been very welcome but now, like all good things, it was coming to an end. Lance was an ex-member of the now defunct IRA. Igor, a rather mean-looking Romanian, had come to the UK on the back of a lorry, asking for asylum which had been granted. Now Igor spent most of his time just making a few pounds enforcing the wishes of anyone that would pay him enough money. Neither man really worried about the law.

'Well, looks like that guy is going to live after all,' remarked Walker. 'In fact I understand he's out of the hospital and has gone home. You should have done a better job.'

'Like to see you do any better,' Igor responded. 'He was moving fast in that Porsche of his!'

'Anyway, it might just work out well for us,' went on Lance. 'The guy that hired us might want us to finish him off, but that would be extra if we have to go to his house and do it.'

'Why don't you give him a call? You still have his mobile number, don't you? Anyway he owes us the balance of the money, another couple of grand.'

'Well, he might not want to cough up as we never finished him off,' Walker replied after a moment's hesitation.

'Well, we'll have to make him an offer he can't refuse.' Igor laughed.

Lance went to a quiet corner in the hotel and pushed the direct call on his mobile. He knew he had to be pleasant; well, at least at first.

Martin Scott pulled at his top pocket as he heard the ring tone of his mobile phone pierce the silence. It was on the loudest setting so it almost shook him off his bar stool. 'Hullo.' He hoped it would not be his son Kevin.

'Martin, my friend,' came a familiar voice, 'I do believe we have some unfinished business.'

211

Martin Scott recognised the caller immediately. 'You've got to be joking, Walker, you messed it up.'

If it wasn't for those two idiots, he would not be sitting here now worrying about having his collar felt, conveniently forgetting that it was he who had blurted out to his son and daughter-in-law just who had arranged the shooting in the first place. Realising he was attracting a little too much attention, Martin slid off his bar stool. Leaving his half full glass of beer, he went out into the pub car park. Lance knew he would have to take a different approach. 'Well, there is an easy way and a hard way as you well know, Mr Scott. It's all the same to us. I understand there's a reward out for the shooting and anyone who might be brought into the frame, so to speak, will have a hard time getting out of it. If you want us to go and finish the job, that will cost you another two grand.'

Martin scoffed at this offer. 'The police are ready for any further attempts, not to mention the private security firm he has hired to look after him.'

'You never mentioned the fact the guy had the same last name as you, Scott.' Lance decided to play another card he had up his sleeve. 'Now there's a coincidence, for sure. In fact, we understand he's your son. Now that was not a fatherly thing to do to your own son.' His Irish brogue seemed to indicate disdain as he emphasised the word 'son'.

Martin was anxious to conclude the discussion and, thinking they had more to lose as they were the two that had carried out the shooting, decided to call their bluff. 'Oh, do what you want, but you're not getting any more money from me.' Pressing 'end call' on his mobile phone he turned it off. Damn the two; he was more concerned if he would survive the next forty-eight hours.

Returning his phone to his jacket pocket, Lance went back

into the bar and the waiting Igor. 'He's playing rough. It looks like we'll need to lean on him a bit. Give me a double whisky in there, luv,' he added, pushing his empty glass across the bar.

Now they would have to make their way back to Oxford and find this Martin guy and change his mind.

The two men sat at the bar for the next hour and then got into their car to drive the short distance to Oxford later that evening.

54

Kevin was now becoming a little alarmed. He had never been one to hobnob with royalty and politicians, and here he was entering the private office of the Prime Minister of the UK. There were two other men sitting around the table with him. They had been introduced as Steven Jones and Rodney Spencer.

'Please sit down, Kevin,' the Prime Minister invited him.

Taking a seat, Kevin looked blankly at the PM as if to say what do you want me for?

'We understand that you acquired a machine that enabled you to look into the past and even into the future.' The Prime Minister came straight to the point. 'This somehow assisted you in making a great amount of wealth, did it not?'

Blimey, Kevin thought, the man doesn't mix his words. 'Well, sir, all I can tell you is that my wealth came from my knowledge of the stock markets,' he replied, trying to appear nonchalant.

The Prime Minister, seeing he was not getting anywhere with that line of questioning, changed his approach. 'Can you at least tell us how you acquired the machine which we understand is called a dream machine.'

Kevin laughed. 'A dream what? No, sir, I can't quite get what you're on about.'

'You haven't told us how you acquired it, whatever it is called or you wish to call it,' Rodney Spencer said.

Kevin knew he was on dodgy ground. If he told them how he had found the machine it would prove it was not his. In fact, it could be construed that it was his father's, if you fell back on the finders keepers rule.

'I got it at a car boot some time ago. I wanted to take up cycling and needed a helmet,' he lied.

'We know that in the past it belonged to three gentlemen who lived close to here and they were quite pleased when it was returned to them.' It was the Prime Minister's turn to tell a white lie because he wanted to see Kevin's reaction. 'If you tell us what you paid for it, I'm sure they would be pleased to reimburse you and some more for your trouble.'

Kevin knew he was being set up. 'No, that's all right, sir. I quite like it and, besides, I've promised it to one of my kids. When he has a bike for his next birthday, he can wear it. As you know, sir, we all have to obey the law and keep them safe. Now, if you would be so kind as to arrange for the return of the helmet...'

The Prime Minister looked at his colleagues and, with a shrug of his shoulders, thanked Kevin for his time, walked to the door and opened it.

Kevin took this as his cue to leave but as he was going out of the door, he addressed his final remark to the Prime Minister. 'Can I take it that I'll have the helmet returned to me then?'

The Prime Minister said what all politicians do at times like this: 'I'll look into it.'

As Kevin walked away he had a spring in his step. He smiled to himself; well, he never voted for them in the last election anyway.

The Prime Minister summed up the situation: 'Steven, this is a national emergency and I want you to deal with it whichever way you feel fit. All I can say is I don't want to read about it in the Daily Express.'

'Yes, sir, I'll get on to it straightaway.' Steven Jones left and returned to his office at MI5.

55

Before returning to the UK, Andrew and Bridget had had many meetings with the family, meetings that brought back bad memories for them all. The ladies particularly were greatly distressed at the news that their husbands had blamed themselves for what they believed they had caused. Why, oh why had they left them so soon and without a proper farewell? They must have had terrible feelings of guilt to even contemplate such a thing. Ray was a Catholic so that would have been an even worse dilemma for him.

The astounding revelations supplied by John, Philip and Ray were still sinking in. The date and time that appeared at the end of their broadcasts was even more startling. Roberto had been the first to spot the significance of the date as he was a bit of a history buff. He calmly announced to the group that the date mentioned could well be correct as this was the date shown centuries ago in the Mayan Calendar.

Andrew could not get the broadcast out of his mind and knew deep down that perhaps, if they had been there, it might have been possible for them to spot the distress their fathers had been going through. After his meeting with the Prime Minister, he had several conversations with Inspector Morris about how his visit went, and they concluded that it was best left to the authorities to sort Kevin Scott out.

Martin Scott was having nightmares about having his collar felt and drank even more, if that was at all possible. It was Saturday night and as usual it was raining. The licensee of the Maypole Arms had decided that there would be no lock-in that night and Martin was making his way very unsteadily to his home nearby. He did not see them coming. Suddenly he was pushed up against a wall and manhandled into a car which was then driven with great haste from the pub car park. He hardly had a chance to draw a breath when the car stopped and he was heaved out of the car and thrown roughly to the wet ground.

Placing his foot on Martin's head, Igor explained that he regretted the fact that Martin had forced them to come and see him again. As they had told him before, they had some unfinished business.

Removing Martin's Rolex watch from his wrist, Lance peered down at him. 'We'll have this instead of interest on the money you owe us.'

'Just take it,' Martin muttered – as if he had any choice. 'Just leave me alone.'

'You're not listening, Mr Scott,' Igor repeated. 'You owe us a couple of grand plus interest.'

Lance laughed. 'Oh, don't forget the watch, Igor. We'll have to deduct that amount from the total. Shall we say a tenner?'

The two men laughed between themselves and turned their attention back to the unfortunate Martin. 'Now, do you wish us to finish the job for say around five grand or do you want to just pay us the three thousand you now owe?'

Martin was about to argue the point about the extra money but he knew in his present predicament he would not get very far. 'Let me up and we'll talk,' he gasped. Lying in the wet grass was not to his liking, and he was sobering up fast.

Pulling him to his feet, the two men started to give him a further lesson in manners hitting him where it would not show but hurting nevertheless. Pulling a gun from his coat, Lance pushed the nozzle right up against Martin's nose, and looked directly into his eyes. Even on that dark night, Martin could see the determination and evil in Lance's eyes and he knew he would have to come up with a solution quickly, and one that would satisfy the two men. Suddenly he saw his opportunity, as Lance glanced at Igor, Martin with a superhuman effort grabbed at the gun which had eased a little from his nose. His sudden movement took Lance completely by surprise, knocking him off balance. As he tried to regain it, the gun went off and a bullet went straight into the amazed face of Igor. His frozen expression was evident in the soft moonlight as he now hit the sodden earth with a thud. Lance was horrified at his friend's sudden demise and for a moment he just stood there stunned. Martin not really knowing what had happened took the chance to shove Lance away from him. Lance fell over Igor's motionless body and was momentarily winded. It was a few seconds before he managed to lift himself up and let off a couple of shots in the direction of the fleeing Martin. The two men's 'offer that Martin Scott could not refuse' had not worked out at all well for them.

Lance bent down and took the keys from the dead Igor's pocket, got into the car and left the scene cursing the escaping Martin.

Martin, for his part, was just thankful to get away in one piece but it was only upon arriving home that he found that his shirt was covered in blood. On closer examination, he found a wound in his right side. Fortunately the bullet had passed right through his side and out the other; nevertheless he knew he had to get to the hospital as soon as possible. Wrapping a bandage around his waist, he hailed a cab and was driven to the Oxford Infirmary. There he walked unsteadily into the A&E Department.

Doctor Brown, the doctor who had treated Kevin, was on duty. He could immediately see that his patient had been shot and tried to stem the bleeding. After using all of his expertise, he was finally satisfied that Martin was as comfortable as possible in the Intensive Care Unit. In accordance with standard procedure with gunshot wounds, he requested a nurse to notify the police.

Inspector Morris arrived at Oxford Infirmary to investigate the shooting that had been reported. It was of great interest to him that the name on the report was Scott, a name he seemed to be plagued by these days.

His talk with Doctor Brown soon allayed his fears that it might have been more serious, but then no shooting is particularly pleasant for the person on the receiving end of a bullet. He would have to wait a couple of hours before he could quiz the now recovering Martin Scott. His first thoughts were that maybe it was part of a family vendetta, with the males of the Scott family being selected by someone that they had seriously upset.

He soon found that Martin was as devious as his son Kevin when it came to answering questions. Martin's version was that he must have walked into the line of fire between two rival gangs. However he seemed unable to recall where this had happened or to describe any members of the gangs.

Morris knew that he was getting nowhere and failing to retrieve the bullet which must be lodged in some tree, was going to make his task much harder. The Scott name was becoming a curse to him.

First Kevin, now his father; Morris realised he would

now have to visit the manor house and question the son. He hated that part as he knew he would probably receive a cool response from him if he had found out that it was he who had given Andrew the dream machine.

Kevin's response to the inspector was one of concern when he found out what had happened to his father. Sarah's was one of indifference. Inspector Morris was satisfied however that neither of them had had anything to do with the incident.

Kevin, upon hearing the news and after being assured that his father was out of any danger, felt that perhaps some poetic justice had been carried out. He did wonder though if perhaps the man who had shot his father might have been involved with his own shooting; perhaps not enough payment passing hands. He did not realise for one moment just how close to the truth he was.

Robert had still not come to terms with the broadcast announcing that the three men were contemplating taking their own lives. This was something he had not bargained for when he sought more details about how they had actually died. Roberto was also having problems. He would be the first to admit that he did not fully understand just how exactly the Dream Room worked or how, when it came to forecasting the future, this was possible.

He decided to talk with his father and cousin and to ask them to try and explain further just how the three men could have discovered about the world coming to an untimely end. It just did not add up, and the more Roberto thought about it, the more confused he became. He would have to arrange another meeting and, as all the answers appeared to be in England, Roberto suggested to the others that it should be held in Oxford so that perhaps Andrew's wife Bridget could attend. Bridget's input had been very beneficial to all of them and she might be able to come up with some solutions that the men had not thought of.

Robert and Roberto arrived at Andrew's manor house and, after resting and dining in the old hall, they retired to the drawing room to go over the events that had disturbed them greatly. Bridget listened to her husband and the others as each of them related their individual concerns and, in return, simply asked each of them just why they thought their individual fathers and grandfather had reacted as they did.

Bridget could tell that the men were disappointed by her questions but she explained that she could not just wave a magic wand and make it all right. After all, they knew their relatives much better than she did. One by one, they gave their own viewpoints on their individual relative's behaviour.

'The answer must still be with the dream machine and what effect it had on the people that used it,' Bridget offered.

The three men sat in silence, trying to make sense of this. Could it be that the dream machine had taken over the actual thoughts of the three men or, even worse, had influenced the men so drastically that their response to the news of the world coming to an end was not really of their own making. Had the dream machine taken over their minds, perhaps in some kind of brainwashing? It all seemed too incredible to believe.

Robert was the first to comment. 'I've been worried about just how my father would actually accept the news of the world ending. It's just not like him to walk away and leave his family whom he adored to face the end without him. After all, as Roberto says the legend of the end of the world has been around for many years and been written about many times.'

'That's right,' joined in Andrew, 'and nobody has started to take it seriously enough to take their own lives.'

'That's correct,' Robert interjected, 'but then nobody has ever had access to a machine which as far as we know has never been found to be wrong!'

Gloom descended upon the group with Bridget trying to come up with a scientific answer that could help her husband and their two friends. 'The answer has to be tied in with the men's response to the machine. What we have to try to establish is if it was at all possible that the machine took over control of their minds and influenced their normal responses.'

The three men nodded. It was Andrew that came up with the next proposal, an idea that Robert and Roberto had some trouble accepting. 'I think we should visit Kevin Scott and see if he has any notions about all this.'

'What on earth for?' exclaimed Roberto. 'He was the one who took the machine from our fathers in the first place.'

'That's not really true,' said Andrew. 'Martin Scott found the machine in the Thames where we know my father threw it from the train. Kevin must have discovered the box in his attic or somewhere where Martin had left it for all those years.'

Bridget summed it up: 'Look, we seemed to have reached a dead end as far as fresh ideas are concerned, but it's better to do something than nothing. Who knows it might just throw up something that will put us on the right path.'

The three men reluctantly agreed.

56

Kevin Scott was watching television when his wife came in to tell him that a Robert Courtney was on the telephone requesting a meeting with him. Kevin was confused at first but his curiosity soon got the better of him and he took the phone from Sarah. Robert explained briefly the reason for a meeting and Kevin eagerly agreed.

Now he had almost recovered completely from his shooting 'accident', he desperately wanted to know the answer to some of the questions concerning the disappearance of his 'helmet'.

The meeting was arranged for the next day and, upon arriving at Kevin and Sarah's manor, Robert was amazed just how much it reminded him of Courtney Manor where he had grown up and had experienced those incredible days when his family were attacked. Days that seemed so far in the past but with one common denominator: the dream machine. Many years had passed but still it was the centre of attention.

The four visitors sat down with coffee served by Sarah who had long forgone the comforts of maids and butlers that had been her husband's way of using their great wealth. She was only too pleased to have some normality in their home and, while she knew they were still extremely wealthy, she preferred to live the simple life as she had all those years ago with her father.

The three men had previously decided to tell Kevin about the Dream Room and its special powers. It seemed rather silly to pretend that the whole story started and ended with the smaller dream machine. So many people already knew about it – one more would make no difference.

Kevin was amazed when he was told about the existence of a Dream Room. At first he denied any knowledge of the old helmet but soon realised that, by doing this, he would not learn any more about the Dream Room which interested him greatly. He decided to cooperate with his newly arrived guests and was soon pouring out his experiences with the strange box found in the Thames by his father all those years ago.

The visitors listened closely, nodding several times in agreement.

'Well, I must admit that we don't totally agree with what

you did after you found the dream machine,' Andrew said. 'You seem to have accomplished some considerable wealth however by your ingenuity.'

Kevin accepted this as a compliment and smiled. However his next comment silenced the visitors: 'It seems that, by letting the Russians, Chinese and French have access to the machine, your fathers changed the possibility of a world catastrophe into one of absolute certainty.'

Surprisingly, Roberto nodded in agreement. 'It would seem that way, but I guess they did so after being convinced by the other scientists that it would only be used to further world peace, not hinder it.'

Kevin then quizzed them about the main reason for their visit. He was secretly enjoying himself, being the centre of attention, and sat waiting patiently for the forthcoming explanation.

Andrew told him how they had found the messages left by the three men and their puzzlement as to why their relatives had decided to take their own lives. This was contrary to what everyone who knew them could believe. It just did not add up.

Kevin pondered for a moment, conscious of the fact that these people wanted an answer that might give them some way of coming to terms with their loss. It did seem rather far-fetched and maybe just a little flattering that they were asking for his advice. 'Well, as far as I can see, and taking into consideration that they were not able to transport forward to the time mentioned itself, I would imagine that the machine actually took over their minds and initiated the thought of ending their own lives into their heads.'

Bridget who had been silent up to this point spoke. 'Well, that's exactly what I thought. It must have been something like that, but why?'

It was the only thing that logically made sense, knowing their relatives as they did. Ray was a hands-on fellow who would not take no for an answer. Philip was certainly a hard man when faced with danger and there had been numerous occasions when he had proved his worth before. John's scientific mind would not have let him succumb to defeat unless an outside influence had convinced him all was lost. He must at least have been aware that the date mentioned was one already recorded in numerous legends and would have made his views known to the other two. The date given as the possible end of the world was thought to be just another unlikely piece of prophecy.

Kevin, seeing his comments had made a marked impact on his visitors, ventured further. 'Just how long were your relatives using the new Dream Room?'

'We gather it could have been at least twenty years give or take,' Robert answered.

Kevin thought for a while. 'Well, I never used the small machine for anything like that, but could it be possible that the large machine was indeed affecting their minds more than they realised?'

'As far as we can see the new Dream Room was designed solely for the three of them to use at the same time or it would not operate correctly.'

'Did the three ever use the dream machine for solo trips back in time and future trips which the machine was originally designed for?'

'As far as we can understand,' Bridget interjected, 'they soon forgot about all that when they started getting involved with new world events and could not possibly have had any time for their own personal enjoyment.'

Andrew then asked Kevin a question that was puzzling him: 'Just how did you make money out of stocks and shares? How did you use the machine to do that?'

'It was simple. I did some research about stocks and shares and eventually set up a hedge fund. I used to just bet on what the shares would do. I then dreamt seeing the Financial Times forty-eight to sixty hours in advance and betted according to what would rise or fall. I had to make several visits to the London Stock Exchange to familiarise myself with everything.'

Roberto could not help smiling. 'Talk about inside information. That just about takes the biscuit. It takes a devious mind to work out that easy and effective way of doing things.'

'Well, operating a hedge fund isn't illegal and a lot of people do have access to advance knowledge and use it to their advantage.' Kevin felt he needed to defend his actions. 'With me I was just lucky enough to be able to have the correct results at the right time. The more I used the machine, the more I found that I understood the stock market and was able to act on what the outcome of the stocks and shares would be. It was almost as if the machine was taking over my thoughts and making my understanding of the market even easier. For a long time, I've been of the opinion that the dream machine had the ability to sharpen my mind and make it easier to understand what I wanted to achieve. It became my own private financial advisor.'

Andrew interrupted, 'Well, that doesn't surprise me. If you remember the Dream Room did something like that to our relatives making everything clearer to understand.'

The others nodded.

'I guess you could have done worse and played the lottery,' said Andrew, 'but maybe that would have drawn too much attention to you.'

Kevin nodded. 'Well you must understand I was penniless and had been for all my life. I was fed up with working in a dead-end job and, after the first time, the rest was easy.'

Robert shook his head. 'We're not here to pass judgement

on you, Kevin, but just to find out how the Dream Room could possibly take over and influence our fathers' and grandfathers' minds, if at all.'

The group decided to conclude the session and, with Sarah's assistance, were soon sitting down to an excellent lunch which Sarah had been preparing in the luxurious kitchens of the manor. While the party ate their lunch, they discussed between themselves just what they had learnt which, although interesting, was not really very much. Kevin had just confirmed Bridget's conclusions that perhaps the machine had influenced the three men's minds enough make them end their lives. All the three men loved their wives and families and, if anything, they would have wanted to stand and see any dangers out with them, and protect them as in the past.

The more the group talked about it, the more convinced they became that the Dream Room had indeed influenced their relatives' deaths. The question was how and why?

It was only a matter of time before Kevin asked if it was possible to visit Italy and see the Dream Room.

'Better than that,' Robert said, 'why don't we try to get you into the British one?'

Kevin looked uncertain. 'Well, I don't really want to meet the PM again and, to be frank, I reckon a visit to Italy for Sarah and me would be better.'

Robert looked at the other three and they all nodded their approval. He could understand Kevin's reluctance to visit the government offices again.

Soon afterwards, the four visitors left and returned to Andrew's home to make plans for the Scotts' visit to Italy which was scheduled to take place within the next five days.

57

Lance Walker had taken a few days off from his quest to get even with Martin Scott. He realised that his shots had clipped his runaway 'benefactor' and had already checked on his condition at the hospital. He had learnt from a helpful porter that Martin would be released shortly and straightaway made plans to be in the area to give him a warm welcome. The porter had promised to inform Lance exactly when that day would be. Money always talks at times like this.

The day dawned when Martin Scott was finally able to put on his street clothes and walk out of the Oxford Infirmary. This was a good day and he headed for the nearest public house to get some liquid refreshment. All the upheaval with the two crooks had made him thirsty and he was grateful to still be alive and kicking. He still had his nice apartment and, as far as he knew, his monthly allowance from Kevin was still being paid into his bank account. He would explain to everyone it was just a small misunderstanding and, as Kevin had obviously decided to not press charges, nothing had changed.

He finished his sixth pint of the local brew and walked unsteadily to the entrance of the public house. He would hail a taxi and return home to his apartment, rest up and then take a well-earned holiday to fully recover. He was in luck; fortuitously a taxi pulled over. Great, he would be home within the hour. The taxi pulled away from the kerb and it was only then, to Scott's horror, that he realised that there was already a passenger: Lance Walker who indicated to Martin that he had a gun tucked into belt and motioned to him to act normally.

'That'll be fine here, cabbie,' Lance said, after a short distance. The taxi driver, although rather annoyed with the short trip, was soon happy enough when the passenger gave him an extremely large tip.

'Thank you, sir,' he said, pulling away and leaving the hapless Martin with Lance.

Lance grinned at Martin who had sobered up extremely quickly. 'I thought we could complete our unfinished business, Martin.'

Martin just looked blankly at his captor. How could he have been so stupid as to get into a taxi without checking it first? A large car then pulled up by the kerb and Lance pushed him inside. He knew he was now helpless and his frustration grew as the car left the town centre of Oxford and drove into the countryside.

The farmhouse was deserted. In the current property market, Lance had had no problems finding somewhere ideally suited to his needs. He had recruited a couple of Eastern bloc friends who, like the poor departed Igor, were happy to assist in anything illegal and dangerous for cash. Brother and sister, Ali and Heidi, were recent arrivals in the UK, claiming political asylum as soon as they had arrived. It was not as easy to get asylum as it had been several years before, but the British government had let the two stay while they investigated their background. This gave Ali and Heidi enough time to disappear into the black economy, hence their employment by the thug Lance Walker.

If caught, Ali and Heidi would soon be deported. Still they already had survived six months and, with Lance's assistance, were only too pleased to assist their new employer. Heidi for one was always ready to keep Lance sweet, with frequent trips to his bedroom at night, just to maintain the newly acquired friendship that the three had.

Pushing the unfortunate Scott down some steps into the

farmhouse cellar was the job of the strongman Ali, a master of many arts which included snapping a man's neck in two places with little effort. Martin feared for his life. He had managed to escape the clutches of Lance and Igor once before, but this man Ali was different. He was huge and as wide as he was tall. He grunted rather than talked which did nothing to allay Martin's fears. Martin had always maintained a quiet life and, as long as he could have his pints in the evening, he was quite happy. That was until his fateful decision to acquire by foul means his son's newly found wealth.

He cursed as he lay on the foul-smelling stone floor which was covered with old matted hay that had not been cleared for many a year. As his eyes grew accustomed to the dim light he managed to see the outline of an old bed which had an equally ancient mattress on it with a shapeless pillow and blanket. It was clear that his new captors had taken a lot of trouble to make sure he would be comfortable during his stay.

How long would he stay? Martin was starting to get worried. Lance's sudden appearance at the top of the stairs enabled Martin to thank him sarcastically for the nice bed and mattress.

'Oh, is there a bed down there?' Lance seemed surprised.

By Martin's watch, he could see that he had been down in the cellar for at least ten hours. It must be dark outside now. There had been no movement from his captors upstairs. Then the door to the cellar opened and Ali appeared carrying a tray of bread and cheese and a cup of coffee. Motioning Martin to move to the other side of the room, he laid the tray down on the floor of the room and retreated upstairs, closing the door. Martin could hear the sound of a bolt being pushed into place and he knew he would be there for the night. Looking at the tray he noticed a box of matches and two large candles. At least he would be able to see to eat and drink. After eating, he lay down wearily on his cot, pulled the grimy blanket over himself and tried to sleep. Fortunately it came more easily than he expected and he was soon snoring loudly.

Upstairs, Lance reached for Martin's mobile phone and dialled the number for Kevin. Now they would know just how much the son thought of his devious father.

Kevin and Sarah had just finished packing their cases and were looking forward to catching the flight out of Heathrow to Rome, Italy. Yes, if you have to travel you need to travel first class, and to a much sunnier climate than they had experienced recently. It was strange that the two were looking forward to the trip as they already owned a couple of sunshine retreats in the Caribbean. It might just be the excitement of seeing the large dream machine or Dream Room as it was now called.

They were about to leave when the telephone rang. Kevin answered it and heard a voice asking him to identify himself. Ignored the request, he asked who the caller was. Again, there was another request for Kevin to identify himself. Kevin ignored this request thinking now that it was some nuisance caller.

Lance passed the phone to Heidi who had already been briefed what to say. She fancied herself as an actress and her words were sharp with a mixture of French and American accents, making her sound rather more amusing than frightening. 'We must talk to you about your father. It is very important.'

'What do you want?' Kevin was curious.

Heidi relayed her message almost as if she was reading it from a script. 'We have your father. If you wish to see him alive you must pay five million pounds.' With that the phone line went dead.

Kevin replaced the receiver and turned to Sarah who had

just walked back into the room, her small carry-on case at the ready. 'Who was that?'

Kevin looked unconcerned. 'Someone who says they have Dad and want five million pounds for his safe return.'

'Oh dear, but we must hurry or we'll miss the plane.'

Kevin agreed and the two left the manor to drive to Heathrow Airport.

58

The large Boeing 747 dropped silently out of the sky, landing effortlessly in the evening sunshine of Rome International Airport. Waiting in the arrivals hall were Robert and Roberto who warmly welcomed Kevin and Sarah and went on to explain that Andrew and Bridget would be joining them shortly after catching a later flight from London.

The Mercedes car drove through the lanes and the two visitors felt quite relaxed for the first time after all the hectic happenings of the past few months. The warm temperature had an extremely restful effect on them.

Robert suggested that they all had a drink when they arrived at the villa and took time to relax before they continued with their visit to the Dream Room. Kevin readily agreed. Certainly he had had enough excitement over the past few months. Getting shot was seemingly the start of it all but since then he had met the Prime Minister, had his father shot and kidnapped – supposedly – and lost the precious machine which had made him a lot of money. Yes, coming into contact with the dream machine was certainly not dull in any sense of the word. Now he was about to experience the wonders of a far more powerful machine and he wondered what the next few days would bring.

When they arrived at the villa, Rena welcomed them on behalf of the rest of the family and they all sat down for a typical Italian meal of pasta and meatballs, accompanied by some Italian wine. Sarah was pleased to talk about their family and it was obvious that the three ladies were extremely interested in everything she told them about her children.

After the meal, the three elderly ladies excused themselves and retired for the evening. Retiring to the lounge for brandy and coffee, the other four were soon joined by Andrew and Bridget. As they had already eaten on the plane, the two latecomers sat down and relaxed.

Robert was the first to start talking. 'I think we should just relax this evening and get an early start in the morning as it's likely going to be quite an exciting day for Kevin and Sarah. We've got a lot to discuss and will need all our faculties to make sense of everything.' He went on to explain for the benefit of Kevin and Sarah that, while they had visited the Dream Room several times, they were still on what they considered 'a steep learning curve'.

Kevin nodded, rather disappointed that he would have to wait until the next day, but acknowledging that he and Sarah would benefit from a good night's rest. Roberto did suggest that they all take a walk in the garden and perhaps visit one of the many vineyards. The golden brown vineyards glowed as the sun dipped beneath the horizon. Italy, it seemed, certainly had a lot to offer even without the dream machine.

Kevin and Sarah slept peacefully in the grand four-poster bed that was the norm in every bedroom in the sumptuous villa.

Lance was getting exasperated. Numerous phone calls were only met by the soft tones of Sarah on the answering machine. He had lost count of the number of calls they had made. It was obvious that the people in the manor were either just not answering or possibly were not even in residence. He sent Ali up to take a look around. Ali arrived back with the news that the grounds were being patrolled as usual by the security company employed to look after the estate. Lance concluded that the original message either had not been taken seriously or maybe the son and his wife just did not care what happened to Martin Scott.

Going down into the cellar, Lance pulled the now extremely scruffy Martin upstairs. 'Here, take this towel and soap, and have a shower. You're stinking the place out.'

After his shower, Lance handed Martin a glass of wine. He looked blankly at Lance. What on earth was going on?

'It would seem that your son doesn't value your miserable life one iota. He seems to have gone off on holiday somewhere and we can't contact him.'

Martin now realised why he had been abducted and was being kept in these filthy conditions – for a ransom. He decided to play along with Lance and his companions. 'I could have told you that. After he found out that I'd hired you, he wasn't too happy.'

'Well, if he won't cough up any cash for you, I can't see any reason why we shouldn't just plug you with lead and drop you off in the nearest river,' Lance sneered.

Martin's face fell. He knew that, after all that had happened with Igor, Lance was in no mood for games. 'Hold on a minute, perhaps we can work something out.'

'What exactly?'

'I don't know – yet. Just give me some time to think.'

'You've got twenty-four hours.' Lance motioned for Ali to return Martin to the cellar.

Martin was wondering what to do next when the door shut and the bolt was pushed across violently on the other side. The pleasant interlude was over for the time being and he had to start working out yet again a way of saving his miserable life.

59

Kevin woke early, showered and dressed leaving Sarah still sleeping. He hurried down to the lounge where they had spent the previous evening only to find it empty. He was about to see if anyone was in the kitchen when he was hailed by Andrew who was sitting with the others outside on the terrace.

'We have been waiting for you to wake. Help yourself to breakfast here – full English or continental.'

Kevin was feeling extremely hungry and helped himself to some eggs and bacon with toast and coffee. He was soon feeling extremely fit and looking forward to the visit to the Dream Room.

Andrew took over the introduction of the day's events. 'Do you want Sarah to be in on this or shall we go ahead and let her sleep? She can eat breakfast with the ladies when they get up.'

'I guess she'll be OK with us proceeding,' Kevin answered. 'She's never been involved much with things like this in the past. I'll leave a note telling her where we are.'

'Fine.' Andrew led the way to the Dream Room.

Bridget took her usual position just inside the room with her customary notebook and small light.

'We always take notes for later,' explained Roberto.

Due to the seating arrangements, Kevin also sat outside the table area and was asked to watch and listen. Any questions would have to wait until the demonstration had finished. He was amazed at the splendour of the room; its glowing lights in the walls all gave it an awesome atmosphere. Kevin suddenly realised just how much the men had accomplished since they had thrown his old dream machine in the Thames. Well, he privately hoped that the machine would still be his. Kevin sat down beside Bridget and watched with anticipation as the three men took their positions that were once occupied by their fathers and grandfather.

The three men sitting at their stations took it in turns to explain to Kevin exactly what they were doing, how the machine responded and what they expected the next step would be. Watching quietly, Kevin made a mental note of what was taking place he did not want to miss a thing.

Bridget also wanted to re-evaluate her first impressions of the Dream Room, and she knew that everyone there was searching for anything that they had possibly missed at the last session with the dream machine. Nothing must be left to chance if the group was to get a fresh look at the recordings that had devastated the whole family.

After the group had watched again Ray's, John's and Philip's broadcasts, Kevin asked to see again the last broadcast by John. This was the one that intrigued him the most. Also, although he had never met the three men before, he felt a kind of empathy with them.

Andrew again turned his head away as his father signed off. It was John's manner which perturbed all of them the most. Why would he throw in the towel when, as a scientist you would think he would be the first to put forward some kind of plan to prevent the end of the world? It all came down to the inescapable possibility that the three men were by now totally convinced of the Dream Room's capabilities. It had to have some bearing.

Robert suggested that they take a break. They were anxious to get Kevin's initial impressions but he remained rather non-committal. They would resume the next day with an actual attempt to use the machine. This was something that the three men had not attempted up to now. It could be extremely dangerous but everyone there knew that, if they were to make progress with their understanding of how all this occurred, they had to take the chance.

Martin awoke from his rather uncomfortable night's sleep and waited for the next visit from Lance and his companions. Ali was the first to show with breakfast for Martin. The toast was cold and the coffee lukewarm. If Ali had made it there had been no thought about serving it hot. With a further glare at Martin, he grunted and left the cellar.

Martin thought he would not get fat on this meagre ration; that was for sure. He had no idea what he could do to prevent Lance carrying out his threat to dispose of him now he had been unable to contact Kevin. A shortage of cash did nothing for Lance's disposition; he was always at his worst when he was in that position.

It was not long before Ali appeared again at the top of the stairs, but this time he gestured with his gun for Martin to come up the stairs. Martin did as he was bid, blinking at the sunlight as he entered the untidy room upstairs. Lance pushed him into an armchair.

'So, have you got any ideas that might save your miserable life?' Lance looked down disdainfully at the cowering figure.

'How about if I produce a machine that will make you all millions,' Martin blurted out.

Ali was about to hit Martin across his head with his gun, when Lance stopped him. 'What do you mean?'

'You know that my son's very wealthy but what you don't know is just how he made his money.'

'OK, you have my interest, but this had better be good or you'll be on the receiving end of this.' Lance pushed the muzzle of his gun against Martin's head to reinforce what he was saying.

'When I worked at Thames Water,' Martin continued, 'one of my men dredged up a box that contained a machine which I took to be a helmet. I put it away in my basement. Then my son found it and discovered it had powers to make money. He used it, hence the wealth he has now.'

'Enough of your fairy stories,' Ali shouted. 'You're playing us for fools. We've never heard such a load of crap. Shoot him, Lance, and let's get on our way.'

'Hold on a minute.' Martin could see that his time was fast running out and he needed to be convincing. 'How do you think I would even have the money to hire you in the first place? I was and am still an alcoholic. Kevin worked at a distribution centre in a dead-end job. Look at him now. He never even went to university!'

Lance looked at Martin who was sweating now. He had always wondered how large amounts of money were made by some people, and, if it was not drugs, he could never understand how people like Kevin had made his cash.

'Tell me more about this machine and make it good. I don't want you to bamboozle me with science.'

Martin relaxed a little and went on to explain as succinctly as possible how the dream machine worked. Of course, he did not know for sure just how it worked but he had enough experience in lying and being creative to put up a plausible account of how his son was able to tap into the stock market and get the results of advanced dealings.

'Oh, he has some kind of computer that hacks into the set-up and relays it back to him,' Lance said.

'That's right,' exclaimed a relieved Martin, just happy that what he had dreamt up had come across as something believable. 'Look, I can get you that machine,' he went on, adding, 'for a small fee.'

Lance smirked. 'Yes, of course, Martin, my old mate, whatever you want.'

Martin with all his years of telling and receiving lies knew for once that he was never ever going to benefit from any promises that Lance made. No, he would have to ensure that, if he could get the machine, he had some distance from him and, for that matter, Kevin as well.

Lance cocked his gun and pointed it at Martin. 'If you don't produce this money-making machine within twenty-four hours, this is what you'll get!' and he released a bullet which passed over Martin's head and lodged in the wall behind him.

Martin instinctively shrunk down in his chair, a look of horror on his face. He realised that Lance had just about run out of patience and he had to be very convincing in the next few minutes or he could well end up with a bullet between his eyes. He explained that firstly he did not know where his son was or when he was returning. However, one thing was for sure: he would return and then Martin would break in and get the machine.

'OK, my friend, you've got seven days to do this. However, change of plans: we will break into the house with you and get it.'

'Yeah, do you think we're thick or something letting you go for it on your own?' Ali added.

Martin looked blankly at the pug-nosed Ali. 'No, of course not!'

Lance looked meaningfully at Martin, a glint in his eye. 'Scott, if I think for one minute you're messing with me, you will be shot – it won't matter where we are.'

Martin nodded. 'I know that – I won't let you down. I want to stay alive.'

'We'll be watching you and if you try to get away we'll find you and deal with you. You won't have another chance.'

'OK, OK.' Martin sounded desperate. 'I told you I got the message. As soon as I find out when Kevin's back, I'll let you know – if you give me your mobile number.'

Lance seemed convinced that he had got his message through and motioned for Martin to leave the house. When Martin reached the nearest road, he started to hitch-hike back to town. A gentle rain was falling but he was oblivious to this – he was free and that was all that mattered.

A car pulled over and he gratefully accepted a lift. As he sat silently in the car, he knew he would have to move fast if he was to save his own skin. He also knew that, if he remembered correctly, the damn machine was in the hands of the local police. He had two choices: go on the run without any money or face Kevin and see if he could make amends. If so Kevin might take pity on him, give him some money and let him stay in one of his Mediterranean villas. However, he did not savour the prospect of trying to tell his son that he was hiding away from the men he had hired to actually kill him! Martin decided that he would have to think it out again.

60

Kevin was oblivious to his father's plight. He had been talking continuously with the other members of the group. He was rather disturbed by the messages from Philip, Ray and John; in another life he would have laughed at it all. Now however was different: he knew what the small dream machine could do after all he had accomplished with it.

It was also plausible that the large Dream Room would accomplish even more, such was its highly advanced technology.

'It all comes down to how the three men came to their decision to end it all,' remarked Kevin to Bridget.

Bridget agreed. She had been the first to raise the possibility of the machine having an extreme influence on the men.

As the evening progressed, the group were becoming increasingly exhausted going over and over again all the possible explanations and counter-arguments. They had eaten dinner with the three senior ladies but kept their talk about the Dream Room to themselves.

Everyone retired for the evening. Kevin and Sarah slept soundly although Kevin's mind was occasionally being transported back and forth in time without the need for a dream machine.

The next morning they assembled at breakfast and, as Sarah had taken the opportunity to get up early as well, they all agreed that she could sit in on the next visit to the room. The three ladies were not present at breakfast which was not unusual due to their senior years.

Robert approached the door and, using his key, opened the door. He was surprised to see the lighting already at a high level, a level which meant that the machine had been or was in use. He wondered at once whether Kevin had managed to get into the room and been trying to use the machine. Those thoughts were quickly dispelled however when he noticed three forms sitting at strange angles in the chairs surrounding the table. He recognised them instantly: his stepmother Christine, Ray's wife Rena and John's wife Gina.

The group stood in silence as they surveyed the scene. The three ladies had faint smiles on their faces, almost as if they had been having a nice time.

'Oh, my God,' exclaimed Andrew and he walked towards the three ladies, gently touching their cheeks in turn, a tear rolling down his own face. They felt cold, but all looked rested and at peace. Their long grey hair was gently pushed back from their faces, almost as if they had planned a photo shoot. However, this was just three elderly ladies who wanted to find closure and rejoin their beloved husbands.

Andrew saw a letter in the centre of the round table. He found it had been written by Christine who, at her younger age, was the most likely to have the better handwriting. As he read aloud, his voice quavered and he was unable to go on. Bridget gently took the letter from his grasp.

She read out loud: 'We have now joined our husbands in a better place and you should all be pleased for us. We have for several days now, while you were all away in England, been visiting the Dream Room and having some very pleasant times with our husbands, sometimes all together and sometimes apart. We have managed to relive parts of our lives again and this in itself has managed to give us some closure after what has happened. It was lovely to see and be with our husbands again and we want you to know that it is our wish to be with them from now on. We have had our lives and the future is now yours. We know you will do the right thing when it comes to the dream machine. We believe it was a good idea at the time but now feel that perhaps it has grown too big and got out of human control. It will be your decisions to make.

'We have taken a small pill that will ensure that we remain asleep. We are extremely tired and miss our menfolk so very much. Goodbye to all of you and God bless. Love from all of us.'

Bridget, tears streaming down her face, placed the letter back on the table and stepped back.

The whole group stood in silence. No one was able to utter a word as the enormity of what had taken place sank in. Kevin and Sarah retreated from the room and sat in the lounge. Sarah was deeply distressed; she had not known the three ladies for long but had been impressed by their dignity and love. In the Dream Room the men were gently kissing their mothers and grandmother. They removed the bodies gently one by one from the rooms, placing them in one of the bedrooms. They knew that maybe they should have left them in the Dream Room but instinct told them to move them to a more discreet place. To have the police questioning them about the Dream Room did not bear thinking about.

The next few hours were filled with visits from the police and then the undertakers who took the bodies away. The doctor had taken some time examining them but felt obliged to offer an open verdict, at least for the time being. The coroner would obviously go into the deaths in more depth but for now the family could be left alone to grieve.

Watching all of this, Kevin and Sarah quietly suggested that they return earlier to England so the family could grieve in peace. Robert thanked them for their consideration and the two bade the group farewell with a promise to return after the funerals.

61

After landing at Heathrow, Kevin and Sarah collected their car from the airport car park and made their way home. It was a sombre trip home, with the two maintaining a dignified silence. What had started out as a welcome, interesting break had turned into yet another tragedy.

Sarah broke the silence. 'I'm the first to admit that I've not really been interested in the dream machine or the room for that matter, but I do feel it must have been nice to revisit all those pleasant times again with their loved ones; to actually experience the nearness and the passion that made up their earlier lives.'

Kevin nodded. This was an entirely different aspect of the dream machine which, up to now, he had not taken into consideration. Yes, the dream machine had actually been used for possibly what Ralph Hess and John Jefferson had invented for – spending time reliving your life in nicer times when all has been lost.

Martin Scott had been keeping an eye on his son's house and, as he still possessed a key, he had been able to enter the manor and look over its many rooms. Not finding the dream machine inside, he left, deciding to look around the spacious grounds. As he made his back to the front of the house, he saw a car pull up. Kevin and Sarah climbed out and went inside. After a few minutes, he ventured to the front door and tapped tentatively. Opening the door, Kevin was startled for a moment but, perhaps influenced by recent events, stepped back to allow his wayward father to enter. Martin was completely gobsmacked by this; he was in the house at Kevin's invitation. Not for one moment had he thought that he would be allowed in again – at least not without an argument.

Kevin and Sarah, following their experience in Italy, now

felt that perhaps, even knowing what Martin had set out to do, he was still Kevin's father. They were not to know that his father might not be as repentant as he could be.

The latest deaths in Italy still hung over all those connected with the dream machine, but how many more deaths might occur before the final episode would take place. It would not be long for the answer to unfold.

Martin knew he had only seven days to come up with a solution to his problem. He either had to throw himself on his son Kevin's mercy or find out where the dream machine was located. He had tried asking Lance for more time, giving the excuse that Kevin and Sarah had only just arrived back and they were expecting the machine back at the manor anytime. Surprisingly, Lance agreed a three-day extension.

Martin continued to stay with his son and daughter-in-law, trying to make himself as useful as possible. He was attentive to everyone's needs even to the extent of doing odd jobs around the grounds. He was getting his feet under the table again and knew this could only be a good thing. He was also conscious of being watched.

He was working in the grounds when he saw a delivery company drive up to the door with a large package for Kevin. He waited for a short time before he went in and made himself a coffee. Looking into the lounge, he noticed Kevin and Sarah had unwrapped the package and he readily recognised the familiar shape of the dream machine. Robert and Andrew had decided that it would be a nice gesture to return the machine to Kevin and Sarah. They had arranged for the police to return the machine. They would have liked to return the machine personally but were all still in Italy. Kevin took one look and walked away. Somehow it had lost its appeal. As far as he was concerned, the machine had provided him and Sarah with millions, yet he also knew now that this particular machine was a prelude to a considerable amount of grief. It would be returned to the locked room and, as far as he was concerned, could stay there forever.

Martin was in the kitchen that evening and could not believe his ears. His son was telling Sarah that he wanted to return the dream machine to the room at the top of the house. Sarah was pleased to hear this and at once collected the machine, taking it upstairs and placing it unceremoniously in the room. Martin knew now what he had to do.

Two days later, he made his way quietly up to the room. Using some clay, he made an impression of the key that Sarah had conveniently left in the door. He was extremely optimistic now that the machine would soon be his. Then he just had to overcome the problem of Lance and his associates. Yes, after all these years it looked as if the man who had discovered the machine was well on the way to having it back. All he had to do was wait until Kevin and Sarah had left the house and he could go to the locked room with his newly made key and, as his old father used to say, 'Bob's your uncle.'

He had already decided that there was no way he was going to give up the machine to Lance. Instead, he started to ask Kevin about how he had used the machine to make so much money. If he was going to use it for his own benefit, he needed to know these things. Surprisingly Kevin gave a detailed account on how he had used the machine to such beneficial effect. After all he would not be using the machine again.

Martin's opportunity came soon enough. One evening, Kevin and Sarah left to go shopping at one of the large malls that had been built just outside the town. Opening the door, he entered the room and picked up the dream machine that was sitting on top of an old filing cabinet. Locking the door afterwards, he left the house via the back door and made his way to the front of the house, desperately trying to see in the gloom if anyone was watching. Finally satisfied that there was no one, he got into his car and made his way quickly to the nearby motorway. It was not long before he was entering the Channel Tunnel. Within a couple of hours he would be in France, putting as much distance as possible between him, his son and the obnoxious Lance.

Kevin and Sarah returned from their evening out a few hours later. When his father did not show for breakfast the next morning, Kevin merely shrugged his shoulders; maybe he had decided to give them some space at last.

A few days later Kevin and Sarah were sitting in their lounge and were recalling what had taken place in Italy, the tragic deaths of those sweet old ladies, the sudden attempt on his own life, the shooting of his own father and... Kevin suddenly had an uneasy feeling. He leapt up from his chair and, hastening to the locked room, gave a gasp of dismay as he saw a space where his precious machine had been. His treacherous father had been up to his tricks again. The dream machine was gone and he knew that his father would not be coming back. Suddenly he experienced a strange feeling of relief, almost as if a load had been lifted from his shoulders. He locked the door again, walked downstairs and informed his waiting wife that perhaps now they could really start a normal life. That was of course until 22nd December 2012.

In Italy the sun was shining, but for the family and friends of the three ladies it was a mournful day and the sun was eclipsed by tears and sorrow as the funeral cortège made its way to the family cemetery that was the final resting place for all of the Barone family.

The huge crowd that followed the three hearses were silent which seemed to enhance the distress that everyone was feeling.

Robert gave the eulogy with Andrew and Roberto following with their own thoughts about the lives of their mothers and grandmother.

Andrew declared that it was not only God's will but the will of the three ladies who wanted to be back with their loved ones. Everyone must respect that and feel happy for them as they bowed out for the last time.

As the sun sank beneath the horizon, the vineyards that seem to stretch forever glowed of orange and brown, a sight which the now departed ladies must have enjoyed immensely and had taken with them on their journey.

62

It was a sombre week that followed with all the family trying to come to terms with the sudden departure of the three senior members. And understandably so, as not since the deaths of Philip, Ray and John had there been such an impact on the family.

It was Roberto who mentioned it first: 'We have to make some decisions about the dream machine and also try to figure out some way of sorting out the uncertain future of the other dream machines which must surely be coming online soon.'

Andrew was decisive: they should all return to the United Kingdom and consult the Prime Minister and his cabinet. With the assistance of MI5 and MI6, they might just be able to come with a solution as to how to deal with the rogue dream machines.

That evening the three men entered the room and activated the procedures to start the crystals. It would be the first time that they had used the machine and they were all feeling nervous. Suddenly the lights in the thirteen crystals intensified and the table opened to expose the centre crystal. Putting on the headphones, they gasped at the kaleidoscope of colour and images that seemed to surround them.

They had decided to attempt to go back to the time their relatives were in before the period of betrayal from the Chinese and the Russians. Their luck was in as they were plunged into a scene that amazed them. They were suddenly witnessing Ray, Philip and John talking about the problems at that time.

It seemed that Philip had just returned from Russia and was upset about his refuse entry into the country. The next few hours seemed to speed up and the three men watching could hardly keep up. It was fantastic, watching the past as if it was actually happening that day.

Ray was speaking with John about the trip to England to see the British authorities. It was also mentioned that they should visit the USA but this was changed to an invitation for the Americans to attend the meeting in London.

It was past midnight when Andrew, Robert and Roberto shut down the dream machine and went to the kitchen to get some refreshments. They had not the benefit of Bridget's notes as she had returned to work in England. The excitement of the evening and the previous week's events took its toll and it was not long before they all retired to bed. It was amazing that any of them were able to sleep, but sleep they did.

The next morning Robert phoned the British Prime Minister and asked him if a meeting had taken place between their fathers, the British and the Americans. After checking, the Prime Minister came back with the answer that no meeting had ever been scheduled or taken place. He did say however that he thought a meeting should be scheduled between the three men and his Cabinet as soon as possible.

Despite the disappointing response from the Prime

Minister, Robert was still insistent that the possible answers to their problems lay with the dream machine.

Again the three entered the room and started the machine. This time they would try to pinpoint the days just before the tragic deaths of their fathers and grandfather. Having arrived at the day before the deaths, they found John speaking of effecting the safeguard which they had built in the other machines. Ray and Philip were cautious as to whether this could be achieved, but John was insistent that he knew how to do it. The problem was it could also mean destroying their own machine, something which Ray and Philip were reluctant to do. How did they know it was a correct date and should they recheck it? Philip agreed and they soon persuaded John to go along with this approach. They rechecked the date and confirmed it was 22nd December 2012.

The scene moved forward to the three men talking about the return to the future and, yes, the date they had was seemingly correct. John reiterated his proposal to destroy all the machines although it meant theirs would also be destroyed. It would mean resetting the crystals so they were in reverse alignment which in turn would create a reverse vortex throwing the machine into such spin it would then destroy itself. Well, that was the theory anyway. It also meant the three men would have to restart the dream machine and that could be dangerous to all three of them. All of them agreed however that it needed to be done. They started writing their wills just in case they did not survive. What happened next was horrifying, seeing their own fathers and grandfather implementing a move that should destroy the dream machine. It seemed that the machine was having a private war with itself, emitting blinding lights and excruciating noises that became too loud for the human brain to endure.

Robert, Roberto and Andrew were experiencing the actual

event that their fathers had endured. It seemed that events of the whole world were going past their eyes in quick flashes; events that they recognised as World War Two and then World War One and even farther back. The collage of episodes spelt out pain and misery which the men could only stare at with horror. All involved were having their own private history lesson and it was not turning out to be at all pleasant. The original three had been experiencing this first-hand so it must have been even more painful for them. Their sons and grandson were more fortunate; theirs flashed by much faster. The nightmare seemed to continue for hours although, in reality, for Andrew, Robert and Roberto it was not that long. It seemed to finish as quickly as it started. Blackness came and the three of them realised that they were experiencing the minds of their fathers. It looked as if they had lapsed into unconsciousness. However, one thing was for sure: they knew they had survived the latest trip but, more to the point, so had the dream machine.

It was Philip that came to first. He opened his eyes and was quickly followed by Ray and then John.

John was the first to speak. 'We've failed. We've not achieved our objectives. It looks like nothing has changed. The dream machine hasn't destroyed itself; it's still functioning. All we've done is to have a history lesson of world events and, as far as I'm concerned, I have the biggest headache ever.'

Philip and Ray agreed.

'I also saw something else as we came back to our senses,' Philip said.

John and Ray looked at him. 'What was that?'

'Our own graves with our names over them.'

John and Ray were stunned. Each of them was in turmoil, each striving to make sense of their trip back in time and into the future.

Andrew, Robert and Roberto felt helpless as they watched. They could do nothing to stop what they knew was going to unfold. Philip, Ray and John were experiencing a total breakdown of reality and their minds were becoming confused. Moreover, Andrew, Robert and Roberto could feel themselves being dragged into this vortex of confusion.

Suddenly Robert let out a shout and, jumping to his feet, pulled off his headphones and stepped back out of the circle, plunging the room into semi-darkness. Roberto and Andrew followed and staggered out into the next room holding their heads in their hands. For God's sake, what had happened in that room?

Robert slammed the door of the Dream Room shut and joined them as they all walked unsteadily out onto the terrace and the evening sunlight. They had been in the Dream Room all day. As the summer sun dipped out of sight and twilight descended, it seemed to the three men as if this truly was the end of the world. After a few minutes, they returned to the lounge, sinking down into the sofas, none of them knowing what exactly had happened. All of them knew however that their relatives had gone through a much more painful and distressing experience. Whatever state their minds were in before, they must have been in an almost vegetative state afterwards. It was no wonder that they had decided the path they took.

Robert looked at Andrew and he in turn looked at Roberto. They knew that they had just witnessed the beginning of the end of their fathers and, what was more, it seemed that the dream machine was powerful enough to affect the minds of people just observing the past. Could it be true that the dream machine had an evil side to it that no one, including Ralph Hess who created the original machine, could have ever realised?

63

Kevin was talking with Sarah about their experiences in Italy. 'I just can't understand the latest communication from the guys. I mean, how was it possible for them to tune into the events that showed their fathers and grandfather actually using the machine? The concept of the dream machine was that you were able to use the machine to go back or forth to your own past, not someone else's. It doesn't make sense. I'll have to talk with Andrew and ask him to let me know how this was possible. It's almost as if the darn machine has developed skills of its own. I'm glad in a way to be shot of the smaller machine. It does seem that the more you use the machines, the more they take over your minds. I can't cope with all this, Sarah. It's beyond my comprehension. If the guys aren't coming back to the United Kingdom, I feel we should return to Italy.'

Sarah nodded her agreement but without much enthusiasm.

Kevin's telephone call was taken by Robert just two days after the terrible experience they had all endured with the dream machine. He sounded vague about everything, almost as if he could not concentrate on what Kevin was trying to tell him.

Turning to Andrew, he asked, 'Are we going back to the England in the near future? Kevin needs to talk with us all urgently.'

'I think we should. After all, we did say we'd meet with the Prime Minister. Tell him we'll be over within the next few days.'

Kevin was pleased to hear that they would be coming back to England and suggested that they stayed with him, bringing Bridget with them as well.

*

Andrew, Bridget, Robert and Roberto arrived at the manor and were welcomed by Kevin. He could see at once that they were not themselves. They looked drawn, their manner subdued. Bridget had also noticed it when they had picked her up on the way to Kevin's. Andrew was reluctant to say anything and she knew it was better not to pursue the matter at that time.

The group sat down to a delicious meal of fish and chips, washed down with some French wine. Kevin apologised to Robert and Roberto for the choice of wine but they said it was a welcome change. Anything that took their minds off Italy was very welcome. Retiring to the lounge for coffee and brandy, the group relaxed for the first time. Kevin listened intently as the three men in turn told him of their terrifying experiences. At the end he had one question: How had they managed to make actual contact with their relatives, albeit only from a distance?

The three men looked at each other. 'I hadn't even thought about that,' Andrew answered. 'How did we do that, Robert?'

Robert was perplexed, shaking his head. No way should have that been possible, accepting the basic principles of how the dream machine had been designed and built.

Roberto was also puzzled but he ventured to go somewhat further than the rest: 'I've been wondering since our last experience with the machine if by some strange occurrence it has developed extra capabilities which no one including Ralph Hess and John had even planned for.'

'It's possible,' Andrew admitted, 'but if this is true it could be that the machine is almost developing its own capabilities and self-control.'

'Good God,' Robert interjected, 'what the hell is happening? This is beyond all of us. We should at least go and see the Prime Minister and his scientists. Perhaps they can throw some light on it.'

Given that no one else came up with an alternative idea, it was agreed and Andrew made the call to arrange an appointment for the following day.

David Carson held an emergency meeting with his Cabinet and the team that were working on the British dream machine. Over thirty people were in attendance. The Prime Minister opened the meeting by outlining some of what had been relayed to him over the phone, but leaving out most of the news about the possible evolution in the operation of the machine. Then most of the Cabinet were excused, reducing the number of attendees to sixteen. As far as Carson was concerned, the fewer people that knew about the new concerns, the better.

The Prime Minister warmly welcomed the three men when they arrived. He was rather surprised to see Kevin also appear in the doorway but he shook his hand. Bridget was to join the group within the hour so, while they were waiting for her, they talked in general about how far the British had got with their Dream Room. The first provisional tests had been carried out. These had been quite promising but, due to the time spent by the security service checking on everyone involved, it seemed that the project was fast becoming bogged down by red tape. The truth was that things had not changed that much since the new government had taken over. Carson apologised for this and said that, depending on how the meeting went, he would ensure that things were speeded up. He asked Andrew to take charge of the meeting and to explain in detail exactly what had happened.

Andrew did this and then waited to see if anyone picked up on the point that Kevin had brought up. He also told how the three ladies had now passed on, but had used the machine to meet their husbands again, something which he knew would interest the group. He also explained Kevin's presence in terms of how he had been able to describe his own experience with the smaller machine. The next hour was taken up by some of the scientists who were working on the British machine. However, none of them could come up with anything different.

In a momentary lull in the discussion, one of the scientists who had said nothing up to that point spoke up. Frank Peterson was an Oxford graduate and had been involved with the British project from the start. 'I hope you don't mind me interrupting but how exactly did you manage to intercept and enter the actual time when your relatives were on the machine?'

'Well, to tell you the truth we don't know,' Robert answered at Andrew's request. 'We just tried to arrive near the date we knew our fathers decided to end their lives.'

'We know that shouldn't have been possible under normal circumstances but should we now assume that the way in which the dream machine is performing has changed, and changed dramatically?' Frank continued. 'For a long time, I've been concerned just how we have delved into mind travel, which is basically what we've been doing all these years. At least, your relatives have. We just don't know the full effect on our brains, and remember, once we enter this procedure we tend to think it's one way but in reality it's two ways as we are opening our inner thoughts to be collected and registered by the machine.'

The group fell silent.

'Has Frank expressed this fear about this before?' the Prime Minister whispered to the minister at his side. 'If so, why wasn't I informed about his fears?'

The minister, John Reed, shrugged his shoulders. 'Yes, Frank has mentioned this before but I decided to push on with the actual completion of the machine. We could worry about that further one when we are online, so to speak.'

The Prime Minister nodded and suggested that they break for lunch. He also took Frank, Andrew, Robert and Roberto to one side and advised them that he wanted to have a further discussion with them afterwards. He wanted to hear more about Frank's concerns. One thing he did not want was the completion of a machine that they could not control.

Four hours later, the group had still reached no firm conclusions, other than all agreeing that the machine appeared to be displaying tendencies to act autonomously. The Prime Minister suggested that the four should stay overnight at the Ritz Hotel and they could meet the next day to continue their meeting.

John Reed was the Secretary of Defence, the man in charge of the armed forces and also the person with overall responsibility for the building of the dream machine. He had listened to the exchanges carefully but was of the opinion that Britain should still go ahead with the final phase of the machine. He left the meeting at Number Ten and headed for the manufacturing centre where the machine was in its last stages.

Calling his work team together, John spoke reassuringly. 'There is nothing to be concerned about. We've been told to continue with the machine and get it operational without delay. I want to keep this top secret. No one else is to enter these premises without my express approval.'

The waiting scientists applauded, happy that their work could continue.

The next day, there were some additional people at the meeting with the Prime Minister. He had invited the American and French counterparts who were in charge of their respective dream machine production. They had been extremely interested in the fact that the machine in Italy had possibly developed a mind of its own.

At the invitation of David Carson, Robert opened the meeting with the news that his group had met with their own scientist Frank Peterson who had been working on the British project from day one. He had come up with some thoughts on how it had all happened. They had concluded that, in the case of the machine accepting the new arrivals of Robert, Andrew and Roberto, it could simply have been because they were closely related to the original three mind travellers. The machine had been unable able to differentiate between them by their DNA.

Andrew tried to sum up what had taken place. 'We know that our relatives attempted to throw the dream machine into reverse which they thought would have a similar effect to winding a clock backwards. However, this didn't seem to have any effect on the machine whatsoever. It does that anyway.'

Robert interjected. 'It seems it was worth a try as we understand that no one actually planned that the machine should be able to go forward in time. It was only designed by Hess and John to go backwards. Isn't that correct?' He looked around the room as if for approval. The majority nodded as if to agree. However, some merely looked blank.

'What your relatives experienced must have been terrifying,' Frank Peterson said. 'They were trying to effect changes that they hoped would shut down the machine. However, it seems that all that happened was that the machine became confused and tried to deal with the sudden changes being forced on it by producing a kaleidoscope of events in fast sequence that was too much for the men's brains to cope with all at once.'

Robert was the first to agree that this was possibly the best answer to what had happened, but it was still only an informed guess at best.

The Prime Minister looked around everyone. 'Well, gentlemen, we all seem to agree that what has taken place in Italy has not in any way interfered with the rest of the machines. But perhaps we should wait and see what state the machine is in when our friends here return to Italy.'

He was about to call the meeting to a close when Roberto interjected and suggested that Frank came to Italy and took a fresh look at the Italian machine. Robert realised what Roberto was concerned about: the fact that they had left the machine in Italy in such a hurry that they could not be sure if any damage had occurred. It would be good to have a professional scientist look at the machine and perhaps test it again to see if all was well.

The Prime Minister, as he was in overall charge of the British project, concurred, giving Frank his blessing for the trip. He also announced that a hold would be placed upon the commissioning of the British machine. It was also agreed on Frank's suggestion that he take one other man with him – his immediate assistant, Richard Wilson.

John Reid put the telephone down, a smile on his face. It was great news that Richard had been invited to visit Italy with Frank Peterson. It would be good to have one of his own men on the spot. Having just received the PM's orders that the British machine's commissioning was now on hold did not seem to worry him; what the PM did not know would not hurt him. He knew he was taking the biggest risk of his career but figured that, when he finished the project, the PM would be happy to accept that he was acting in the country's best interest. After all, he also felt that the PM would not be around after the next election. He returned to his workforce, laying off those considered surplus to requirements but keeping a chosen few with the strict instruction to them that they were not to divulge to anyone that they were continuing with the work.

Robert invited Kevin to join the group which he willingly accepted. Sarah and Bridget would remain in England but in the meantime, everyone was invited to Kevin's home while they made the arrangements for the trip back to Italy. They were happy to be away from the eyes of the Prime Minister. Pleasant as he appeared to be, politicians are politicians and have the effect of holding people to their word while not actually giving anyone their own.

That evening at dinner everyone talked excitedly about the forthcoming trip. Frank and Richard were quite intrigued to hear about the old helmet which turned out to be a time mind machine. Richard also remarked that he would have liked to have seen Kevin putting it on his head and attempting to ride his bike.

Kevin accepted all this in good humour. 'At least I benefited from it,' he responded, opening his arms to show them the luxurious surroundings of his home. There was not a lot anyone could say in response to that.

The large group travelled to Italy and made their way to the villa. Upon their arrival they made themselves comfortable in the spacious rooms that had been allocated to them. Frank joked about how the other half lived and Richard Wilson looked on with some envy. He had come up the hard way and the fact that Kevin had made considerable amounts of money from the dream machine was of great interest to him.

It was decided that Frank and Richard should look at the operation of the Italian machine to determine if any changes might have occurred with the reversing of the crystals .The fact that it had apparently reverted to its prior form was of interest to them. Or had it? Was it possible that the machine could operate even with a reversal? It suddenly dawned on the two men that they could not measure the state of crystals. They did not know what the actual position of the dream machine was – had it stayed in its reversed state or had it reverted to its original state? If they turned on the machine, they did not know what to expect – perhaps something that they could not control?

The group wished they had the wisdom of John, or even Christopher who had recently passed away. They concluded that the only way they could resolve it was to turn the machine on and see what happened.

It was decided that they work in teams of three to try and get a clearer picture of how things were. The two teams would be Robert, Frank and Roberto going first, with Andrew, Kevin and Richard the second time; that is, if there was going to be a second time.

With Robert and his team taking up their positions in the three chairs in the Dream Room, the trio of Andrew, Kevin and Richard positioned themselves outside the triangle. The first team put on their headphones and started the operation of the machine. The thirteen revolving outside lights came on as normal. Robert turned around and gave Andrew the thumbs-up sign.

The three men then tried to access the day and date from the last operation. They wanted to know if any damage or anything untoward had happened after they left. Instead of clear pictures of that period, they were surprised to see only swirls of clouds. It seemed that, as far as that time was concerned, the machine was having some difficulty in operating correctly. Did this mean it was indeed damaged? Had John's theory of reversing the alignment of the crystals worked? For the next hour, the three men tried to make the machine operate normally but all they got was swirls of cloud – nothing else. The thirteen smaller crystals seemed to work as usual but when it came to the large centre one only the clouds filled the crystal.

Frank and Richard were disappointed. Here had been a chance to see the dream machine working to its full capacity and all they could see was this clouded dome. All warnings of a world catastrophe were momentarily forgotten as they looked glumly at the machine. Andrew, Robert and Roberto, on the other hand, were satisfied they could do no more, but immediately wondered if what had happened here in Italy had affected the rest of the machines being built.

As they shut down the machine, Frank offered to notify the PM in London so that he could make some urgent enquiries. Within the hour, he came back with the news that the French had been making enquiries, asking whether the British had any problem with their Dream Room. He had also tried to reach the Chinese and Russian governments but, even at that crucial time, they still denied having such a machine.

The PM also confirmed that the British machine, after finally coming online, was also experiencing the swirls of cloud. He had been furious to discover that work had continued on the British effort and had told the Defence Minister, John Reid, to clear his desk. A replacement for him had already been appointed.

Robert and Frank were discussing the latest turn of events. While they knew what had taken place with the Italian machine had affected the British and obviously the French, it could be rightly assumed that both the Russian and Chinese had also been closed down. However, how on how on earth had the malfunction of the Italian machine affected the other machines all those thousand of miles away? It was a question that no one present including Frank Peterson had the answer to.

Andrew suddenly had grave doubts that their earlier sense of euphoria of succeeding in shutting down the dream machine was correct. After all he explained, with his limited knowledge of the working of dream machines, was it now possible that all they had done was to blow a gigantic fuse? If this is all that they had achieved then it was possible that the machine could be repaired and if the Italian one could be then so could the others.

He looked frantically at Frank Peterson. 'Frank, tell us what you think.'

Frank nodded. 'The only thing we can do is to check to see if we can manage to revert back to the original alignment of the machine.'

It had to be done. Frank and Richard were charged with the task of trying to realign the crystals, but what would happen if they had been damaged beyond repair. It could take weeks to find out and, to the waiting men that would feel like an eternity. Had the Dream Room's long and eventful existence now come to an untimely end?

Robert managed to find two men who, although retired, had worked on the dream machine when it was first built. With their rather limited assistance, the four men started to dismantle the dream machine. It did seem ironic that after all the desperate efforts of all of them to close down the machine here they were trying to repair it. The first find which the two men uncovered when they started to dismantle, it was that the thirteen smaller crystals were now white and smoky like blown light bulbs. The larger crystal seemed to be untouched and was still clear, but then it would have only been receiving what the thirteen smaller crystals had sent to it. The best scenario was that they would have to replace all the outside crystals to have even an outside chance of getting the machine back online – if that was what everyone wanted. They assumed that the Russians and Chinese would certainly want to do this but first they had to discover what had caused their machines to malfunction.

Numerous questions were raised as the six men tried to figure out their next step. If they managed to repair the machine, would they be repairing the other four machines as well? Always one to delve into the unusual, Roberto had another question: how did the three ladies manage to use the machine and visit their husbands when at that time it would appear that the dream machine was already in the process of meltdown, if that was the correct expression?

Frank came up with a plausible answer: 'When Philip and the others effected the reversal and you all experienced that ordeal with time flashing by, what was actually happening was that it was starting the closing down of its time portals that it had established all those years ago when it was first made. It's quite possible that, once the Dream Room was created, it started registering all past and future events, perhaps from the beginning of time.'

'God,' Robert exclaimed, 'when Ralph Hess and John invented the first machine, they most likely never realised that they were opening the gates to a time portal the world could never even dream of.'

Frank smiled. 'Yes, dream is the operative word but John activating the closing-down mechanism by putting into reverse must have had a real effect on its operation.'

'You mean it was actually closing down,' answered Roberto.

'Exactly,' confirmed Frank. 'It just went back to its earliest recollection whenever that was and started phasing it out of its memory banks. It took a considerable amount of time for it to make its way back to the twenty-first century. Perhaps it wanted to give those lovely ladies enough time to experience the machine. After all, that was what it was first intended for.'

Andrew and Robert smiled. Roberto agreed. 'Yes, it certainly looks that way.'

'It also must have been a surprise to the owners of the other machines which had just come online to have them go into what can only be described as a reverse action. They never knew what was happening. Your relatives must have known what they had done, interfering with the normal functioning of the machine. They reasoned that, if they remained alive, the other countries would eventually demand that they repair the damage caused. That could have put all their loved ones in danger, including you. If they weren't alive then it would be obvious that there was nobody left on this earth that would be able to repair the damage caused. The fail-safe method that they built into all the machines must have been fantastic. I can only salute John Jefferson. He must have been a great scientist.'

'Yes, I do believe he was,' said Andrew proudly.

'Look, we know that your fathers created the first Dream Room and subsequently built in safeguards in the others when they produced the new plans.' The question of how the Italian machine had managed to influence and have such a drastic effect on the others was another theory put forward by Frank who had been dwelling on this for some time. 'It is quite possible that they also realised that spread all over the world are other crystals capable of interacting with each other, including in the Dream Rooms. This would make sense if you believe the legend of the crystal skulls that are purported to be spread over all the continents of the world. It would also make sense for the dream machine to then be able to produce accurate visions of past and future events from all over the world. Otherwise it's quite possible that the Italian one on its own could not have worked so effectively. It always had some unknown assistance, perhaps even without John and Ralph Hess realising it at the time. Perhaps John never realised it at all.'

'So when our machine was made to malfunction,' Roberto

exclaimed, 'the other crystals picked it up and relayed it to the other Dream Rooms as usual.'

Frank nodded. 'They could well have done just that. If the original skulls were constructed in the way the legend goes, it is quite possible that they also have a fail-safe system which, realising that all was not well, added their own contribution to the shut-down. They could do this without affecting themselves, which would be a good thing if, as the legend says, when the thirteen skulls do come together it will be for the benefit of mankind. Perhaps this was just the start of it.'

It was Andrew that summed it all up: if all this was actually true, even if the other machines were repaired, it would probably be impossible for them to function as the Italian one did. It had taken many years to accumulate all the knowledge in that Dream Room.

'Oh God,' Robert frowned, 'let's not go down that road. Anyway, we all have to survive December 22nd 2012.'

'What will be, will be,' Roberto added.

Hearing all this, Frank gave an enigmatic smile. 'If that fellow John Reid had done what Dave Carson had told him and kept the British machine non-commissioned, the chances are that the British machine would have remained undamaged.'

Richard Wilson looked up to the sky and cursed his luck. He would never be able to make his millions now, not with his chief benefactor gone.

The final decision made after consultation with the British Prime Minister was to delay doing anything at this time and, with some regret, the team locked up the Dream Room. Robert and Roberto would be staying at the villa for a long earned rest and Andrew, Kevin and the two scientists made plans to return to the UK.

Andrew returned to Bridget and to pick up the pieces of

running the company his father had started all those years ago. Kevin returned to his Oxfordshire country estate and the ever-doting Sarah. He too felt the Dream Room had run its course and was glad it had. As he poured himself a large glass of cognac, he chuckled and wondered just where his wayward father was at that time.

Lance and his friends set out to find the elusive Martin Scott but gave up after a few months. It was like looking for a needle in a haystack. If Martin did not want to be found, there was a good chance he would not be – well not just yet.

Gordon the butler came to the side of the swimming pool of the swish villa in Altea, Spain and served his master his usual pint of English ale that had been imported specially for the person lying on his sun lounger.

'Will that be all, sir?'

'Yes thanks, Gordon, but wake me up in two hours as I need to check the American stock market,' breezed Martin Scott as he relaxed.

In the Spanish countryside, nothing stirred. It seemed that some dreams do come true!

Lightning Source UK Ltd.
Milton Keynes UK
UKOW051351040512

192021UK00001B/8/P